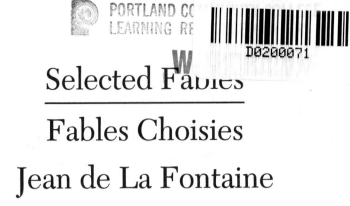

# Selected Fables

## Fables Choisies
## Jean de La Fontaine

### A Dual-Language Book

Edited and Translated by
STANLEY APPELBAUM

DOVER PUBLICATIONS, INC.
Mineola, New York

## Bibliographical Note

The present edition, first published by Dover in 1997, contains the full French text of 75 poems from the *Fables* of La Fontaine (see Introduction for bibliographic details), reprinted from a standard edition, plus new translations of each by Stanley Appelbaum, who also made the selection, wrote the Introduction and prepared all the other apparatus in the volume.

## Library of Congress Cataloging-in-Publication Data

La Fontaine, Jean de, 1621–1695.
    [Fables. English & French. Selections]
    Selected fables : a dual-language book / Jean de La Fontaine ; translated by Stanley Appelbaum = Fables choisies.
       p.    cm.
    ISBN 0-486-29574-5 (pbk.)
    1. Fables, French—Translations into English.   I. Appelbaum, Stanley.   II. Title.
PQ1811.E3A64     1997
841'.4—dc20
                                         96-35538
                                            CIP

Manufactured in the United States of America
Dover Publications, Inc., 31 East 2nd Street, Mineola, N.Y. 11501

# Contents and Key to Sources

The numbers in parentheses following the title of each fable indicate its original placement in La Fontaine's definitive edition; thus, "(I, 1)" stands for "Book I, Fable 1." The symbol in square brackets at the end of each entry, such as ["Ab"], refers to the Key to Sources located at the end of the table of contents; it indicates from which earlier piece(s) of writing La Fontaine derived the bare incidents of the fable in question; where no source is indicated, it is known or presumed that La Fontaine originated the entire fable.

## Key to Sources

**Ab**      Abstemius (pseudonym of Lorenzo Bevilacqua), published
            Latin fables in Venice in 1495 (*Hecatomythion*).

**Ae**      Aesop, or Aesopic collections. The legendary Aesop is said
            to have lived in the sixth century B.C., but no collection of
            fables attributed to him is even mentioned earlier than ca.
            300 B.C. The Greek prose of the various Aesopic collections
            is extremely straightforward and unadorned.

**Ap**      Aphthonius, Greek rhetorician, ca. 400 A.D., wrote *Progym-
            nasmata* (rhetorical exercises).

**Ar**      Aristotle, great Greek philosopher (384–322 B.C.)

**Av**      Avianus, Roman author of fables in verse, ca. 400 A.D.

**Bi**      Bidpai, legendary author of fables in India. Fables attributed
            to him were collected in the early centuries A.D., and rapidly
            spread, in translation, to the Middle East and then eventually
            to Europe. A French translation was published in 1644; one
            into Latin, in 1666.

**Bo**      Nicolas Boileau (-Despréaux; 1636–1711), major poet of sat-
            ires, epistles, literary criticism; his rather plain oyster fable was
            the stimulus for La Fontaine's superior version (IX, 9).

**Com**     Philippe de Commynes (ca. 1447–1511), French historian
            (*Mémoires*).

**Ré 2**    Mathurin Régnier (1573–1613), major satirical poet.

**Sa**    Sa'di (Muslih al-Din; 1194–ca. 1282), Persian poet, author of the *Gulistan* (Rose Garden). A French translation appeared in 1634.

***SM***    *La Satire Ménippée*, 1594, a collective political pamphlet favorable to King Henri IV during his struggles with the Catholic faction.

**So**    Jan III Sobieski (1624–1696), became king of Poland in 1674.

**Tab**    Tabarin (Antoine Girard; 1584–1626), performer of farces outdoors.

**Tav**    Jean-Baptiste Tavernier (1605–1689), great French traveler, who crossed Asia all the way to Java.

**Ve**    Giovanni Mario Verdizotti (1530–1607? 1525–1600?), a Venetian who published *Cento favole morali* in 1570.

***VSPD***    *Les vies des saints pères des déserts* (The Lives of the Holy Desert Fathers), a collection accessible to La Fontaine in a translation by Robert Arnauld d'Andilly made in 1647–1653.

# Introduction

**The Poet.** Jean de La Fontaine was born in 1621 at Château-Thierry,[1] on the Marne River halfway between Paris and Reims; the house in which this occurred is now a museum. His father was a royal counselor and a forestry official. After a flirtation with a religious calling (1641–2), Jean studied law in Paris (1645–7), where he made many lasting friendships with literarily inclined colleagues. Becoming a lawyer, he also married to please his father, but seems never to have been particularly devoted to his wife; later he neglected the upbringing of their one son; it was to friends and patrons that he would display staunch loyalty and affection.

In 1652, La Fontaine purchased a forestry commission in Château-Thierry similar to his father's, but soon got into financial difficulties. He was never really assiduous at his work, and was even to receive official reprimands. When his father died in 1658, the poet inherited his post, but also his considerable debts. (It was only in 1671 that La Fontaine sold his commission; by that time he was being supported by his patrons.)

In La Fontaine's day, patronage was necessary for a writer who was neither wealthy nor highly placed in society. In 1657, the poet, who had already begun publishing (anonymously) as early as 1654, was brought to the attention of Nicolas Fouquet, the all-powerful minister of finances (since 1653), who maintained an all-but-royal court and was building a magnificent château at Vaux-le-Vicomte, southeast of Paris. In 1658, La Fontaine dedicated his major poem *Adonis* to Fouquet, and became attached to his service the following year, writing *Le Songe de Vaux* (The Dream of Vaux), a poetic foretaste of the château's wonders.

This idyllic existence was brutally interrupted in 1661, when Louis XIV, at age 23, assumed personal control of the highest power on the death of Cardinal Mazarin, the chief minister during his minority. Smarting from the nobles' rebellion called the Fronde (the last—up to the 1789 revolution—of a long series of civil conflicts), during which he had been driven from Paris, Louis immediately began his absolutistic program of ruling without a chief minister and of reducing the nobility to the role of mere courtiers. Fouquet was a thorn in his side; in September 1661, only weeks after a fête at Vaux in the king's honor, Louis

---

[1] Site of a spectacular victory for the doughboys in 1918.

had Fouquet suddenly arrested for peculation; the accuser was Jean-Baptiste Colbert, who succeeded Fouquet as finance minister. (Later, Louis, to whom residence in the Louvre had become distasteful, started the construction of the Vaux-like château at Versailles, where the court moved in 1682.)

La Fontaine courageously wrote important poems in favor of his patron, but he himself was in new trouble, being fined for usurping a title of nobility. In 1663 he accompanied an uncle, implicated in the Fouquet affair, to Limoges, where the older man was exiled. In the following year the poet entered the service of the dowager Duchess of Orléans in Paris, and remained with her until her death in 1672. (The poet's wife was relegated to Château-Thierry.)

Now an important series of publications followed: in 1665, the first set of *Contes et nouvelles en vers* (Tales and Novellas in Verse), licentious anecdotes narrated with suggestive humor, the plots drawn extensively from Boccaccio and his imitators; in 1666, the second set of *Contes*, even bawdier and more anticlerical; in 1668, the first set (the future Books I through VI)[2] of *Fables choisies mises en vers par M. de La Fontaine* (Selected Fables Versified by M. de La Fontaine), published by Claude Barbin and Denys Thierry in Paris, a book that gained immediate widespread popularity and is still the basis for the poet's lasting worldwide fame; in 1669, *Les amours de Psyché et de Cupidon* (The Love Story of Psyche and Cupid), a brilliant retelling in prose and verse of the allegorical fairy tale from *The Golden Ass* of the Roman novelist Apuleius; and, in 1671, the third set of *Contes* as well as the volume *Fables nouvelles et autres poésies de M. de La Fontaine* (New Fables and Other Poems by M. de La Fontaine), which included eight new fables that were later to be incorporated into the second set.

After the death of the Duchess of Orléans, La Fontaine became the guest of Madame de la Sablière in Paris from 1673 to 1693. This distinguished patroness maintained a literary salon frequented by a variety of scholarly and artistic people (the practice of salons presided over by society ladies had begun with the Marquise de Rambouillet in 1608, and had already made incalculable contributions to French culture in the course of the century). In his new surroundings, La Fontaine would be introduced to the philosophy of Gassendi and would meet diplomats and ambassadors, as well as travelers who had been in Russia and Asia

---

[2] The present standard numbering of the books dates from a posthumous edition of 1709.

and could disclose to him the marvels of Indian and Persian storytelling. All these experiences were immeasurably to enrich the second set of fables (the future Books VII through XI), which were published (same city and publishers as for the first set) in 1678 (the future Books VII and VIII) and 1679 (the future Books IX–XI).

The last set of fables (now Book XII) was published by Claude Barbin in Paris in 1693 (volume dated 1694); all but ten had appeared separately earlier. Other important writings of the poet between 1673 and his death in 1695 included a religious poem about Saint Malc (whose temptation is of a drastically erotic nature), various unsuccessful plays and opera librettos, the fourth set of *Contes* (seized by the police), a scientific poem about Peruvian bark (cinchona) and a number of delightful occasional poems, outstanding among which are the autobiographical "Discours à Madame de la Sablière" of 1684 (not to be confused with the poem of the same name included in Book IX of the *Fables* and translated in the present volume) and the 1687 "A Mgr l'Évêque de Soissons" (generally called the "Épître à Huet"), La Fontaine's chief contribution to the Battle of the Ancients and the Moderns, the celebrated, long-running literary feud about the relative merits of current vs. Greco-Roman authors, which erupted in that year.

In 1683, the poet's election to the Académie Française was personally blocked by the king. One might attribute this to La Fontaine's reputation for impiety, or to his numerous unobliging references to kings (per se, or as represented by lions) in the *Fables;* but, the following year, his election was made final only one week after the election of the king's favored candidate, the satirist and critic Nicolas Boileau-Despréaux. After the death of Madame de la Sablière in 1693, La Fontaine spent the last two years of his life, addicted to piety, as the guest of the d'Hervart family in Paris.

It is saying the very least to call La Fontaine the major French lyric poet of the second half of the seventeenth century; this still controversial figure—already an enigma to his contemporaries—has also been called everything from "not a poet at all" to the greatest French poet of all time, the one most fully embodying such French ideals as wit, clarity, grace and ease of expression, and a broad, humane outlook. To those who are now studying the earlier poets of the century with a more open mind (untrammeled by the long-canonical strictures of Boileau and others), La Fontaine's work can be seen as an ingenious summation of such trends as François de Malherbe's rhetorical but mellifluous "classical" poems; the more personal and quirky productions of such so-called libertine poets as Théophile de Viau and Marc-Antoine de Saint Amant (he derives from them his constant theme of happiness in rural seclusion, and his descriptions of gardens and estates); the trifling but highly polished witticisms of such salon favorites as Vincent Voiture and Jacob Benserade; the pastoral poets and many, many others. (The only major area he leaves aside, except for brief parodistic references, is the epic poem, in which no one really succeeded in the seventeenth century.)

Part of the everlasting freshness of La Fontaine's work is due to the contradictions in his own nature and to the vastly differing evaluations and interpretations of him by others, up to the present day. Was he a naïve, flighty dreamer or a supremely conscious craftsman shrewdly cloaking dangerous thoughts in "safe" poetic forms? Did he have a real knowledge of rural conditions, or did he derive all his peasant scenes from genre paintings and tapestries? The list of such questions could go on and on; more will be raised in the discussion of the *Fables* that follows. For generations La Fontaine's name was kept alive in schoolbooks that featured a few of his simplest, earliest fables, among those most accessible to children. Today he is an unassailable classic on many grounds, in the view of most critics. But, however his content and "message" are judged, no careful reader can fail, at the very least, to be overwhelmed by the sheer marvel of his poetic technique, exemplified above all by the *Fables*.

**The *Fables*.** The genre of the fable, including the use of anthropomorphized animals as characters, extends far back into the literary traditions of India, both Buddhist and Hindu, from which it spread westward across Asia. The notorious difficulty of dating older Indian material makes it impossible to say whether the European fable, legendarily credited to the Greek Aesop in the sixth century B.C., was a separate invention or not. At any rate, we do not hear of any Greek fable collection actually in existence until about 300 B.C., and those that have come down to us, attributed to Aesop, date from even later; they are written in a severely simple, unornamented prose style. The first extant important poetic treatment of fables is in Latin, the work of the freedman Phaedrus in the early first century A.D.

There were several other fable collections, both Greek and Latin, in late antiquity, and the genre became extremely popular in the Middle Ages all over Europe. After the invention of printing, a good number of translations, adaptations and new versions continued to appear in Latin, Italian and French right up to La Fontaine's day, although these were generally volumes by and for academics, and none had the resonance or influence of his exceptional personal treatment.

La Fontaine may have been experimenting with the genre by the early 1660s, even before the catastrophic fall of his patron Fouquet, but it is irresistibly tempting to associate his wholesale adoption of the fable form with those traumatic events—especially since the fable has often served as a vehicle for veiled protests, both before and after La Fontaine's time (its origins in Europe point that way: the self-consolations of the ugly slave Aesop, the political slings of the ex-slave Phaedrus during the oppressive reign of Tiberius).[3] An alternative explanation for La Fontaine's awakened interest in the genre has also been offered: the birth of the Dauphin (crown prince) in 1661 induced the favor-currying poet to attempt juvenile literature that could be dedicated to the royal child.

Indeed, the three sets of La Fontaine's *Fables* (Books I–VI; Books VII–XI; Book XII) are quite different from one another, and their dedicatees are symptomatic of those differences. The first set, published in 1668 when the Dauphin (Louis de France) was seven, and dedicated to him,[4] consists largely of poems whose "plots" are derived directly from Aesop, Phaedrus or other well-known Roman authors. Generally speaking, in this first set the poems are short and La Fontaine hews fairly closely to the traditional narratives. These are the plots best known to children and the La Fontaine pieces most often used for pedagogical purposes. Even here, of course, his wit and charm are everywhere in evidence, as are his gift for dialogue and narration, his skill with a variety of meters, and his penchant for self-referential reflections on literary matters. It is already clear from the first set that, for whatever reasons the poet developed the fable genre, he soon found it the most congenial form for his own talents and mind-set, and that there is no injustice in deeming his fables the summit of his production.

And yet the second set, published in 1678–9 and dedicated to the king's beautiful and intelligent official mistress, the Marquise de Montespan (thus distinctly not associated with pedagogy), widens the poet's horizons in every direction. Here, in all ways, he is at the peak of his powers. He turns his fables into pastorals, orations, epistles, treatises or novelettes just as he pleases. He introduces his own feelings,

---

[3] Does La Fontaine support this theory when he calls his fables *feintes* (ruses), as well as referring to them deprecatingly as *fictions* and *mensonges* (lies)?

[4] This crown prince was never to reign; Louis XIV was succeeded on the throne not by a son, but by a great-grandson!

wishes and opinions at any time. He weds the content to the form with breathtaking ease, at times achieving a naturalness and lightness of expression, within the constraints of the verse, that are all the more remarkable in his era, with its frequent preference for pompous rhetoric. In this second set he taps a much greater variety of sources, including India, and is even inspired by current events. The poems are generally longer and infinitely richer in beauty and wisdom.

The third set, published in 1693, was dedicated to the Duke of Burgundy, a grandson of the king's who was later to become the father of Louis XV; the Duke was then eleven. A few of the fables are strictly juveniles, custom-written for the young dedicatee; the rest, a number of which had been previously published separately, continue the features of the second set. There is some falling off in tightness and control, but the final fable, "Le juge arbitre, l'hospitalier, et le solitaire," has been called the finest of all by more than one qualified critic.

How carefully did La Fontaine arrange the fables within each book and each set? Even a cursory first consecutive reading reveals the existence here and there of meaningful pairings of fables, and the poet obviously gave great weight to the choice of the first and last fable in each book; but the scholars Alain-Marie Bassy and Yves Le Pestipon (in their 1995 GF-Flammarion edition of the *Fables*) suggest an extensive, complex interlocking of motifs and a cunningly contrived sequence of poems throughout books and sets. Their theory may perhaps be carried to extremes but is worthy of careful consideration.

Some of the fables are written in regular short stanzas or in unbroken successions of one and the same meter, but most of them are in *vers libres*, or *vers irréguliers*, in which lines of varying meters occur without a fixed pattern. This not only adds to the narrative charm, it sometimes allows the poet to achieve a unique effect. Perhaps the most famous example is the two-word, three-syllable line "Le berger" in the fable "Les animaux malades de la peste": by this scanty reference to the shepherd, the lion king, hypocritically confessing his crimes, manages to minimize the most flagrant one of all—eating the shepherd along with the sheep. The poet's sparing, but telling, use of such devices as alliteration and onomatopoeia deserve close attention.

Fables traditionally have morals. La Fontaine plays with this tradition. Often in his fables the moral is at the end, where you would expect it, but sometimes at the very beginning. Sometimes the moral, or rather the poet's reflections on the "plot," take over the poem, relegating the plot to the status of a secondary pretext. Sometimes there is no plot at all, as in "Contre ceux qui ont le goût difficile." Much more often, no moral is expressed at all, as in the ultra-famous first fable, "La cigale et la fourmi," in which you can imagine La Fontaine siding with both the cicada *and* the ant.

As much as the poet obviously loved his animals (see his ardent defense of their intelligence in the "Discours à Madame de la Sablière"), he was no great naturalist; he confuses rats and mice indiscriminately and he generally follows his sources in all their time-honored grotesque mistakes about animals' actual habits: foxes and crows don't really eat cheese, turtles don't have teeth, deer don't really weep when their life is threatened. On the other hand, loving personal observation can be detected in such pieces as the "Discours à Monsieur le duc de La Rochefoucauld."

La Fontaine uses the widest vocabulary of any seventeenth-century French poet (compare the dramatic poet Racine, for instance, who in his sublime plays restricts himself to some two thousand "dignified" words): The *Fables* contain a number of words dating from the sixteenth century (especially from François Rabelais's *Pantagruel* and *Gargantua*), as well as many technical terms derived from such professions or pursuits as gardening and hunting. Especially frequent are expressions from the law (remember the poet's own legal training) and the military (a quite pervasive influence during the king's unending expansionist campaigns, which bankrupted the country).

By La Fontaine's day the French language had basically attained the form known as modern French, and his poetry can be readily understood today with only a little effort (remember, he wrote at the same time as John Dryden). Aside from the few borrowed from Rabelais, there are hardly any obsolete words (one is "semondre" in "Le satyre et le passant"). On the other hand, there have been numerous semantic changes in the connotations of words since his time; these are reflected in the translations in the present volume and should be carefully observed. Those wishing a brief overview of the chief differences in grammar and syntax between La Fontaine's day and ours would do well to consult a French textbook such as *XVIIe Siècle*, by André Lagarde and Laurent Michard, published by Bordas, Paris, 1985; or *Recueil de textes littéraires français: XVIIe siècle*, by A. Chassaing and Ch. Senninger, Hachette, Paris, 1966. With regard to pronunciation, the most important difference is that the dipthong *oi*, now pronounced like the *wa* in the English word "watch," was then pronounced like the *we* in the English word "wet"; thus, in the fable "Le berger et le roi," the words "froid" and "fouet" form a perfect rhyme.

The sensational popularity of La Fontaine's *Fables* elicited a rash of imitations almost at once, and their influence has not abated over the centuries. Among the most important sets of fables inspired by his example are those of John Gay in England and Gotthold Ephraim Lessing in Germany (both eighteenth century) and especially those written in the early nineteenth century in Russia by Ivan Andreyevich Krylov, with their unmistakable aim of satirizing the oppressive social and political milieu after the Napoleonic wars.

   **The Present Edition.** This volume contains, in their entirety, 75 poems out of the 244 contained in modern French editions of the *Fables.*[5] The selection is distributed fairly evenly over the 12 books and includes poems of every length and representatives of every type, whether from the point of view of poetic form, content or approach. Criteria for inclusion were: regular appearance in French anthologies, critical acclaim, famous quotations—and this editor's preferences. The exclusion of any poem from this introductory volume is no reflection on its merit; indeed, the reader is warmly urged to continue with all the fables and with other works of La Fontaine as well.

   The French text, reprinted from a standard edition, follows the current practice of modernizing spelling and punctuation while changing not a word of the original.

   The source of the "plot" of each fable included (not all editors agree on each and every source) is indicated by an abbreviation at the end of each entry in the table of contents, and that table is immediately followed by an explanatory key to the abbreviations. (La Fontaine seems to have depended on Latin and French versions of his sources that originated in other languages.)

   There are alphabetical lists of French titles and French first lines at the end of the volume.

   In accordance with the goals of this Dover dual-language series, the new translation is literal, in English prose, line for line. (It is absolutely impossible to translate literally while following the original meters and rhyme schemes.) In places the translation is slightly wordier than the

---

   [5] The first set (Books I–VI) is preceded by a dedicatory poem to the Dauphin (as well as a prose dedication to him, a prose preface and a prose biography of Aesop); Book I contains 22 numbered fables; Book II, 20; Book III, 18; Book IV, 22; Book V, 21; Book VI, 21 and the Epilogue to the first set. The second set (Books VII–XI) is preceded by a dedicatory poem to Madame de Montespan (as well as a prose preface); Book VII contains 18 numbered fables; Book VIII, 27; Book IX, 19 and, at the end, the unnumbered "Discours à Madame de la Sablière"; Book X, 15; Book XI, 9 and the Epilogue to the second set. The third set (Book XII) includes a prose dedication to the Duke of Burgundy and 24 numbered fables; modern editions tack on 3 uncollected fables.

original, since it attempts to be somewhat interpretative (spelling out certain metaphors more fully, for instance) and tries to avoid all ambiguity of expression. It is thus an idea-for-idea rather than a word-for-word translation, but not one idea has been omitted, added or falsified. Certain French idioms could, of course, not be translated word for word into what would have been nonsensical English. In most cases, animals have been deliberately referred to as "he" or "she" depending on their grammatical gender in French; "it" would have destroyed their personality. La Fontaine frequently uses the so-called historical present tense in narrative, adding variety and a feeling of immediacy. This practice, though much less common and natural-sounding in English than in French, has been generally adopted in the present translation, chiefly for pedagogical reasons. But present and past tenses are never mixed in the same English sentence, and a degree of regularization has been consciously sought.

The translator has also supplied over a hundred explanatory footnotes.

# Selected Fables

## Fables Choisies

# La cigale et la fourmi

La cigale, ayant chanté
    Tout l'été,
Se trouva fort dépourvue
Quand la bise fut venue.
Pas un seul petit morceau
De mouche ou de vermisseau.
Elle alla crier famine
Chez la fourmi sa voisine,
La priant de lui prêter
Quelque grain pour subsister
Jusqu'á la saison nouvelle.
«Je vous paierai, lui dit-elle,
Avant l'oût, foi d'animal,
Intérêt et principal.»
La fourmi n'est pas prêteuse;
C'est lá son moindre défaut.
«Que faisiez-vous au temps chaud?
Dit-elle à cette emprunteuse.
—Nuit et jour à tout venant
Je chantais, ne vous déplaise.
—Vous chantiez? j'en suis fort aise.
Eh bien! dansez maintenant.»

# Le corbeau et le renard

Maître corbeau, sur un arbre perché,
    Tenait en son bec un fromage.
Maître renard, par l'odeur alléché,
    Lui tint à peu près ce langage:

## The Cicada and the Ant

The cicada,[1] after singing
   all summer long,
found she was very low on provisions
when the wintry north wind arrived.
Not a single little bit
of fly or wormlet.
She went crying hunger
to the home of her neighbor, the ant,
asking her to lend her
a few grains to live on
until springtime.
"I'll pay you," she said to her,
"before harvest time, on my word as an animal,
both interest and principal."
The ant wasn't the lending kind;
if she had any fault, it wasn't that one.
"What were you doing during the warm weather?"
she asked that borrower.
"Night and day I would sing
to all and sundry, if it please you, ma'am."
"You were singing? I'm very glad to hear it.
Well, then, now dance."

## The Crow and the Fox

   Master Crow,[2] perched on a tree,
     was holding a cheese in his beak.
   Master Fox, allured by the aroma,
     spoke to him more or less like this:

---

  [1] Not "grasshopper," which is *sauterelle* in French.
  [2] *Corbeau* might better be translated as "raven," but designations of members of the crow family can be vague in French.

«Hé! bonjour, Monsieur du Corbeau.
Que vous êtes joli! que vous me semblez beau!
    Sans mentir, si votre ramage
    Se rapporte à votre plumage,
Vous êtes le phénix des hôtes de ces bois.»
A ces mots, le corbeau ne se sent pas de joie;
    Et pour montrer sa belle voix,
Il ouvre un large bec, laisse tomber sa proie.
Le renard s'en saisit, et dit: «Mon bon monsieur,
    Apprenez que tout flatteur
    Vit aux dépens de celui qui l'écoute.
Cette leçon vaut bien un fromage sans doute.»
    Le corbeau honteux et confus,
Jura, mais un peu tard, qu'on ne l'y prendrait plus.


# La grenouille qui se veut faire aussi grosse que le bœuf

    Une grenouille vit un bœuf
    Qui lui sembla de belle taille.
Elle qui n'était pas grosse en tout comme un œuf,
Envieuse s'étend, et s'enfle, et se travaille
    Pour égaler l'animal en grosseur,
    Disant: «Regardez bien, ma sœur;
Est-ce assez? dites-moi. N'y suis-je point encore?
—Nenni.—M'y voici donc?—Point du tout.—M'y voilà?
—Vous n'en approchez point.» La chétive pécore
    S'enfla si bien qu'elle creva.

Le monde est plein de gens qui ne sont pas plus sages:
Tout bourgeois veut bâtir comme les grands seigneurs;

    Tout petit prince a des ambassadeurs;
    Tout marquis veut avoir des pages.

"Hello! Good day, Sir Crow.
How good-looking you are! How handsome you seem to me!
　　It's no lie; if your singing
　　is any match for your plumage,
you are the phoenix among the inhabitants of this forest."
At those words, the crow is beside himself with joy;
　　and, to show his beautiful voice,
he opens his beak wide and drops his catch.
The fox seizes it and says: "My dear sir,
　　　　learn that every flatterer
　　makes his living at the expense of those who listen to him.
This lesson is surely well worth a cheese."
　　The crow, ashamed and embarrassed,
swore, though a bit too late, that he would never again be fooled
　　　　　　　　　　　　　　　　　　　　　　　　that way.


# The Frog Who Wanted to Become as Large as the Ox

　　A frog saw an ox
　　who seemed to her to be of a lovely size.
She, who was altogether not as big as an egg,
in her envy stretched and swelled and strained
　　in order to equal that animal in bulk,
　　　　saying: "Take a good look, sister;
is this enough? Tell me. Am I not there yet?"
"No." "Is this it?" "Not at all." "What about this?"
"You're nowhere near." The puny creature
　　swelled up until she burst.

The world is full of people who are no wiser than that:
every member of the middle class wants to build palaces like great
　　　　　　　　　　　　　　　　　　　　　　　　　　　lords;
　　every petty princeling has ambassadors;
　　every minor nobleman wants to have pages.

## La besace

Jupiter dit un jour: «Que tout ce qui respire
S'en vienne comparaître aux pieds de ma grandeur.
Si dans son composé quelqu'un trouve à redire,
    Il peut le déclarer sans peur:
    Je mettrai remède à la chose.
Venez, singe, parlez le premier, et pour cause.
Voyez ces animaux, faites comparaison
    De leurs beautés avec les vôtres.
Êtes-vous satisfait?–Moi, dit-il, pourquoi non?
N'ai-je pas quatre pieds aussi bien que les autres?
Mon portrait jusqu'ici ne m'a rien reproché;
Mais pour mon frère l'ours, on ne l'a qu'ébauché.
Jamais, s'il me veut croire, il ne se fera peindre.»
L'ours venant là-dessus, on crut qu'il s'allait plaindre.
Tant s'en faut: de sa forme il se loua très fort,
Glosa sur l'éléphant; dit qu'on pourrait encor
Ajouter à sa queue, ôter à ses oreilles;
Que c'était une masse informe et sans beauté.
    L'éléphant étant écouté,
Tout sage qu'il était, dit des choses pareilles.
    Il jugea qu'à son appétit
    Dame baleine était trop grosse.
Dame fourmi trouva le ciron trop petit,
    Se croyant, pour elle, un colosse.
Jupin les renvoya s'étant censurés tous,
Du reste contents d'eux. Mais, parmi les plus fous,

Notre espèce excella: car tout ce que nous sommes,
Lynx envers nos pareils et taupes envers nous,

Nous nous pardonnons tout, et rien aux autres hommes.
On se voit d'un autre œil qu'on ne voit son prochain.

# The Double Shoulder-Bag [3]

Jupiter[4] said one day: "Let all creatures who draw breath
come and appear at the foot of my glorious throne.
If any of them finds fault with his physical make-up,
    he can declare it without fear:
    I will remedy the matter.
Come, monkey, you speak first, and rightly so.
Look at these animals and compare
    their beautiful features with yours.
Are you satisfied?" "I?" he said. "Why not?
Don't I have four feet just like the rest?
Up to now my portrait hasn't reproached me in any way;
but as for my brother, the bear, he has been merely blocked roughly.
If he takes my word for it, he'll never have his picture painted."
The bear arriving thereupon, they thought he was going to complain.
Far from it: he expressed great satisfaction with his shape,
but carped at the elephant, said that it was still possible
to add something to his tail and take something away from his ears,
that he was a shapeless mass devoid of beauty.
    When the elephant was heard,
as wise as he was, he said similar things.
    He deemed that, to his liking,
    Madame Whale was too big.
Madame Ant found the mite too small,
    thinking she herself was a giant in comparison.
Jupiter dismissed them after they had all criticized one another,
while remaining contented with themselves. But among the most
                        foolish
our species excelled: for, each and every one of us,
lynx-eyed with regard to our fellows and mole-blind with regard
                        to ourselves,
we forgive ourselves everything and other men nothing.
We see ourselves with other eyes than we see our neighbors with.

---

[3] A bag with two pouches slung over one's back and chest, carried by beggars and mendicant monks.

[4] Roman name for the king of the gods. In the *Fables,* La Fontaine frequently uses ancient mythology in place of Christian terminology.

    Le fabricateur souverain
Nous créa besaciers tous de même manière,
Tant ceux du temps passé que du temps d'aujourd'hui.
Il fit pour nos défauts la poche de derrière,
Et celle de devant pour les défauts d'autrui.

## Le rat de ville, et le rat des champs

Autrefois le rat de ville
Invita le rat des champs,
D'une façon fort civile,
A des reliefs d'ortolans.

Sur un tapis de Turquie
Le couvert se trouva mis.
Je laisse à penser la vie
Que firent ces deux amis.

Le régal fut fort honnête,
Rien ne manquait au festin;
Mais quelqu'un troubla la fête
Pendant qu'ils étaient en train.

A la porte de la salle
Ils entendirent du bruit.
Le rat de ville détale,
Son camarade le suit.

Le bruit cesse, on se retire:
Rats en campagne aussitôt;
Et le citadin de dire:
«Achevons tout notre rôt.

–C'est assez, dit le rustique;
Demain vous viendrez chez moi:
Ce n'est pas que je me pique
De tous vos festins de roi;

Mais rien ne vient m'interrompre:
Je mange tout à loisir.
Adieu donc, fi du plaisir
Que la crainte peut corrompre!»

The supreme artisan
created all of us as shoulder-bag carriers in the same way,
those of bygone days as well those of the present day.
He made the back pouch for our own faults
and the front pouch for the faults of others.


## The City Rat and the Country Rat

Once upon a time the city rat
invited the country rat
most politely
to some leftovers of ortolans.

On an Oriental carpet
the table was spread.
I leave it to you to imagine the good time
these two friends had.

The banquet was quite a respectable one;
nothing was lacking at the feast;
but someone spoiled their enjoyment
while they were in the midst of it.

At the door to the room
they heard some noise.
The city rat scooted away,
his comrade followed him.

The noise stopped, whoever it was withdrew:
the rats took the field again at once;
and the city dweller said:
"Let's finish all of our roast."

"This is enough," said the country fellow;
"tomorrow you'll visit me:
it's not that I can boast
of all your royal feasts;

but nothing interrupts me:
I eat in complete peace of mind.
Farewell, then, I scorn the pleasure
that can be ruined by fear!"

## *Le loup et l'agneau*

La raison du plus fort est toujours la meilleure,
        Nous l'allons montrer tout à l'heure.
        Un agneau se désaltérait
        Dans le courant d'une onde pure.
Un loup survient à jeun qui cherchait aventure,
        Et que la faim en ces lieux attirait.
«Qui te rend si hardi de troubler mon breuvage?
        Dit cet animal plein de rage:
Tu seras châtié de ta témérité.
–Sire, répond l'agneau, que Votre Majesté
        Ne se mette pas en colère;
        Mais plutôt qu'elle considère
        Que je me vas désaltérant
        ⋅ Dans le courant,
        Plus de vingt pas au-dessous d'Elle,
Et que par conséquent en aucune façon
        Je ne puis troubler sa boisson.
–Tu la troubles, reprit cette bête cruelle,
Et je sais que de moi tu médis l'an passé.
–Comment l'aurais-je fait, si je n'étais pas né?
        Reprit l'agneau, je tette encor ma mère.
        –Si ce n'est toi, c'est donc ton frère.
        –Je n'en ai point.–C'est donc quelqu'un des tiens:
        Car vous ne m'épargnez guère,
        Vous, vos bergers et vos chiens.
On me l'a dit: il faut que je me venge.»
        Là-dessus au fond des forêts
        Le loup l'emporte, et puis le mange
        Sans autre forme de procès.

# The Wolf and the Lamb

The stronger man's reasoning always carries the day,
    as we shall demonstrate at once.
    A lamb was quenching his thirst
    in the current of a clear stream.
Along came a starving wolf out to try his luck;
    hunger had drawn him to that spot.
"Who makes you so bold as to muddy my drinking water?"
    said that animal, full of rage:
"You'll be punished for your rashness."
"Sire," the lamb replied, "may it please your Majesty
    not to get angry;
    rather, consider
    that I am drinking
        from the flowing current
    more than twenty paces downstream from you,
and that consequently there is no way
    in which I can muddy your drinking water."
"You *are* muddying it," replied that cruel beast,
"and I know that you slandered me last year."
"How could I have, since I wasn't born yet?"
    replied the lamb; "I'm still suckling my mother."
      "If it wasn't you, then it was your brother."
    "I have none." "Then it was some relative of yours:
    for all of you show me no mercy,
    you, your shepherds and your dogs.
I was told about it: I must take revenge for it."
    Thereupon the wolf carried him off
    deep into the forest, and then ate him
    without any other form of due process.

## La mort et le bûcheron

Un pauvre bûcheron, tout couvert de ramée,
Sous le faix du fagot aussi bien que des ans
Gémissant et courbé marchait à pas pesants,
Et tâchait de gagner sa chaumine enfumée.
Enfin, n'en pouvant plus d'effort et de douleur,
Il met bas son fagot, il songe à son malheur.
Quel plaisir a-t-il eu depuis qu'il est au monde?
En est-il un plus pauvre en la machine ronde?
Point de pain quelquefois, et jamais de repos.
Sa femme, ses enfants, les soldats, les impôts,
      Le créancier et la corvée,
Lui font d'un malheureux la peinture achevée.
Il appelle la mort; elle vient sans tarder,
      Lui demande ce qu'il faut faire.
      «C'est, dit-il, afin de m'aider
A recharger ce bois; tu ne tarderas guère.»

      Le trépas vient tout guérir;
      Mais ne bougeons d'où nous sommes.
      Plutôt souffrir que mourir,
      C'est la devise des hommes.

## Le chêne et le roseau

      Le chêne un jour dit au roseau:
«Vous avez bien sujet d'accuser la nature:
Un roitelet pour vous est un pesant fardeau.
      Le moindre vent qui d'aventure
      Fait rider la face de l'eau
      Vous oblige à baisser la tête:
Cependant que mon front, au Caucase pareil,
Non content d'arrêter les rayons du soleil,

# Death and the Woodcutter

An impoverished woodcutter, completely covered with branches,
bending and groaning beneath the double burden of his bundle
and his years, was walking with heavy steps,
and was trying to reach his smoke-blackened hovel.
Finally, totally worn out with the strain and the ache,
he sets down his bundle and meditates on his unhappy situation.
What pleasure has he had ever since he was born into the world?
Is there anyone poorer than he on the entire globe?
No bread at times and never any rest.
His wife, his children, the soldiers,[5] the taxes,
　　　the creditor and the forced labors
make him the perfect picture of a miserable wretch.
He calls upon Death, who appears without delay
　　　and asks him what he wants.
　　　He says: "It's to help me
load this wood on my shoulders again; it'll take you no time at all."

　　　Death comes as a cure for everything;
　　　but we don't stir a step from where we are.
　　　"Rather suffer than die"
　　　is the motto of mankind.

# The Oak and the Reed

　　　The oak said to the reed one day:
"You have every right to blame nature:
for you a wren is a heavy burden.
　　　The slightest breeze that happens
　　　to ripple the surface of the water
　　　makes you bow your head:
while my brow, like unto the Caucasus range,
not content with halting the rays of the sun,

---

[5] Marauders, or else soldiers sent to enforce the peasants' payments or their labor services.

Brave l'effort de la tempête.
Tout vous est aquilon, tout me semble zéphyr.

Encor si vous naissiez à l'abri du feuillage
    Dont je couvre le voisinage,
    Vous n'auriez pas tant à souffrir:
    Je vous défendrais de l'orage.
    Mais vous naissez le plus souvent
Sur les humides bords des royaumes du vent.
La nature envers vous me semble bien injuste.
–Votre compassion, lui répondit l'arbuste,
Part d'un bon naturel; mais quittez ce souci.
   Les vents me sont moins qu'à vous redoutables.
Je plie, et ne romps pas. Vous avez jusqu'ici
    Contre leurs coups épouvantables
    Résisté sans courber le dos;
Mais attendons la fin.» Comme il disait ces mots,
Du bout de l'horizon accourt avec furie
    Le plus terrible des enfants
Que le Nord eût portés jusque-là dans ses flancs.
    L'arbre tient bon, le roseau plie;
    Le vent redouble ses efforts,
    Et fait si bien qu'il déracine
Celui de qui la tête au ciel était voisine,
Et dont les pieds touchaient à l'empire des morts.

## Contre ceux qui ont le goût difficile

Quand j'aurais, en naissant, reçu de Calliope
Les dons qu'à ses amants cette muse a promis,
Je les consacrerais aux mensonges d'Ésope:
Le mensonge et les vers de tout temps sont amis.
Mais je ne me crois pas si chéri du Parnasse
Que de savoir orner toutes ces fictions.
On peut donner du lustre à leurs inventions;
On le peut, je l'essaie: un plus savant le fasse.
Cependant jusqu'ici d'un langage nouveau

braves the assault of the tempest.
Everything is a north wind to you, everything seems a gentle zephyr
                                               to me.
If you could only grow beneath the shelter of the foliage
    with which I cover the vicinity,
      you would not have to suffer so much:
    I would protect you from the storm.
    But most often you grow
on the moist banks of the kingdoms of the wind.
Nature seems to me to be very unfair to you."
"Your pity," replied the small plant,
"shows a good heart; but put aside those worries.
  I have less to fear from the winds than you do.
I bend and don't break. Up to now
    you have withstood their frightful blows
    without bending your back;
but let's wait until the end." As he spoke those words,
from the end of the horizon there came blowing with fury
    the most terrible of the offspring
that the north had hitherto carried in its womb.
    The tree held fast, the reed bent;
    the wind doubled its efforts
    and blew so hard that it uprooted
the one whose head had been close to heaven
and whose feet once reached to the realm of the dead.

## Against the Hard-to-Please

If I had received from Calliope[6] at birth
the gifts which that muse has promised to her adorers,
I would devote them to Aesop's fancies:
fancies and poetry have always been friends.
But I do not think myself so dear to Parnassus
that I am capable of ornamenting all those fictions.
It is possible to lend luster to their inventions;
it is possible, and I am trying to: let someone more scholarly do so.
Nevertheless, up to now, with novelty of language,

[6] The muse of epic poetry. The muses lived on Mount Parnassus.

J'ai fait parler le loup et répondre l'agneau;
J'ai passé plus avant: les arbres et les plantes
Sont devenus chez moi créatures parlantes.
Qui ne prendrait ceci pour un enchantement?
        «Vraiment, me diront nos critiques,
        Vous parlez magnifiquement
        De cinq ou six contes d'enfant.»
Censeurs, en voulez-vous qui soient plus authentiques
Et d'un style plus haut? En voici. Les Troyens,
Après dix ans de guerre autour de leurs murailles,
Avaient lassé les Grecs, qui, par mille moyens,
        Par mille assauts, par cent batailles,
N'avaient pu mettre à bout cette fière cité;
Quand un cheval de bois par Minerve inventé
        D'un rare et nouvel artifice,
Dans ses énormes flancs reçut le sage Ulysse,
Le vaillant Diomède, Ajax l'impétueux,
        Que ce colosse monstrueux
Avec leurs escadrons devait porter dans Troie,
Livrant à leur fureur ses dieux mêmes en proie.
Stratagème inouï, qui des fabricateurs
        Paya la constance et la peine.
«C'est assez, me dira quelqu'un de nos auteurs;
La période est longue, il faut reprendre haleine.
        Et puis votre cheval de bois,
        Vos héros avec leurs phalanges,
        Ce sont des contes plus étranges
Qu'un renard qui cajole un corbeau sur sa voix.
De plus, il vous sied mal d'écrire en si haut style.»
Eh bien! baissons d'un ton: La jalouse Amarylle
Songeait à son Alcippe, et croyait de ses soins
N'avoir que ses moutons et son chien pour témoins.
Tircis, qui l'aperçut, se glisse entre des saules;
Il entend la bergère adressant ces paroles
        Au doux Zéphire, et le priant
        De les porter à son amant.
        «Je vous arrête à cette rime,
        Dira mon censeur à l'instant,
        Je ne la tiens pas légitime,

I have made the wolf speak and the lamb reply;
I've gone further: in my pieces, trees and plants
have become creatures endowed with speech.
Who wouldn't take this to be a magic spell?
        "Truly," our critics will tell me,
        "you are speaking in a high and mighty way
        about five or six children's stories."
Carping critics, do you want some that are more legitimate
and in a loftier style? Here are some: "The Trojans,
after ten years of combat outside their walls,
had wearied the Greeks, who, in a thousand ways,
        by a thousand attacks, by a hundred battles,
had been unable to overcome that haughty city;
when a wooden horse invented by Minerva[7]
        with rare new skill
received within its enormous flanks the crafty Ulysses,
the brave Diomedes and the impulsive Ajax,
        whom this monstrous colossus
was to carry into Troy along with their squadrons,
handing over its very gods as a prey to their fury.
An unheard-of stratagem, which repaid
        the steadfastness and trouble of its builders."
"That's enough," one of our authors will tell me;
"the period is long, it's necessary to stop for breath.
        And, besides, your wooden horse,
        your heroes with their phalanxes,
        are tales even stranger
than a fox flattering a crow about his voice.
Furthermore, it ill becomes you to write in such a lofty style."
All right! Let's lower our tone one degree: "Jealous Amaryllis
was daydreaming about her Alcippus, and thought she had
only her sheep and her dog as witnesses of her affection.
Tircis, who noticed her, hid himself among willow trees;
he heard the shepherdess addressing these words
        to gentle Zephyr, asking him
        to carry them to her lover."
        "I won't let you get past that rhyme,"
        my critic will immediately say;
        "I don't consider it an acceptable one,

---

[7] Goddess of wisdom, equivalent to the Greek Athene.

Ni d'une assez grande vertu.
Remettez, pour le mieux, ces deux vers à la fonte.»
Maudit censeur, te tairas-tu?
Ne saurais-je achever mon conte?
C'est un dessein très dangereux
Que d'entreprendre de te plaire.
Les délicats sont malheureux:
Rien ne saurait les satisfaire.

# Les deux taureaux et une grenouille

Deux taureaux combattaient à qui posséderait
Une génisse avec l'empire.
Une grenouille en soupirait.
«Qu'avez-vous? se mit à lui dire
Quelqu'un du peuple croassant.
– Et ne voyez-vous pas, dit-elle,
Que la fin de cette querelle
Sera l'exil de l'un; que l'autre, le chassant,
Le fera renoncer aux campagnes fleuries?
Il ne régnera plus sur l'herbe des prairies,
Viendra dans nos marais régner sur les roseaux,
Et, nous foulant aux pieds jusques au fond des eaux,

Tantôt l'une, et puis l'autre, il faudra qu'on pâtisse
Du combat qu'a causé madame la génisse.»
Cette crainte était de bon sens.
L'un des taureaux en leur demeure
S'alla cacher à leurs dépens:
Il en écrasait vingt par heure.
Hélas! on voit que de tout temps
Les petits ont pâti des sottises des grands.

and I don't find it forceful enough.
To improve things, recast those two lines."
    Accursed critic, won't you be still?
    Can't I finish my story?
    It's a very dangerous plan
    to undertake to please you.
    Fastidious people are unfortunate:
    nothing can satisfy them.


## *The Two Bulls and a Frog*

Two bulls were fighting for the possession
    of a heifer and control of their territory.
    A frog was heaving sighs over this.
    "What's wrong with you?" one of the croaking folk
    started saying to her.
    "Don't you see," she said,
    "that the upshot of this dispute
will be the exile of one of them; that the other, driving him away,
will make him give up the flowery countryside?
He will no longer reign over the grass of the meadows,
he will come to our marshes to reign over the reeds;
and, when he tramples us underfoot down to the very bottom of
                                                    the water,
now one of us and now another, we will have to suffer
from the fight brought on by Madame Heifer."
    That fear was well founded.
    One of the bulls went off to hide
    in their home to their cost:
    he would crush twenty of them every hour.
    Alas! It's clear that at all times
humble folk have suffered from the follies of the great.

# Le lion et le moucheron

«Va-t'en, chétif insecte, excrément de la terre!»
    C'est en ces mots que le lion
    Parlait un jour au moucheron.
    L'autre lui déclara la guerre.
«Penses-tu, lui dit-il, que ton titre de roi
    Me fasse peur, ni me soucie?
    Un bœuf est plus puissant que toi,
    Je le mène à ma fantaisie.»
    A peine il achevait ces mots
    Que lui-même il sonna la charge,
    Fut le trompette et le héros.
    Dans l'abord il se met au large,
    Puis prend son temps, fond sur le cou
    Du lion, qu'il rend presque fou.
Le quadrupède écume, et son œil étincelle;
Il rugit, on se cache, on tremble à l'environ;
    Et cette alarme universelle
    Est l'ouvrage d'un moucheron.
Un avorton de mouche en cent lieux le harcèle,
Tantôt pique l'échine, et tantôt le museau,
    Tantôt entre au fond du naseau.
La rage alors se trouve à son faîte montée.
L'invisible ennemi triomphe, et rit de voir
Qu'il n'est griffe ni dent en la bête irritée
Qui de la mettre en sang ne fasse son devoir.
Le malheureux lion se déchire lui-même,
Fait résonner sa queue à l'entour de ses flancs,
Bat l'air, qui n'en peut mais; et sa fureur extrême
Le fatigue, l'abat; le voilà sur les dents.
L'insecte du combat se retire avec gloire:
Comme il sonna la charge, il sonne la victoire,
Va partout l'annoncer, et rencontre en chemin
    L'embuscade d'une araignée:
    Il y rencontre aussi sa fin.

# The Lion and the Gnat

"Off with you, puny insect, scum of the earth!"
    It was in those terms that the lion
    spoke to the gnat one day.
    The other declared war on him.
"Do you think," he said to him, "that your title of king
    frightens me or worries me?
    An ox is more powerful than you are,
    and I can lead him around just as I like."
    Hardly had he finished uttering those words
    when he sounded the charge himself,
    acting as both bugler and hero.
    When first facing the enemy, he keeps at a distance,
    then, seeing his opportunity, he swoops onto the neck
    of the lion, whom he drives nearly crazy.
The quadruped foams at the mouth, and his eyes flash;
he roars; all around other animals hide and tremble.
    And that universal alarm
    is the doing of a gnat.
An undersized fly torments him in a hundred spots,
now stinging his back, now his muzzle,
    now entering deep into his nostril.
Then his rage rises to its peak.
The invisible enemy triumphs, and laughs to see
that there is no claw or tooth in the harassed beast
that is not doing its job of making him bleed.
The miserable lion tears himself apart,
makes his tail slap both his sides noisily,
thrashes the air, which is not to blame; and his extreme furor
tires him, fells him; there he is, completely worn out.
The insect withdraws from battle covered with glory:
just as he sounded the charge, now he blows a victory call,
goes off to announce it everywhere, and on his path meets with
    a spider's ambush:
    there he also meets with his end.

Quelle chose par là nous peut être enseignée?
J'en vois deux, dont l'une est qu'entre nos ennemis,
Les plus à craindre sont souvent les plus petits;
L'autre, qu'aux grands périls tel a pu se soustraire
  Qui périt pour la moindre affaire.


# *Le lion et le rat*

Il faut autant qu'on peut obliger tout le monde:
On a souvent besoin d'un plus petit que soi.
De cette vérité deux fables feront foi,
  Tant la chose en preuves abonde.
  Entre les pattes d'un lion
Un rat sortit de terre assez à l'étourdie.
Le roi des animaux, en cette occasion,
Montra ce qu'il était, et lui donna la vie.
  Ce bienfait ne fut pas perdu.
  Quelqu'un aurait-il jamais cru
  Qu'un lion d'un rat eût affaire?
Cependant il avint qu'au sortir des forêts
  Ce lion fut pris dans des rets
Dont ses rugissements ne le purent défaire.
Sire rat accourut, et fit tant par ses dents
Qu'une maille rongée emporta tout l'ouvrage.

  Patience et longueur de temps
  Font plus que force ni que rage.

What can be taught us by this?
I see two lessons, of which one is that, among our enemies,
the smallest are often the most to be feared;
the second is that men have been able to escape great dangers
    and have then succumbed to the merest trifle.

## *The Lion and the Rat*

One ought as far as possible to do favors for everyone:
one often has need of someone smaller than oneself.
Two fables attest to this truth,[8]
    so abundant are the proofs of the matter.
    Between the paws of a lion
a rat emerged from the ground quite thoughtlessly.
The king of beasts on this occasion
showed the stuff he was made of, and granted him his life.
    This good deed wasn't wasted.
    Would anyone ever have thought
    that a lion might have need of a rat?
All the same it came about that, on leaving the forest,
    this lion was caught in some nets
that his roars were unable to tear apart.
Sir Rat came to his aid and applied his teeth so effectively
that a gnawed-through mesh put the whole contraption out of
                    commission.[9]

    Patience and the passing of time
    do more than strength or fury.

---

[8] The companion fable on this theme, "The Dove and the Ant," is not included in the present selection.

[9] A very literal rendering might be: "captured the entire outworks of the fortification."

# La chatte métamorphosée en femme

Un homme chérissait éperdument sa chatte;
Il la trouvait mignonne, et belle, et délicate,
    Qui miaulait d'un ton fort doux.
    Il était plus fou que les fous.
Cet homme donc, par prières, par larmes,
    Par sortilèges et par charmes,
    Fait tant qu'il obtient du destin
    Que sa chatte en un beau matin
    Devient femme, et le matin même
    Maître sot en fait sa moitié.
    Le voilà fou d'amour extrême,
    De fou qu'il était d'amitié.
    Jamais la dame la plus belle
    Ne charma tant son favori
    Que fait cette épouse nouvelle
    Son hypocondre de mari.
    Il l'amadoue, elle le flatte;
    Il n'y trouve plus rien de chatte,
    Et poussant l'erreur jusqu'au bout,
    La croit femme en tout et partout,
Lorsque quelques souris qui rongeaient de la natte
Troublèrent le plaisir des nouveaux mariés.
    Aussitôt la femme est sur pieds:
    Elle manqua son aventure.
Souris de revenir, femme d'être en posture.
  Pour cette fois elle accourut à point:
    Car, ayant changé de figure,
    Les souris ne la craignaient point.
    Ce lui fut toujours une amorce,
    Tant le naturel a de force.
Il se moque de tout, certain âge accompli:
Le vase est imbibé, l'étoffe a pris son pli.
    En vain de son train ordinaire
    On le veut désaccoutumer.
    Quelque chose qu'on puisse faire,
    On ne saurait le réformer.
    Coups de fourche ni d'étrivières

# *The Cat Transformed into a Woman*

A man was excessively fond of his female cat;
he found her dainty, and beautiful, and delicate,
    and thought her meowing was very sweet.
    He was madder than any madman.
Well, this man, by dint of praying, weeping,
    spells and charms,
    perseveres until he obtains his wish from Destiny
    and one fine morning his cat
    becomes a woman; and that very morning
    the supreme fool makes her his better half.
    There he is, crazy with extreme love,
    just as he was formerly crazy with fondness.
    Never did the most beautiful lady
    charm her favored lover as much
    as this new bride
    charms her eccentric husband.
    He wheedled her, she flattered him;
    he found nothing catlike in her any more,
    and, carrying his folly to extremes,
    he believed she was a woman totally in all ways,
when some mice who were gnawing a mat
disturbed the bliss of the newlyweds.
    At once the woman rose to her feet:
    she was out of luck.
The mice returned, the woman remained poised.
  This time she dashed over at just the right moment:
    for, since she had changed her shape,
    the mice had no fear of her.
    They were always a lure for her,
    so much strength is there in one's inborn nature.
When one has reached a certain age, it defies all else:
the vessel is impregnated, the crease won't come out of the cloth.
    It is in vain that one tries to break it of its habits
    and abandon its customary routine.
    Whatever one may do,
    one can't reform it.
    Neither pitchfork blows nor blows from leather straps

Ne lui font changer de manières;
Et, fussiez-vous embâtonnés,
Jamais vous n'en serez les maîtres.
Qu'on lui ferme la porte au nez,
Il reviendra par les fenêtres.

# Le meunier, son fils, et l'âne

A. M. D. M.

L'invention des arts étant un droit d'aînesse,
Nous devons l'apologue à l'ancienne Grèce.
Mais ce champ ne se peut tellement moissonner
Que les derniers venus n'y trouvent à glaner.
La feinte est un pays plein de terres désertes.
Tous les jours nos auteurs y font des découvertes.
Je t'en veux dire un trait assez bien inventé;
Autrefois à Racan Malherbe l'a conté.
Ces deux rivaux d'Horace, héritiers de sa lyre,
Disciples d'Apollon, nos maîtres, pour mieux dire,
Se rencontrant un jour tout seuls et sans témoins,
(Comme ils se confiaient leurs pensers et leurs soins)
Racan commence ainsi: «Dites-moi, je vous prie,
Vous qui devez savoir les choses de la vie,
Qui par tous ses degrés avez déjà passé,
Et que rien ne doit fuir en cet âge avancé,
A quoi me résoudrai-je? Il est temps que j'y pense.
Vous connaissez mon bien, mon talent, ma naissance.
Dois-je dans la province établir mon séjour,
Prendre emploi dans l'armée, ou bien charge à la cour?
Tout au monde est mêlé d'amertume et de charmes.
La guerre a ses douceurs, l'hymen a ses alarmes.

make it change its ways;
and, even if you were armed with sticks,
you'd never get the better of it.
Shut the door in its face
and it'll come back in through the window.


# *The Miller, His Son and the Donkey*

TO M[ONSIEUR] D[E] M[AUCROIX][10]

Since the invention of the arts is a function of seniority,
we owe the fable to ancient Greece.
But this field cannot be so thoroughly reaped
that the newest comers can find nothing to glean.
Fiction is a land full of unexplored territory.
Every day our authors make discoveries there.
I want to tell you one such story that was finely conceived;
Malherbe told it to Racan.[11]
Those two rivals of Horace,[12] inheritors of his lyrical skill,
disciples of Apollo[13]—our masters, to state it more properly—
finding themselves one day all alone and without witnesses
(for they confided their thoughts and concerns to each other),
Racan began as follows: "Tell me, I beg you,
you who ought to know about everything in life,
since you have already passed through all its stages
and nothing should elude you at your advanced age,
what course should I resolve on? It's time for me to think about it.
You know what property I own, my talent, my birth.
Should I take up residence in the provinces,
buy a rank in the army or a position at court?
Everything in the world is a mixture of bitterness and attractiveness.
War has its pleasures, marriage has its battles.

---

[10] François de Maucroix, a lifelong friend of the poet.

[11] Two eminent poets of the early seventeenth century: François de Malherbe (1555–1628) and his chief disciple, Honorat de Bueil, Marquis de Racan (1589–1670).

[12] Roman poet (65–8 B.C.)

[13] God of poetry, as (at the end of the poem) Mars is god of war, and Cupid is god of love.

Si je suivais mon goût, je saurais où buter;
Mais j'ai les miens, la cour, le peuple à contenter.»
Malherbe là-dessus: «Contenter tout le monde!
Écoutez ce récit avant que je réponde.

«J'ai lu dans quelque endroit qu'un meunier et son fils,
L'un vieillard, l'autre enfant, non pas des plus petits,
Mais garçon de quinze ans, si j'ai bonne mémoire,
Allaient vendre leur âne un certain jour de foire.
Afin qu'il fût plus frais et de meilleur débit,
On lui lia les pieds, on vous le suspendit;
Puis cet homme et son fils le portent comme un lustre:
Pauvres gens, idiots, couple ignorant et rustre.
Le premier qui les vit de rire s'éclata.
«Quelle farce, dit-il, vont jouer ces gens-là?
«Le plus âne des trois n'est pas celui qu'on pense.»
Le meunier à ces mots connaît son ignorance.
Il met sur pieds sa bête, et la fait détaler.
L'âne, qui goûtait fort l'autre façon d'aller,
Se plaint en son patois. Le meunier n'en a cure.
Il fait monter son fils, il suit, et d'aventure
Passent trois bons marchands. Cet objet leur déplut.
Le plus vieux au garçon s'écria tant qu'il put:
«Oh là! oh! descendez, que l'on ne vous le dise,
«Jeune homme qui menez laquais à barbe grise.
«C'était à vous de suivre, au vieillard de monter.
«—Messieurs, dit le meunier, il vous faut contenter.»
L'enfant met pied à terre, et puis le vieillard monte,
Quand, trois filles passant, l'une dit: «C'est grand'honte
«Qu'il faille voir ainsi clocher ce jeune fils,
«Tandis que ce nigaud, comme un évêque assis,
«Fait le veau sur son âne, et pense être bien sage.
«—Il n'est, dit le meunier, plus de veaux à mon âge.
«Passez votre chemin, la fille, et m'en croyez.»
Après maints quolibets coup sur coup renvoyés,
L'homme crut avoir tort, et mit son fils en croupe.

Au bout de trente pas, une troisième troupe
Trouve encore à gloser. L'un dit: «Ces gens sont fous,
«Le baudet n'en peut plus, il mourra sous leurs coups.
«Hé quoi! charger ainsi cette pauvre bourrique!
«N'ont-ils point de pitié de leur vieux domestique?

If I followed my own preference, I'd know what to aim at;
but I have to satisfy my family, the court and the public."
Whereupon Malherbe says: "Satisfy everybody!
Listen to this tale before I give my answer.

I've read somewhere that a miller and his son,
one an old man, the other a child—not of the youngest,
but a lad of fifteen, if I recall correctly—
were going to sell their donkey on a certain market day.
To keep him healthier and easier to sell,
they tied his feet and hung him up;
then that man and his son carried him like a chandelier:
poor people, fools, an ignorant hayseed pair.
The first person who saw them burst out laughing.
'What farce,' he said, 'are those people going to act?
The biggest donkey of the three isn't the one you might think.'
Hearing these words, the miller recognizes his ignorance.
He sets his animal on its feet and makes it scurry along.
The donkey, who really liked the other way of traveling,
complains in his dialect. The miller pays it no heed.
He has his son mount, he walks behind, and by chance
three well-to-do merchants come along. That sight displeased them.
The oldest one shouted to the boy as loud as he could:
'Hey there! Hey! Get down, you shouldn't need to be told,
you youngster leading a graybearded lackey!
It was your place to follow behind, the old man's to ride.'
'Gentlemen,' said the miller, 'it behooves us to satisfy you.'
The child sets foot on the ground and then the old man mounts,
when, three girls passing by, one of them says: 'It's an awful shame
for us to have to see that young boy limping behind that way
while this fool, sitting like a bishop,
lolls on his donkey like a calf, and think he's really wise.'
The miller says: 'There are no more calves at my age.
Get along with you, you lady, and take my word for it.'
After many exchanges of sarcastic remarks one after the other,
the man was convinced he was wrong and made his son ride
                              behind him.
After they had ridden thirty paces, a third group
still found something to criticize. One said: 'These people are crazy;
the donkey is worn out, he'll die from their exactions.
How do you like that! Loading down that poor ass that way!
Don't they have any compassion for their old servant?

«Sans doute qu'à la foire ils vont vendre sa peau.
«—Parbieu, dit le meunier, est bien fou du cerveau
«Qui prétend contenter tout le monde et son père.
«Essayons toutefois si par quelque manière
«Nous en viendrons à bout.» Ils descendent tous deux.
L'âne, se prélassant, marche seul devant eux.
Un quidam les rencontre, et dit: «Est-ce la mode
«Que baudet aille à l'aise, et meunier s'incommode?

«Qui de l'âne ou du maître est fait pour se lasser?
«Je conseille à ces gens de le faire enchâsser.
«Ils usent leurs souliers, et conservent leur âne:
«Nicolas au rebours, car, quand il va voir Jeanne,
«Il monte sur sa bête; et la chanson le dit.
«Beau trio de baudets!» Le meunier repartit:
«Je suis âne, il est vrai, j'en conviens, je l'avoue;
«Mais que dorénavant on me blâme, on me loue;
«Qu'on dise quelque chose, ou qu'on ne dise rien,
«J'en veux faire à ma tête.» Il le fit, et fit bien.

«Quant à vous, suivez Mars, ou l'Amour, ou le Prince;
Allez, venez, courez, demeurez en province;
Prenez femme, abbaye, emploi, gouvernement:
Les gens en parleront, n'en doutez nullement.»

# Le renard et le bouc

Capitaine renard allait de compagnie
Avec son ami bouc des plus haut encornés.
Celui-ci ne voyait pas plus loin que son nez;
L'autre était passé maître en fait de tromperie.
La soif les obligea de descendre en un puits.
        Là chacun d'eux se désaltère.
Après qu'abondamment tous deux en eurent pris,
Le renard dit au bouc: «Que ferons-nous, compère?
Ce n'est pas tout de boire, il faut sortir d'ici.

They must surely be going to sell his hide at the market.'
'Damn me,' says the miller, 'you've got to be crazy in the head
if you try to satisfy everybody and his father.
All the same, let's try and see if there's any way
for us to manage the matter.' Both of them dismount.
The donkey, striding majestically, walks alone in front of them.
Some fellow or other meets up with them and says: 'Is it the fashion
for Mister Donkey to walk free and easy and Mister Miller to be
                                        inconvenienced?
Which one is made for getting tired out, the donkey or his master?
I advise these people to have him enshrined like a relic.
They're wearing out their shoes and preserving their donkey:
Nicolas in reverse, because, when he goes to see Jeanne,
he mounts his animal; and the song says so.[14]
Fine trio of donkeys!' The miller replied:
'I'm a donkey, it's true, I agree, I admit it;
But from now on, whether they blame me or praise me;
Whether they say something or say nothing,
I want to do just as I please.' He did so, and was right to do so.

As for you, follow Mars or Cupid or our ruler;
go, come, run, stay in the provinces;
take a wife, an abbey, a position or a governorship:
people will discuss it, have not the slightest doubt about it."


## *The Fox and the Billygoat*

Captain Fox was walking in company
with his friend, the goat of very lofty horns.
The latter saw no further than the end of his nose;
the former was a past master when it came to deceit.
Thirst compelled them to go down into a well.
      There each of them quenched his thirst.
After both had drunk from it copiously,
the fox said to the goat: "What shall we do, friend?
Drinking isn't everything, we've got to get out of here.

---

[14] Refers to a humorous song of the day, in which a rejected lover states that he will
ride away to his death on a donkey.

Lève tes pieds en haut, et tes cornes aussi:
Mets-les contre le mur. Le long de ton échine
  Je grimperai premièrement;
  Puis sur tes cornes m'élevant,
  A l'aide de cette machine
  De ce lieu-ci je sortirai.
  Après quoi je t'en tirerai.
—Par ma barbe, dit l'autre, il est bon; et je loue
  Les gens bien sensés comme toi.
  Je n'aurais jamais, quant à moi,
  Trouvé ce secret, je l'avoue.»
Le renard sort du puits, laisse son compagnon
  Et vous lui fait un beau sermon
  Pour l'exhorter à patience.
«Si le Ciel t'eût, dit-il, donné par excellence
Autant de jugement que de barbe au menton,
  Tu n'aurais pas à la légère
Descendu dans ce puits. Or adieu, j'en suis hors.
Tâche de t'en tirer, et fais tous tes efforts:
  Car, pour moi, j'ai certaine affaire
Qui ne me permet pas d'arrêter en chemin.»
En toute chose il faut considérer la fin.

# Le renard et les raisins

Certain renard gascon, d'autres disent normand,
Mourant presque de faim, vit au haut d'une treille
  Des raisins mûrs apparemment
  Et couverts d'une peau vermeille.
Le galant en eût fait volontiers un repas;
  Mais, comme il n'y pouvait atteindre:
«Ils sont trop verts, dit-il, et bons pour des goujats.»
  Fit-il pas mieux que de se plaindre?

Raise your feet up, and your horns, too:
place them against the wall. I shall climb up
      first along your spine;
      then, raising myself on your horns,
      with the aid of that device
      I shall get out of this place.
      After that I'll pull you out."
"By my beard," said the other, "that's good; and I praise
      people with good sense like you.
      As for me, I would never have
      thought of that stratagem, I admit it."
The fox gets out of the well, abandons his companion
      and preaches a lovely sermon
      to encourage him to be patient.
"If," he said, "heaven had given you in the highest degree
as much common sense as you have beard on your chin,
      you wouldn't have so carelessly
descended into this well. Goodbye now, I'm on the outside.
Try to pull yourself out, make every effort:
      because, as for me, I have a certain piece of business
that won't allow me to tarry along the way."
In every matter one has to take the outcome into account.


## The Fox and the Grapes

A certain fox from Gascony, others say from Normandy,[15]
nearly dying of hunger, saw at the top of an arbor
      grapes that were clearly ripe,
      covered with a vermilion skin.
The sharpster would gladly have made a meal of them;
      but, since he couldn't reach them:
"They're too green," he said, "and only good for clodhoppers."
      Wasn't that better than just lamenting?

---

[15] One of La Fontaine's witty attempts to give an ancient fable a French setting. According to traditional stereotypes, if the fox were a Gascon, he would be boastful and blustering; if a Norman, canny and devious.

## Le lion devenu vieux

Le lion, terreur des forêts,
Chargé d'ans, et pleurant son antique prouesse,
Fut enfin attaqué par ses propres sujets,
　　Devenus forts par sa faiblesse.
Le cheval s'approchant lui donne un coup de pied,
Le loup un coup de dent, le bœuf un coup de corne.
Le malheureux lion, languissant, triste et morne,
Peut à peine rugir, par l'âge estropié.
Il attend son destin, sans faire aucunes plaintes,
Quand, voyant l'âne même à son antre accourir:
«Ah! c'est trop, lui dit-il: je voulais bien mourir;
Mais c'est mourir deux fois que souffrir tes atteintes.»

## Le lion amoureux

### A Mademoiselle de Sévigné

Sévigné de qui les attraits
Servent aux Grâces de modèle,
Et qui naquîtes toute belle,
A votre indifférence près,
Pourriez-vous être favorable
Aux jeux innocents d'une fable,
Et voir sans vous épouvanter
Un lion qu'amour sut dompter?
Amour est un étrange maître.
Heureux qui peut ne le connaître
Que par récit, lui ni ses coups!
Quand on en parle devant vous,
Si la vérité vous offense,
La fable au moins se peut souffrir.

# The Lion Who Had Grown Old

The lion, terror of the forest,
laden with years and lamenting his former prowess,
was finally attacked by his own subjects,
    who had become strong through his weakness.
The horse came up to him and gave him a kick;
the wolf gave him a bite; the ox, a blow with his horn.
The wretched lion, weak with illness, sad and gloomy,
could barely roar, crippled as he was with age.
He awaited his fate without making further lament,
when, seeing even the donkey come running to his den:
"Oh, that's too much," he said to him; "I was willing to die;
but to undergo your mistreatment is like dying twice."

# The Lion in Love

## TO MADEMOISELLE DE SÉVIGNÉ[16]

Sévigné, whose charms
are a model for the Graces,
born totally beautiful
with the exception of your aloofness,
could you look with favor
on the innocent sport of a fable,
and, without being frightened, see
a lion that love was able to tame?
Love is a strange master.
Happy the man who can know him
only by hearsay, him and his deeds!
When someone speaks of him in your presence,
if the reality offends you,
a fable at least can be tolerated.

---

[16] The beautiful daughter (not yet married at this time) of the famous letter writer Madame de Sévigné (Marie de Rabutin-Chantal; 1626–1696).

Celle-ci prend bien l'assurance
De venir à vos pieds s'offrir,
Par zèle et par reconnaissance.

Du temps que les bêtes parlaient,
Les lions, entre autres, voulaient
Etre admis dans notre alliance.
Pourquoi non? puisque leur engeance
Valait la nôtre en ce temps-là,
Ayant courage, intelligence,
Et belle hure outre cela.
Voici comment il en alla.
Un lion de haut parentage,
En passant par un certain pré,
Rencontra bergère à son gré.
Il la demande en mariage.
Le père aurait fort souhaité
Quelque gendre un peu moins terrible.
La donner lui semblait bien dur;
La refuser n'était pas sûr;
Même un refus eût fait, possible,
Qu'on eût vu quelque beau matin
Un mariage clandestin:
Car outre qu'en toute manière
La belle était pour les gens fiers,
Fille se coiffe volontiers
D'amoureux à longue crinière.
Le père donc ouvertement
N'osant renvoyer notre amant,
Lui dit: «Ma fille est délicate;
Vos griffes la pourront blesser
Quand vous voudrez la caresser.
Permettez donc qu'à chaque patte
On vous les rogne, et pour les dents,
Qu'on vous les lime en même temps.
Vos baisers en seront moins rudes,
Et pour vous plus délicieux;
Car ma fille y répondra mieux,
Étant sans ces inquiétudes.»
Le lion consent à cela,
Tant son âme était aveuglée.
Sans dents ni griffes le voilà

This one summons up the boldness
to come and lay itself at your feet,
out of ardor and out of gratitude.

In the days when animals spoke,
the lions, among others, wished
to be allowed to intermarry with us.
Why not, since their species
was as good as ours in those days,
possessing courage, intelligence,
and good looks besides?
Here's how it came about.
A lion of noble birth,
passing through a certain meadow,
met a shepherdess he liked.
He asked for her hand in marriage.
Her father would greatly have wished
for some son-in-law a little less frightening.
To grant her hand seemed very harsh to him;
to refuse to grant it wasn't safe;
a rejection might even possibly have led
to the occurrence one fine morning
of a secret marriage:
for, besides the fact that in every way
the lovely girl favored proud and bold young men,
girls easily become infatuated
with lovers who wear a long mane.
Therefore the father, not daring
to reject our suitor openly,
said to him: "My daughter is delicate;
your claws may wound her
whenever you wish to caress her.
Thus, allow us, on each paw,
to clip them for you, and as for your teeth,
to file them down for you at the same time.
That will make your kisses less rough
and more delightful to you;
for my daughter will respond to them more warmly,
being free of those worries."
The lion consented to that,
so blinded was his soul.
There he was without teeth or claws

Comme place démantelée.
On lâcha sur lui quelques chiens,
Il fit fort peu de résistance.
Amour, amour, quand tu nous tiens,
On peut bien dire: Adieu prudence.

## Le jardinier et son seigneur

Un amateur du jardinage,
Demi-bourgeois, demi-manant,
Possédait en certain village
Un jardin assez propre, et le clos attenant.
Il avait de plant vif fermé cette étendue;
Là croissait à plaisir l'oseille et la laitue,
De quoi faire à Margot, pour sa fête, un bouquet,
Peu de jasmin d'Espagne, et force serpolet.

Cette félicité par un lièvre troublée
Fit qu'au seigneur du bourg notre homme se plaignit.
«Ce maudit animal vient prendre sa goulée
Soir et matin, dit-il, et des pièges se rit:
Les pierres, les bâtons y perdent leur crédit.
Il est sorcier, je crois. – Sorcier? je l'en défie,
Repartit le seigneur. Fût-il diable, Miraut,
En dépit de ses tours, l'attrapera bientôt.
Je vous en déferai, bon homme, sur ma vie.
– Et quand? – Et dès demain, sans tarder plus longtemps.»
La partie ainsi faite, il vient avec ses gens:
«Çà, déjeunons, dit-il; vos poulets sont-ils tendres?
La fille du logis, qu'on vous voie, approchez.
Quand la marierons-nous? quand aurons-nous des gendres?
Bon homme, c'est ce coup qu'il faut, vous m'entendez,
        Qu'il faut fouiller à l'escarcelle.»
Disant ces mots, il fait connaissance avec elle,
        Auprès de lui la fait asseoir,
Prend une main, un bras, lève un coin du mouchoir;
        Toutes sottises dont la belle

like a razed fortification.
Several dogs were set upon him;
he offered very little resistance.
Love, love, when you have hold of us,
one may well say: "Farewell, prudence."

# The Gardener and the Squire

A lover of gardening,
  living part of the time in the city and part in the country,
  possessed in a certain village
a very neat garden and the cultivated land adjacent to it.
He had enclosed this expanse with live hedges;
there, there grew freely sorrel and lettuce,
and the makings of a birthday bouquet for Margot,
not much in the way of Spanish jasmine, but a great deal of wild
                                       thyme.

The disturbance of this felicity by a hare
led our man to complain to the local squire.
"That cursed animal comes and eats his fill
evening and morning," he said, "and makes a mockery of my traps:
stones and sticks lose their prestige where he's concerned.
He's a magician, I think." "A magician? I'll show him!"
replied the squire. "Even if he were the devil, Miraut[17]
will soon catch him, despite his tricks.
I'll rid you of him, my good man, I stake my life on it."
"When?" "As soon as tomorrow, without waiting longer."
The arrangement thus made, he arrives with his men:
"Now let's have lunch," he says; "are your chickens tender?
Young lady of the house, let's see you, come near.
When will we marry her off? When will we have sons-in-law?
My good man, you get me, now is the time one must
    dig down deep into one's purse."
Saying these words, he makes her acquaintance
    and makes her sit down beside him,
takes her hand, her arm, lifts a corner of her neckerchief:
    all foolish actions which the lovely girl

---

[17] The name of a hound.

Se défend avec grand respect;
Tant qu'au père à la fin cela devient suspect.
Cependant on fricasse, on se rue en cuisine.
«De quand sont vos jambons? Ils ont fort bonne mine.
—Monsieur, ils sont à vous.—Vraiment! dit le Seigneur;
    Je les reçois, et de bon cœur.»
Il déjeune très bien, aussi fait sa famille,
Chiens, chevaux et valets, tous gens bien endentés;
Il commande chez l'hôte, y prend des libertés,
    Boit son vin, caresse sa fille.
L'embarras des chasseurs succède au déjeuné.
    Chacun s'anime et se prépare:
Les trompes et les cors font un tel tintamarre
    Que le bon homme est étonné.
Le pis fut que l'on mit en piteux équipage
Le pauvre potager; adieu planches, carreaux;
    Adieu chicorée et porreaux;
    Adieu de quoi mettre au potage.
Le lièvre était gîté dessous un maître chou.
On le quête, on le lance, il s'enfuit par un trou,
Non pas trou, mais trouée, horrible et large plaie
    Que l'on fit à la pauvre haie
Par ordre du seigneur: car il eût été mal
Qu'on n'eût pu du jardin sortir tout à cheval.

Le bon homme disait: «Ce sont là jeux de prince.»
Mais on le laissait dire; et les chiens et les gens
Firent plus de dégât en une heure de temps
    Que n'en auraient fait en cent ans
    Tous les lièvres de la province.

Petits princes, videz vos débats entre vous:
De recourir aux rois vous seriez de grands fous.
Il ne les faut jamais engager dans vos guerres,
    Ni les faire entrer sur vos terres.

wards off, but very respectfully;
this goes on so long that the father finally grows suspicious.
Meanwhile there is fricasseeing and a mad rush in the kitchen.
"How fresh are your hams? They really look good."
"Sir, they are yours." "Really?" says the squire;
      "I accept them from the bottom of my heart."
He makes a very good lunch, and so do his followers,
dogs, horses and servants, all folk with a hearty appetite;
he gives orders in his host's house, he takes liberties there,
      drinks his wine and fondles his daughter.
The nuisance caused by the hunters follows that of the luncheon.
      Everyone becomes lively and prepares:
the various hunting horns make such a din
      that our good man is stunned.
The worst of it was that the poor kitchen garden was reduced
to a piteous state: farewell to flowerbeds and gridrule plantings;
      farewell to chicory and leeks;
      farewell to all that goes into a hearty soup.
The hare had his burrow under a gigantic cabbage.
They sought him, they started him, he escaped through a hole,
not a hole but a breach, a terrible, wide wound
      made in the poor hedge
by order of the squire: because it would have been unseemly
if they hadn't been able to exit from the garden while still on
                                                    horseback.
The good man said: "Those are princely pastimes."
But they just let him talk: both the dogs and the men
did more damage in an hour's time
      than all the hares in the province
      could have done in a hundred years.

Petty rulers, settle your disputes between yourselves:
you'd be raving mad to have recourse to kings.
You should never involve them in your wars,
      or let them enter your territory.

# Le chameau et les bâtons flottants

Le premier qui vit un chameau
S'enfuit à cet objet nouveau;
Le second approcha; le troisième osa faire
Un licou pour le dromadaire.
L'accoutumance ainsi nous rend tout familier.
Ce qui nous paraissait terrible et singulier
S'apprivoise avec notre vue,
Quand ce vient à la continue.
Et puisque nous voici tombés sur ce sujet,
On avait mis des gens au guet,
Qui, voyant sur les eaux de loin certain objet,
Ne purent s'empêcher de dire
Que c'était un puissant navire.
Quelques moments après, l'objet devint brûlot,
Et puis nacelle, et puis ballot,
Enfin bâtons flottant sur l'onde.
J'en sais beaucoup de par le monde
A qui ceci conviendrait bien:
De loin c'est quelque chose, et de près ce n'est rien.

# Le cheval s'étant voulu venger du cerf

De tout temps les chevaux ne sont nés pour les hommes.
Lorsque le genre humain de gland se contentait,
Ane, cheval, et mule aux forêts habitait;
Et l'on ne voyait point, comme au siècle où nous sommes,
Tant de selles et tant de bâts,
Tant de harnais pour les combats,
Tant de chaises, tant de carrosses;
Comme aussi ne voyait-on pas

# The Camel and the Floating Sticks

The first man who ever saw a camel
ran away at that unaccustomed sight;
the second man approached; the third was bold enough to make
    a halter for the dromedary.
Thus familiarization puts us totally at ease.
What formerly appeared terrible and unusual
    becomes ordinary when we observe it
    regularly over a period of time.
And since we have happened upon this topic:
    Men stationed on lookout duty by the ocean,
seeing a certain object on the water at a distance,
    couldn't refrain from announcing
    that it was a mighty warship.
A few moments later, the object became a fire-ship,[17a]
    and then a dinghy, and then a bundle,
    finally some sticks floating on the waves.
    I know many people in society
    to whom this could be fittingly applied:
from a distance they're something, but, up close, nothing at all.

# The Horse Who Had Wanted to Take Revenge on the Deer

Horses haven't always been created for man.
When the human race was satisfied with acorns,
the donkey, horse and mule lived in the woods;
and one didn't see, as one does in the age in which we live,
    so many riding saddles and so many pack saddles,
    so much harness for battle,
    so many coaches, so many carriages,
    just as one didn't see

---

[17a] A vessel set adrift to destroy other ships with the inflammable materials it contains.

Tant de festins et tant de noces.
Or un cheval eut alors différend
    Avec un cerf plein de vitesse:
Et ne pouvant l'attraper en courant,
Il eut recours à l'homme, implora son adresse.
L'homme lui mit un frein, lui sauta sur le dos,
    Ne lui donna point de repos
Que le cerf ne fût pris et n'y laissât la vie.
    Et cela fait, le cheval remercie
L'homme son bienfaiteur, disant: «Je suis à vous,
Adieu. Je m'en retourne en mon séjour sauvage.
– Non pas cela, dit l'homme, il fait meilleur chez nous:
    Je vois trop quel est votre usage.
    Demeurez donc, vous serez bien traité,
    Et jusqu'au ventre en la litière.»

    Hélas! que sert la bonne chère
    Quand on n'a pas la liberté?
Le cheval s'aperçut qu'il avait fait folie;
Mais il n'était plus temps: déjà son écurie
    Était prête et toute bâtie.
    Il y mourut en traînant son lien.
Sage s'il eût remis une légère offense.
Quel que soit le plaisir que cause la vengeance,
C'est l'acheter trop cher, que l'acheter d'un bien
    Sans qui les autres ne sont rien.

## Le renard et le buste

Les grands, pour la plupart, sont masques de théâtre;
Leur apparence impose au vulgaire idolâtre.
L'âne n'en sait juger que par ce qu'il en voit.
Le renard au contraire à fond les examine,
Les tourne de tous sens; et quand il s'aperçoit
    Que leur fait n'est que bonne mine,
Il leur applique un mot qu'un buste de héros
    Lui fit dire fort à propos.
C'était un buste creux, et plus grand que nature.
Le renard, en louant l'effort de la sculpture,
*Belle tête,* dit-il, *mais de cervelle point.*
Combien de grands seigneurs sont bustes en ce point!

so many feasts and parties.
  Now, at that time a horse had a quarrel
    with a deer who was extremely swift:
  and, unable to catch up with him by running,
he sought the aid of the man and begged him to lend his skill.
The man put a bit in his mouth, leaped onto his back,
    and gave him no rest
until the deer was caught and paid with his life.
  And when that was done, the horse thanked
the man, his benefactor, saying: "I'm at your service,
goodbye. I'm returning to my wild haunts."
"Not at all," said the man, "life is better with us:
    I see all too well what use can be made of you.
  And so, stay, you'll be well treated,
    and up to your belly in stable litter."

    Alas! What use is good food
    when you don't have your freedom?
The horse realized that he had acted foolishly;
but by then it was too late: already his stable
    was ready and all built.
  He died there dragging his tether behind him.
How wise if he had forgiven that slight annoyance!
Whatever pleasure is derived from revenge,
it is too dearly bought when paid for with a blessing
    without which all others count for nothing.

## The Fox and the Bust

For the most part, the great of this world are masqueraders;
their outward appearance impresses hero-worshipping commoners.
The donkey can judge them only from what he sees of them.
The fox, on the other hand, examines them thoroughly,
turns them around and around; and when he perceives
    that their only strong point is their fine show,
he designates them by a phrase that the bust of a hero
    suggested to him most appropriately.
It was a hollow bust, and larger than life.
The fox, while praising the sculptor's skill,
said: "A lovely head, but no trace of a brain."
How many great lords are busts on that score!

## *Le loup, la chèvre, et le chevreau*

La bique allant remplir sa traînante mamelle
    Et paître l'herbe nouvelle,
    Ferma sa porte au loquet,
    Non sans dire à son biquet:
    «Gardez-vous sur votre vie
    D'ouvrir, que l'on ne vous die,
    Pour enseigne et mot du guet:
    «Foin du loup et de sa race!»
    Comme elle disait ces mots,
    Le loup, de fortune passe.
    Il les recueille à propos,
    Et les garde en sa mémoire.
    La bique, comme on peut croire,
    N'avait pas vu le glouton.
Dès qu'il la voit partie, il contrefait son ton;
    Et d'une voix papelarde,
Il demande qu'on ouvre, en disant: «Foin du loup!»,
    Et croyant entrer tout d'un coup.
Le biquet soupçonneux par la fente regarde.
«Montrez-moi patte blanche, ou je n'ouvrirai point»,
S'écria-t-il d'abord (patte blanche est un point
Chez les loups, comme on sait, rarement en usage).
Celui-ci, fort surpris d'entendre ce langage,
Comme il était venu s'en retourna chez soi.
Où serait le biquet s'il eût ajouté foi
    Au mot du guet, que de fortune
    Notre loup avait entendu?
    Deux sûretés valent mieux qu'une;
Et le trop en cela ne fut jamais perdu.

# The Wolf, the Goat and the Kid

The nannygoat, going out to refill her slack udder
    and graze on the fresh grass,
    locked her door with the latch,
    not without saying to her kid:
    "On peril of your life make sure not to
    open the door, unless someone says to you,
    as a rallying cry and password:
    'To hell with the wolf and his breed!' "
    While she was saying these words,
    the wolf just happened to come by.
    He heard them at the right moment,
    and stored them in his memory.
    The goat, as is easy to believe,
    hadn't seen the glutton.
As soon as he saw that she was gone, he imitated her voice,
    and in sanctimonious tones
he asked to be let in, saying, "To hell with the wolf!"
    and thinking he'd be admitted at once.
The kid, suspicious, looked through the crack.
"Show me a white paw or I won't open up,"
he shouted first (white paws are a feature
rarely found among wolves, as is well known).
The wolf, extremely surprised to hear words of the sort,
went back home just as he had come.
Where would the kid be if he had lent credence
    to the password, which by mere accident
    our wolf had heard?
    Two safety measures are better than one;
and extra attention in such matters has never been wasted.

# *L'œil du maître*

Un cerf s'étant sauvé dans une étable à bœufs
    Fut d'abord averti par eux
    Qu'il cherchât un meilleur asile.
«Mes frères, leur dit-il, ne me décelez pas:
Je vous enseignerai les pâtis les plus gras;
Ce service vous peut quelque jour être utile;
    Et vous n'en aurez point regret.»
Les bœufs, à toutes fins, promirent le secret.
Il se cache en un coin, respire, et prend courage.
Sur le soir on apporte herbe fraîche et fourrage
    Comme l'on faisait tous les jours.
    L'on va, l'on vient, les valets font cent tours,

    L'intendant même: et pas un d'aventure
      N'aperçut ni cors ni ramure,
    Ni cerf enfin. L'habitant des forêts
Rend déjà grâce aux bœufs, attend dans cette étable
Que chacun retournant au travail de Cérès,
Il trouve pour sortir un moment favorable.
L'un des bœufs ruminant lui dit: «Cela va bien;
Mais quoi! l'homme aux cent yeux n'a pas fait sa revue.
    Je crains fort pour toi sa venue.
Jusque-là, pauvre cerf, ne te vante de rien.»
Là-dessus le maître entre et vient faire sa ronde.
    «Qu'est-ce ci? dit-il à son monde.
Je trouve bien peu d'herbe en tous ces râteliers.
Cette litière est vieille; allez vite aux greniers.
Je veux voir désormais vos bêtes mieux soignées.
Que coûte-t-il d'ôter toutes ces araignées?
Ne saurait-on ranger ces jougs et ces colliers?»
En regardant à tout, il voit une autre tête
Que celles qu'il voyait d'ordinaire en ce lieu.
Le cerf est reconnu; chacun prend un épieu;
    Chacun donne un coup à la bête.

# *The Eye of the Proprietor*

A deer, having taken refuge in a shed of oxen,
    was at first warned by them
    to look for a better hiding place.
"My brothers," he said to them, "don't give me away:
I'll show you where to find the lushest grazing grounds;
this favor may be useful to you some day;
    and you'll never regret it."
The oxen, all things considered, promised to keep his secret.
He hides in a corner, draws a free breath and takes courage.
Toward evening fresh grass and fodder are brought
    according to the daily routine.
  People come and go, the farmhands walk around a hundred
                                times,
    and even the steward: and not one, even by accident,
      notices either antlers or tines,
    let alone the deer. The forest dweller
is already thanking the oxen and waiting in that shed
until everyone returns to the labors of Ceres[18]
and he can find an opportune moment to leave.
One of the oxen, ruminating, said to him: "It's going well;
but, you know, the man with a hundred eyes hasn't checked up yet.
    For your sake I greatly fear his arrival.
Until that time, my poor stag, don't boast of anything."
Thereupon the proprietor enters and makes his tour of inspection.
    "What's this?" he says to his people.
"I find very little grass in all these racks.
This litter is old; go to the storehouse quickly.
From now on I want to see your animals better cared for.
What does it cost you to get rid of these cobwebs?
Don't any of you know how to put away these yokes and collars?"
While observing everything, he sees a head other
than those he usually sees in this place.
The deer is recognized; each man takes a hunting spear;
    each man gives the animal a thrust.

---

[18] Their farm work; Ceres was the goddess of agriculture.

Ses larmes ne sauraient la sauver du trépas.
On l'emporte, on la sale, on en fait maint repas,
    Dont maint voisin s'éjouit d'être.
Phèdre, sur ce sujet, dit fort élégamment:
    Il n'est pour voir que l'œil du maître.
Quant à moi, j'y mettrais encor l'œil de l'amant.


# L'alouette et ses petits, avec le maître d'un champ

Ne t'attends qu'à toi seul, c'est un commun proverbe.
    Voici comme Ésope le mit
        En crédit.

    Les alouettes font leur nid
    Dans les blés quand ils sont en herbe,
    C'est-à-dire environ le temps
Que tout aime, et que tout pullule dans le monde:
    Monstres marins au fond de l'onde,
Tigres dans les forêts, alouettes aux champs.
    Une pourtant de ces dernières
Avait laissé passer la moitié d'un printemps
Sans goûter le plaisir des amours printanières.
A toute force enfin elle se résolut
D'imiter la nature, et d'être mère encore.
Elle bâtit un nid, pond, couve et fait éclore
A la hâte; le tout alla du mieux qu'il put.
Les blés d'alentour mûrs, avant que la nitée
    Se trouvât assez forte encor
    Pour voler et prendre l'essor,
De mille soins divers l'alouette agitée
S'en va chercher pâture, avertit ses enfants
D'être toujours au guet et faire sentinelle.
    «Si le possesseur de ces champs
Vient avecque son fils (comme il viendra), dit-elle,

His tears can't save him from death.
He is carried out, salted and provides many a meal,
     which many a neighbor is happy to be invited to.
On this theme Phaedrus[19] says, most elegantly:
     "Only the eye of the proprietor can see clearly."
As for me, I'd also add: "the eye of the lover."


# The Lark and Her Young, with the Owner of a Field

"Rely on yourself alone" is a common proverb.
     Here is how Aesop[20] gave it
          widespread recognition.

     Larks make their nest
     amid grain when it is still green,
          that is, more or less in the season
when all creatures make love and multiply:
     sea monsters at the bottom of the ocean,
tigers in the jungles, larks in the fields.
     However, one of those last-mentioned birds
had let half a spring season go by
without tasting the pleasure of vernal love.
In spite of that she finally resolved
to follow nature and still become a mother.
She built a nest, laid eggs, sat on them and hatched them out,
all in great haste: everything went as well as it could.
Since the grain all around had ripened before the nestful
          was strong enough yet
          to fly and take wing,
the lark, a prey to a thousand different concerns,
went out to seek nourishment, warning her children
to be always on guard as if on sentry duty.
     "If the owner of these fields
comes with his son (and he *will* come)," she said,

---

[19] The Roman fabulist (first century A.D.), a major source of "plots" for La Fontaine.
[20] This fable is not derived from Aesop, however, but from the *Attic Nights* of the Roman writer Aulus Gellius (second century A.D.)

Écoutez bien: selon ce qu'il dira,
    Chacun de nous décampera.»
Sitôt que l'alouette eut quitté sa famille,
Le possesseur du champ vient avecque son fils.
«Ces blés sont mûrs, dit-il, allez chez nos amis
Les prier que chacun, apportant sa faucille,
Nous vienne aider demain dès la pointe du jour.»
    Notre alouette, de retour,
    Trouve en alarme sa couvée.
L'un commence: «Il a dit que, l'aurore levée,
L'on fît venir demain ses amis pour l'aider.
–S'il n'a dit que cela, repartit l'alouette,
Rien ne nous presse encor de changer de retraite;
Mais c'est demain qu'il faut tout de bon écouter.
Cependant soyez gais; voilà de quoi manger.»
Eux repus, tout s'endort, les petits et la mère.

L'aube du jour arrive; et d'amis point du tout.
L'alouette à l'essor, le maître s'en vient faire
    Sa ronde ainsi qu'à l'ordinaire.
«Ces blés ne devraient pas, dit-il, être debout.
Nos amis ont grand tort, et tort qui se repose
Sur de tels paresseux à servir ainsi lents.
    Mon fils, allez chez nos parents
    Les prier de la même chose.»
L'épouvante est au nid plus forte que jamais.
«Il a dit ses parents, mère, c'est à cette heure . . .
    –Non, mes enfants, dormez en paix;
    Ne bougeons de notre demeure.»
L'alouette eut raison, car personne ne vint.
Pour la troisième fois le maître se souvint
De visiter ses blés. «Notre erreur est extrême,
Dit-il, de nous attendre à d'autres gens que nous.
Il n'est meilleur ami ni parent que soi-même.
Retenez bien cela, mon fils; et savez-vous
Ce qu'il faut faire? Il faut qu'avec notre famille
Nous prenions dès demain chacun une faucille:
C'est là notre plus court, et nous achèverons
    Notre moisson quand nous pourrons.»
Dès lors que ce dessein fut su de l'alouette:
«C'est ce coup qu'il est bon de partir, mes enfants.»

"listen carefully: according to what he says,
   we will all get out of here."
As soon as the lark had left her family,
the owner of the field came with his son.
"This grain is ripe," he said, "let's visit our friends
and ask each of them to bring his sickle
and come to help us tomorrow at daybreak."
   Our lark, back home,
   found her brood in a panic.
One of them began: "He said that, as soon as dawn arrives,
someone should ask his friends to come help him tomorrow."
"If that's all he said," replied the lark,
"we do not yet have any urgent need to change our residence;
but it's tomorrow that you must listen very sharply.
Meanwhile, cheer up; here's something to eat."
When they were full, they all fell asleep, the young ones and their
                            mother.

The dawn arrived, but not a single friend.
The lark flew off, the owner came to make
   his inspection as usual.
"This grain," he said, "should not remain standing.
Our friends are very wrong, and so is anyone who depends
on people who are so lazy and slow to give aid.
   Son, go to our relatives
   and make the same request of them."
In the nest the scare is greater than ever.
"He said his relatives, Mother, this is the time . . ."
   "No, children, sleep peacefully;
   let's not stir from our home."
The lark was right, because no one came.
For a third time the owner remembered
to visit his grain. "We're extremely foolish,"
he said, "to rely on anyone else but ourselves.
There's no better friend or relative than oneself.
Remember this well, son; and do you know
what we must do? Along with our own people
we must each of us take a sickle no later than tomorrow:
that's the shortest and simplest way for us, and we'll finish
   harvesting whenever we can."
As soon as that plan was known to the lark:
"This is the time it's good to leave, children."

Et les petits en même temps,
Voletants, se culebutants,
Délogèrent tous sans trompette.

## Le bûcheron et Mercure

A M.L.C.D.B.

Votre goût a servi de règle à mon ouvrage.
J'ai tenté les moyens d'acquérir son suffrage.
Vous voulez qu'on évite un soin trop curieux
Et des vains ornements l'effort ambitieux.
Je le veux comme vous; cet effort ne peut plaire.
Un auteur gâte tout quand il veut trop bien faire.
Non qu'il faille bannir certains traits délicats:
Vous les aimez, ces traits, et je ne les hais pas.
Quant au principal but qu'Ésope se propose,
        J'y tombe au moins mal que je puis.
Enfin si dans ces vers je ne plais et n'instruis,
Il ne tient pas à moi, c'est toujours quelque chose.
        Comme la force est un point
        Dont je ne me pique point,
Je tâche d'y tourner le vice en ridicule,
Ne pouvant l'attaquer avec des bras d'Hercule.
C'est là tout mon talent; je ne sais s'il suffit.
        Tantôt je peins en un récit
La sotte vanité jointe avecque l'envie,
Deux pivots sur qui roule aujourd'hui notre vie.
        Tel est ce chétif animal
Qui voulut en grosseur au bœuf se rendre égal.
J'oppose quelquefois, par une double image,
Le vice à la vertu, la sottise au bon sens,
        Les agneaux aux loups ravissants,
La mouche à la fourmi, faisant de cet ouvrage
Une ample comédie à cent actes divers,

And at the same time the young ones,
fluttering, knocking one another over,
all moved out quietly, without fanfare.[21]


## *The Woodcutter and Mercury*

TO M[ONSIEUR THE] C[OUNT] D[E] B[RIENNE][22]

Your taste has acted as a set of rules for my work.
I've tried every means to win its approbation.
You want writers to avoid an excessively affected style
and a pompous straining for trivial ornamentation.
I want the same thing you do; such efforts can't be entertaining.
An author spoils everything when he wants to write too fastidiously.
Not that he is obliged to outlaw certain delicate features:
you like those features, and I am no enemy to them.
As for the principal aim that Aesop sets for himself,
    I strive to achieve it as successfully as I can.
In short, if in my verses I fail to give pleasure and instruction,
it's not that I don't try—that's something at least.
    Since forceful expression is a trait
    of which I cannot boast,
I attempt in my poetry to make vice look ridiculous,
being unable to attack it with muscles like those of Hercules.
That is the extent of my talent; I don't know if it's enough.
    At times I depict in a narrative
foolish vanity in league with envy,
two pivots on which our life turns nowadays.
    An example of this is that puny animal
who wanted to become equal to the ox in bulk.
Sometimes, using two opposed characters, I contrast
vice with virtue, folly with common sense,
    lambs with ravaging wolves,
the fly with the ant, transforming my production into
a wide-ranging play in a hundred varied acts

---

21 A military image: an encampment moving out secretly without a regular trumpet
signal, in order to deceive the enemy.
22 Probably Henri-Auguste de Loménie, comte de Brienne (1595–1666), writer of
memoirs.

Et dont la scène est l'univers.
Hommes, dieux, animaux, tout y fait quelque rôle:
Jupiter comme un autre. Introduisons celui
Qui porte de sa part aux belles la parole:
Ce n'est pas de cela qu'il s'agit aujourd'hui.

Un bûcheron perdit son gagne-pain:
C'est sa cognée; et la cherchant en vain,
Ce fut pitié là-dessus de l'entendre.
Il n'avait pas des outils à revendre.
Sur celui-ci roulait tout son avoir.
Ne sachant donc où mettre son espoir,
Sa face était de pleurs toute baignée.
«O ma cognée! ô ma pauvre cognée!
S'écriait-il, Jupiter, rends-la moi;
Je tiendrai l'être encore un coup de toi.»
Sa plainte fut de l'Olympe entendue.
Mercure vient. «Elle n'est pas perdue,
Lui dit ce dieu, la connaîtrais-tu bien?
Je crois l'avoir près d'ici rencontrée.»
Lors une d'or à l'homme étant montrée,
Il répondit: «Je n'y demande rien.»
Une d'argent succède à la première;
Il la refuse. Enfin une de bois.
«Voilà, dit-il, la mienne cette fois;
Je suis content si j'ai cette dernière.
— Tu les auras, dit le dieu, toutes trois.
Ta bonne foi sera récompensée.
— En ce cas-là je les prendrai», dit-il.
L'histoire en est aussitôt dispersée;
Et boquillons de perdre leur outil,
Et de crier pour se le faire rendre.
Le roi des dieux ne sait auquel entendre.
Son fils Mercure aux criards vient encor,
A chacun d'eux il en montre une d'or.
Chacun eût cru passer pour une bête
De ne pas dire aussitôt: «La voilà!»
Mercure, au lieu de donner celle-là,
Leur en décharge un grand coup sur la tête.

with the entire universe for a stage.
Men, gods, animals, all play some part in it:
Jupiter just like anyone else. Let us bring on the one
who carries messages for him to beautiful women:[23]
that is not the duty he's performing today.

A woodcutter lost his means of livelihood:
his axe; and, as he sought it in vain,
it was pitiful to hear him on the subject.
He had no tools to spare.
All his fortune depended on that one.
So, since he didn't know what to hope for any longer,
his face was completely wet with tears.
"Oh, my axe! Oh, my poor axe!"
he shouted; "Jupiter, give it back to me;
for a second time I shall have received my life at your hands."
His lament was heard on Olympus.
Mercury came. "It isn't lost,"
that god said to him; "would you recognize it again?
I think I found it near here."
Then, when a golden axe was shown to the man,
he replied: "That's not what I'm asking for."
A silver one follows the first;
he refuses it. Finally a wooden one.
"There," he said, "this time it's mine;
I'm satisfied if I have this last one."
The god said: "You'll have all three.
Your honesty will be rewarded."
"In that case I'll take them," he said.
The story spread abroad at once;
and woodcutters started losing their tools
and crying out to get them back again.
The king of the gods didn't know which one to listen to first.
His son Mercury once again came to see the shouters;
he showed each of them a golden axe.
Each of them thought he would be considered an imbecile
unless he immediately said: "That's it!"
Mercury, instead of bestowing that one,
dealt them a smart blow on the head with it.

---

[23] Mercury, Jupiter's messenger, one of the gods of Mount Olympus.

Ne point mentir, être content du sien,
C'est le plus sûr: cependant on s'occupe
A dire faux pour attraper du bien.
Que sert cela? Jupiter n'est pas dupe.

## Le petit poisson et le pêcheur

Petit poisson deviendra grand,
Pourvu que Dieu lui prête vie.
Mais le lâcher en attendant,
Je tiens pour moi que c'est folie;
Car de le rattraper il n'est pas trop certain.
Un carpeau qui n'était encore que fretin
Fut pris par un pêcheur au bord d'une rivière.
«Tout fait nombre, dit l'homme, en voyant son butin;
Voilà commencement de chère et de festin;
Mettons-le en notre gibecière.»
Le pauvre carpillon lui dit en sa manière:
«Que ferez-vous de moi? je ne saurais fournir
Au plus qu'une demi-bouchée.
Laissez-moi carpe devenir:
Je serai par vous repêchée.
Quelque gros partisan m'achètera bien cher,
Au lieu qu'il vous en faut chercher
Peut-être encor cent de ma taille
Pour faire un plat. Quel plat? croyez-moi: rien qui vaille.
–Rien qui vaille? Eh bien, soit, repartit le pêcheur;
Poisson, mon bel ami, qui faites le prêcheur,
Vous irez dans la poêle; et vous avez beau dire,
Dès ce soir on vous fera frire.»

Un tiens vaut, ce dit-on, mieux que deux tu l'auras.
L'un est sûr, l'autre ne l'est pas.

Not to lie, to be satisfied with one's own possessions,
is the surest practice: nevertheless, people make use
of false statements to get their hands on property.
What's the good of that? Jupiter isn't taken in by it.


## *The Little Fish and the Fisherman*

A little fish will grow up
as long as God lets him live.
But to let him go while you wait
is folly in my opinion;
because you can't be too sure of catching him again.
A young carp who was still only small fry
was taken by a fisherman on the bank of a stream.
"Every little bit helps," said the man when he saw his catch;
"this is the beginnings of a good meal and feast;
let's put him in our creel."
The poor little carp said to him in his own fashion:
"What will you do with me? I couldn't supply
more than half a mouthful at most.
Let me become a full-grown carp:
I'll be fished out by you again.
Some wealthy tax-farmer will pay you a very good price for me,
instead of your having to keep on looking
for perhaps a hundred more of my size
to make one dish. What dish? Believe me: nothing worthwhile."
"Nothing worthwhile? Well, that may be," replied the fisherman;
"fish, my good friend, although you're preaching sermons,
you're going into the pan; and, no matter what you say,
this very evening you'll be fried."

It's said that one "you've got it" is better than two "you'll get its."
One is a sure thing, the other isn't.

# Le satyre et le passant

Au fond d'un antre sauvage,
Un satyre et ses enfants
Allaient manger leur potage
Et prendre l'écuelle aux dents.

On les eût vus sur la mousse,
Lui, sa femme, et maint petit;
Ils n'avaient tapis ni housse,
Mais tous fort bon appétit.

Pour se sauver de la pluie
Entre un passant morfondu.
Au brouet on le convie:
Il n'était pas attendu.

Son hôte n'eut pas la peine
De le semondre deux fois:
D'abord avec son haleine
Il se réchauffe les doigts;

Puis sur le mets qu'on lui donne,
Délicat il souffle aussi.
Le satyre s'en étonne:
«Notre hôte, à quoi bon ceci?

– L'un refroidit mon potage,
L'autre réchauffe ma main.
– Vous pouvez, dit le sauvage,
Reprendre votre chemin.

Ne plaise aux dieux que je couche
Avec vous sous même toit.
Arrière ceux dont la bouche
Souffle le chaud et le froid!»

# The Satyr and the Passer-by

Deep in a wild cave,
A satyr[23a] and his children
were about to eat their soup
and begin their meal.

They could be seen seated on the moss,
he, his wife and many a little one;
they had neither carpet nor furniture cover,
but all had a very good appetite.

To escape from the rain
a passer-by entered, chilled through.
They invited him to share their broth:
he was unexpected.

His host was spared the trouble
of asking him twice:
at first with his breath
he warmed his fingers;

then on the food they gave him,
being a particular man, he also blew.
The satyr was amazed at this:
"Guest, what is that for?"

"One of those actions cools my soup,
the other warms my hands."
The forest dweller said, "You may
resume your journey.

May the gods not grant that I lie
under the same roof with you.
Away with those whose mouth
blows both hot and cold!"

---

[23a] One of the forest-dwelling man/goat hybrids of Greek mythology.

# Le laboureur et ses enfants

Travaillez, prenez de la peine.
C'est le fonds qui manque le moins.
Un riche laboureur, sentant sa mort prochaine,
Fit venir ses enfants, leur parla sans témoins.
«Gardez-vous, leur dit-il, de vendre l'héritage
    Que nous ont laissé nos parents.
    Un trésor est caché dedans.
Je ne sais pas l'endroit; mais un peu de courage
Vous le fera trouver, vous en viendrez à bout.
Remuez votre champ dès qu'on aura fait l'oût.
Creusez, fouillez, bêchez, ne laissez nulle place
    Où la main ne passe et repasse.»
Le père mort, les fils vous retournent le champ,
Deçà, delà, partout; si bien qu'au bout de l'an
    Il en rapporta davantage.
D'argent, point de caché. Mais le père fut sage
    De leur montrer, avant sa mort,
    Que le travail est un trésor.

# Le serpent et la lime

On conte qu'un serpent voisin d'un horloger
(C'était pour l'horloger un mauvais voisinage)
Entra dans sa boutique, et cherchant à manger
    N'y rencontra pour tout potage
Qu'une lime d'acier qu'il se mit à ronger.
Cette lime lui dit, sans se mettre en colère:
   «Pauvre ignorant! et que prétends-tu faire?
    Tu te prends à plus dur que toi.
    Petit serpent à tête folle,
    Plutôt que d'emporter de moi
    Seulement le quart d'une obole,
    Tu te romprais toutes les dents.
    Je ne crains que celles du temps.»

# The Farmer and His Children

Work hard, take pains.
That's the investment that disappoints you the least.
A wealthy farmer, feeling his death near,
called for his children and spoke to them without witnesses.
He said to them: "Take care not to sell the inheritance
    our forefathers have left us.
    A treasure is hidden on the property.
I don't know the spot; but a little hard work
will allow you to find it, and you'll succeed in your goal.
Turn up your field as soon as the reaping is over.
Plough, dig, delve, don't leave any place
    that your hands haven't passed over time and again."
After their father died, the sons ploughed up the field,
here, there, everywhere; with the result that, at the end of the year,
    it was more fertile on that account.
Money? There was none hidden. But the father acted wisely
    in showing them, before his death,
    that hard work is a treasure.

# The Snake and the File

It's told that a snake who lived next to a clockmaker
(this was not a good neighbor for the clockmaker to have)
entered his shop and, looking for something to eat,
    found as his only "soup"
a steel file, which he began to gnaw on.
This file said to him, without getting angry:
    "Poor ignorant creature! What do you imagine you're doing?
    You're taking on someone tougher than you are.
    Little snake with a silly head,
    before you could bite off from me
    even two grams' weight,
    you would break all your teeth.
    I fear only the teeth of time."

Ceci s'adresse à vous, esprits du dernier ordre,
Qui n'étant bons à rien cherchez sur tout à mordre.

    Vous vous tourmentez vainement.
Croyez-vous que vos dents impriment leurs outrages
      Sur tant de beaux ouvrages?
Ils sont pour vous d'airain, d'acier, de diamant.


# L'ours et les deux compagnons

    Deux compagnons pressés d'argent
    A leur voisin fourreur vendirent
    La peau d'un ours encor vivant,
Mais qu'ils tueraient bientôt, du moins à ce qu'ils dirent.
C'était le roi des ours au compte de ces gens.
Le marchand à sa peau devait faire fortune.
Elle garantirait des froids les plus cuisants.
On en pourrait fourrer plutôt deux robes qu'une.
Dindenaut prisait moins ses moutons qu'eux leur ours:
Leur, à leur compte, et non à celui de la bête.
S'offrant de la livrer au plus tard dans deux jours,
Ils conviennent de prix, et se mettent en quête,
Trouvent l'ours qui s'avance, et vient vers eux au trot.
Voilà mes gens frappés comme d'un coup de foudre.
Le marché ne tint pas; il fallut le résoudre:
D'intérêts contre l'ours, on n'en dit pas un mot.
L'un des deux compagnons grimpe au faîte d'un arbre;
    L'autre, plus froid que n'est un marbre,
Se couche sur le nez, fait le mort, tient son vent,
    Ayant quelque part ouï dire
    Que l'ours s'acharne peu souvent
Sur un corps qui ne vit, ne meut, ni ne respire.
Seigneur ours, comme un sot, donna dans ce panneau.
Il voit ce corps gisant, le croit privé de vie,
    Et de peur de supercherie
Le tourne, le retourne, approche son museau,
    Flaire aux passages de l'haleine.

This is meant for you lowest-class intelligences
who, good for nothing yourselves, strive to bite all others with your
                                                                criticism.
     You torment yourselves in vain.
Do you believe that your teeth leave their damaging imprint
          on all those fine works of art?
For you those works are made of bronze, steel and diamond.


# *The Bear and the Two Companions*

     Two companions in need of money
          sold to their neighbor, a furrier,
          the skin of a bear who was still alive,
but whom they'd soon kill, at least to hear them tell it.
He was the king of bears according to those people.
The merchant would make a fortune from his skin.
It would protect people from the most biting cold.
Two robes, not one, could be made from it.
Dindenaut[24] didn't praise his sheep as much as they did their bear:
"their" bear, as *they* saw it, but not as the animal did.
Promising to deliver the skin in two days at the latest,
they agreed on a price, and set out on their search;
they found the bear advancing and coming toward them at a trot.
Whereupon my people were smitten as by a lightning bolt.
Their contract didn't hold water; it had to be canceled:
no one said a word about collecting damages from the bear.
One of the two companions climbed to the top of a tree;
          the other one, colder than a slab of marble,
stretched out face down, pretended to be dead and held his breath,
          having heard somewhere
          that bears very seldom attack
a lifeless body that neither moves nor breathes.
Sir Bear, like a fool, fell for this ruse.
He saw the body lying there, thought it was bereft of life,
          and, out of fear of being tricked,
turned it over, and over again, brought his muzzle up close
          and sniffed at the places from which breath escapes.

---

24 A character in Rabelais.

«C'est, dit-il, un cadavre; ôtons-nous, car il sent.»
A ces mots, l'ours s'en va dans la forêt prochaine.
L'un de nos deux marchands de son arbre descend,
Court à son compagnon, lui dit que c'est merveille
Qu'il n'ait eu seulement que la peur pour tout mal.
«Eh bien, ajouta-t-il, la peau de l'animal?
     Mais que t'a-t-il dit à l'oreille?
     Car il s'approchait de bien près,
     Te retournant avec sa serre.
    –Il m'a dit qu'il ne faut jamais
Vendre la peau de l'ours qu'on ne l'ait mis par terre.»

## Phébus et Borée

Borée et le Soleil virent un voyageur
     Qui s'était muni par bonheur
Contre le mauvais temps. On entrait dans l'automne,
Quand la précaution aux voyageurs est bonne:
Il pleut; le soleil luit; et l'écharpe d'Iris
     Rend ceux qui sortent avertis
Qu'en ces mois le manteau leur est fort nécessaire.
Les Latins les nommaient douteux pour cette affaire.
Notre homme s'était donc à la pluie attendu:
Bon manteau bien doublé; bonne étoffe bien forte.
«Celui-ci, dit le vent, prétend avoir pourvu
A tous les accidents; mais il n'a pas prévu
     Que je saurai souffler de sorte
Qu'il n'est bouton qui tienne: il faudra, si je veux,
     Que le manteau s'en aille au diable.
L'ébattement pourrait nous en être agréable:
Vous plaît-il de l'avoir?–Eh bien, gageons nous deux,
     Dit Phébus, sans tant de paroles,
A qui plutôt aura dégarni les épaules
     Du cavalier que nous voyons.
Commencez. Je vous laisse obscurcir mes rayons.»
Il n'en fallut pas plus. Notre souffleur à gage
Se gorge de vapeurs, s'enfle comme un ballon,

"It's a corpse," he said; "let's get away, because it stinks."
Saying this, the bear departed into the nearby forest.
One of our two merchants descended from his tree,
ran over to his companion and told him that it was a miracle
that he had suffered nothing more than a scare.
"Well?" he added; "the animal's skin?
    But what did he say in your ear?
    Because he came up really close,
    turning you over with his claws."
    "He told me that one should never
sell the skin of a bear one hasn't killed yet."


## *Phoebus and Boreas*

Boreas[25] and the Sun saw a traveler
    who fortunately had protected himself
against bad weather. It was the beginning of autumn,
a time when it's good for travelers to take precautions:
it rains; the sun shines; and Iris' rainbow sash
    informs those who go out
that in these months they have great need of a coat.
The Romans called them "uncertain months" on that account.
Therefore our man had set out expecting rain:
a good coat, well lined; good material and very strong.
"This man," said the wind, "imagines he has provided
against all eventualities: but he did not foresee
    that I intend to blow so hard
that not a single button will hold; if I wish it,
    his coat will have to go to the devil.
This pastime might be amusing for us:
do you want to go ahead with it?" "All right, let's make a bet,"
    said Phoebus, "without wasting so many words,
as to which of us will sooner uncover the shoulders
    of this rider whom we see.
Begin. I allow you to darken my beams."
No more was needed. Our blower, laboring for his wager,
crammed himself with vapors, swelled up like a balloon,

---

25 Phoebus is another name for Apollo, as god of the sun. Boreas is the north wind.

Fait un vacarme de démon,
Siffle, souffle, tempête, et brise en son passage
Maint toit qui n'en peut mais, fait périr maint bateau;
        Le tout au sujet d'un manteau.
Le cavalier eut soin d'empêcher que l'orage
        Ne se pût engouffrer dedans.
Cela le préserva; le vent perdit son temps:
Plus il se tourmentait, plus l'autre tenait ferme;
Il eut beau faire agir le collet et les plis.
        Sitôt qu'il fut au bout du terme
        Qu'à la gageure on avait mis,
        Le soleil dissipe la nue,
Récrée, et puis pénètre enfin le cavalier,
        Sous son balandras fait qu'il sue,
        Le contraint de s'en dépouiller.
Encor n'usa-t-il pas de toute sa puissance.
        Plus fait douceur que violence.


## Le cochet, le chat et le souriceau

Un souriceau tout jeune, et qui n'avait rien vu,
        Fut presque pris au dépourvu.
Voici comme il conta l'aventure à sa mère:
«J'avais franchi les monts qui bornent cet État,
        Et trottais comme un jeune rat
        Qui cherche à se donner carrière,
Lorsque deux animaux m'ont arrêté les yeux:
        L'un doux, bénin et gracieux,
Et l'autre turbulent, et plein d'inquiétude.
        Il a la voix perçante et rude,
        Sur la tête un morceau de chair,
Une sorte de bras dont il s'élève en l'air
        Comme pour prendre sa volée,
        La queue en panache étalée.»
Or c'était un cochet dont notre souriceau

made a demonic racket,
whistled, blew, stormed, and, as he passed through, broke
many an innocent roof and sank many a boat,
all for the sake of a coat.
The rider carefully prevented the storm
from penetrating his coat.
That saved him; the wind wasted his time.
The more he strained himself, the more the other stood firm;
it was of no use to him to make the collar and the pleats fly.
As soon as he had reached the time limit
that had been set for the wager,
the sun dispersed the clouds,
warmed up the traveler and then finally got through to him,
making him sweat underneath his long coat
and forcing him to take it off.
Even so, he didn't use all his power.
Gentleness accomplishes more than violence.

# The Cockerel, the Cat and the Young Mouse

A very young mouse, who had seen nothing of the world,
was nearly caught unawares.
Here is how he recounted the adventure to his mother:
"I had crossed the mountains that form this country's boundary,
and I was trotting along like a young rat[26]
who wishes to give himself free rein,
when two animals caught my attention:
one gentle, kindly and gracious;
the other, turbulent and full of nervousness.
He has a piercing, harsh voice,
a bit of flesh on his head,
a kind of arm with which he rises into the air
as if to take flight,
and a tail spread out into a plume."
Now, it was a cockerel whose portrait our young mouse

---

26 La Fontaine seems to use "mouse" and "rat" interchangeably, here and elsewhere. The present translation is literal in this regard, preserving the word actually used on each occasion.

Fit à sa mère le tableau
Comme d'un animal venu de l'Amérique.
«Il se battait, dit-il, les flancs avec ses bras,
  Faisant tel bruit et tel fracas,
Que moi, qui grâce aux dieux de courage me pique,
  En ai pris la fuite de peur,
  Le maudissant de très bon cœur.
  Sans lui j'aurais fait connaissance
Avec cet animal qui m'a semblé si doux.
  Il est velouté comme nous,
Marqueté, longue queue, une humble contenance;
Un modeste regard, et pourtant l'œil luisant:
  Je le crois fort sympathisant
Avec messieurs les rats; car il a des oreilles
  En figure aux nôtres pareilles.
Je l'allais aborder, quand d'un son plein d'éclat
  L'autre m'a fait prendre la fuite.
–Mon fils, dit la souris, ce doucet est un chat,
  Qui, sous son minois hypocrite,
  Contre toute ta parenté
  D'un malin vouloir est porté.
  L'autre animal tout au contraire,
  Bien éloigné de nous mal faire,
Servira quelque jour peut-être à nos repas.
Quant au chat, c'est sur nous qu'il fonde sa cuisine.
  Garde-toi, tant que tu vivras,
  De juger des gens sur la mine.»


# Le lièvre et la tortue

Rien ne sert de courir; il faut partir à point.
Le lièvre et la tortue en sont un témoignage.
«Gageons, dit celle-ci, que vous n'atteindrez point
Sitôt que moi ce but.–Sitôt? Êtes-vous sage?
  Repartit l'animal léger.
  Ma commère, il vous faut purger
  Avec quatre grains d'ellébore.

thus painted for his mother
as if it were some exotic animal from the New World.
He continued: "He was beating his sides with his arms,
      making so much noise and such a din
that I, who, thanks to the gods, pride myself on my courage,
      ran away in fear,
      cursing him from the bottom of my heart.
      If it hadn't been for him, I'd have struck up an acquaintance
with that animal who seemed so gentle to me.
      He has velvety fur like us,
spotted, with a long tail and a humble bearing;
a modest look in his eyes, which nevertheless are gleaming:
      I think he has a lot in common
with rat gentlemen; because he has ears
      shaped like ours.
I was about to accost him, when with a most raucous sound
      that other one made me run away."
"Son," said the mouse, "that meek character is a cat,
      who, underneath his hypocritical sweet face,
      is animated by an evil will
      against all of your kind.
      On the contrary, the other animal,
      far from doing us harm,
may perhaps come in handy as a meal for us some day.
As for the cat, he bases his diet on us.
      As long as you live, be careful not to
      judge people by their appearance."

## The Hare and the Tortoise

Running is of no use; one must set out at the right time.
The hare and the tortoise bear witness to this.
The latter said, "Let's bet that you won't reach
that goal as soon as I will." "As soon? Are you in your right mind?"
      replied the swift animal.
      "My friend, you need a purge
      with four grains of hellebore."[27]

---

[27] Hellebore is a plant-derived drug once used to combat mental illness. A grain is a
measure of weight equivalent to about five centigrams.

–Sage ou non, je parie encore.»
Ainsi fut fait: et de tous deux
On mit près du but les enjeux.
Savoir quoi, ce n'est pas l'affaire,
Ni de quel juge l'on convint.
Notre lièvre n'avait que quatre pas à faire;
J'entends de ceux qu'il fait lorsque prêt d'être atteint
Il s'éloigne des chiens, les renvoie aux calendes
    Et leur fait arpenter les landes.
Ayant, dis-je, du temps de reste pour brouter,
    Pour dormir, et pour écouter
  D'où vient le vent, il laisse la tortue
    Aller son train de sénateur.
    Elle part, elle s'évertue;
    Elle se hâte avec lenteur.
Lui cependant méprise une telle victoire,
    Tient la gageure à peu de gloire,
    Croit qu'il y va de son honneur
  De partir tard. Il broute, il se repose,
    Il s'amuse à tout autre chose
  Qu'à la gageure. A la fin quand il vit
Que l'autre touchait presque au bout de la carrière,
Il partit comme un trait; mais les élans qu'il fit
Furent vains: la tortue arriva la première.
«Hé bien! lui cria-t-elle, avais-je pas raison?
    De quoi vous sert votre vitesse?
    Moi, l'emporter! Et que serait-ce
    Si vous portiez une maison?»

# Le chartier embourbé

    Le Phaéton d'une voiture à foin
Vit son char embourbé. Le pauvre homme était loin
De tout humain secours. C'était à la campagne,
Près d'un certain canton de la basse Bretagne

"Sane or not, I still make the wager."
It was thus settled: and the stakes put up by both of them
were placed near the goal.
To know what they were doesn't concern us here,
    nor whom they agreed on to judge the race.
Our hare had only four hops to make;
I mean the kind he makes when, nearly about to be reached,
he moves away from the hounds, puts them off indefinitely
    and makes them roam the heath.
Having, I say, more than enough time to nibble grass,
        to take a nap and to listen
    for the direction of the wind,[28] he allows the tortoise
        to proceed at her majestic senator's pace.
    She starts, she exerts herself;
    she "hastens slowly."
He, meanwhile, scorns such a victory,
        takes little pride in the wager,
        and believes that it's a point of honor
    to start out late. He nibbles, he rests,
        he wastes time on everything
    but the wager. Finally, when he saw
that the other was nearly at the end of the course,
he set out like a shot; but his bursts of speed
were in vain: the tortoise arrived first.
"Well!" she shouted to him; "wasn't I right?
    What use is your velocity to you?
    To think that *I* won the day! How would it be
    if *you* were carrying a house on your back?"


## The Carter Stuck in the Mud

    The Phaethon[29] of a haywagon
found that his vehicle was stuck in the mud. The poor man was far
from any human aid. It was in the country,
near a certain district in Lower Brittany

---

    [28] That is, to idle the time away.
    [29] Jocular designation of the rustic teamster: Phaethon was the son of Apollo who was
unable to drive his father's solar chariot correctly and came to grief.

Appelé Quimper-Corentin.
On sait assez que le destin
Adresse là les gens quand il veut qu'on enrage.
Dieu nous préserve du voyage!
Pour venir au chartier embourbé dans ces lieux,
Le voilà qui déteste et jure de son mieux,
Pestant, en sa fureur extrême,
Tantôt contre les trous, puis contre ses chevaux,
Contre son char, contre lui-même.
Il invoque à la fin le dieu dont les travaux
Sont si célèbres dans le monde.
«Hercule, lui dit-il, aide-moi; si ton dos
A porté la machine ronde,
Ton bras peut me tirer d'ici.»
Sa prière étant faite, il entend dans la nue
Une voix qui lui parle ainsi:
«Hercule veut qu'on se remue,
Puis il aide les gens. Regarde d'où provient
L'achoppement qui te retient.
Ote d'autour de chaque roue
Ce malheureux mortier, cette maudite boue,
Qui jusqu'à l'essieu les enduit.
Prends ton pic, et me romps ce caillou qui te nuit.
Comble-moi cette ornière. As-tu fait?—Oui, dit l'homme.
—Or bien je vas t'aider, dit la voix: prends ton fouet.
—Je l'ai pris. Qu'est ceci? mon char marche à souhait.
Hercule en soit loué.» Lors la voix: «Tu vois comme
Tes chevaux aisément se sont tirés de là.
Aide-toi, le Ciel t'aidera.»


## La jeune veuve

La perte d'un époux ne va point sans soupirs.
On fait beaucoup de bruit, et puis on se console.
Sur les ailes du Temps la tristesse s'envole;
Le Temps ramène les plaisirs.

called Quimper-Corentin.[30]
It's well known that destiny
directs people there when it wants them to go crazy.
May God preserve us from that journey!
To come back to the carter who got bogged down in that vicinity,
there he was cursing and swearing with all his might,
and, in his extreme fury, railing
now at potholes, now at his horses,
at his wagon and at himself.
Finally he called upon the god whose labors
are so universally famous.
"Hercules," he said, "help me; if your back
once supported the entire globe,[31]
your arms can get me out of here."
When his prayer was finished, he heard in the clouds
a voice speaking to him as follows:
"Hercules wants people to bestir themselves,
then he helps them. Look and see the source
of the obstacle that is retaining you.
Remove from around each wheel
that unfortunate mortar, that accursed mud
which is coating them up to the axle.
Take your pickaxe and break up that stone which is distressing you.
Fill in that rut. Have you done so?" "Yes," said the man.
"Now, then, I'm going to help you," said the voice; "take your whip."
"I've taken it. What's this? My wagon is moving perfectly.
Hercules be praised!" Then the voice: "You see how
easily your horses have pulled out of that spot.
Help yourself and Heaven will help you."

## The Young Widow

The loss of a husband does not occur without much sighing.
Women make a great fuss and then console themselves.
Sadness flies away on the wings of Time;
Time brings back pleasures.

---

30 A place of exile at the time.
31 Hercules once supported the sky, taking over temporarily from the giant Atlas.

Entre la veuve d'une année
Et la veuve d'une journée
La différence est grande: on ne croirait jamais
　　Que ce fût la même personne.
L'une fait fuir les gens, et l'autre a mille attraits.

Aux soupirs vrais ou faux celle-là s'abandonne;
C'est toujours même note et pareil entretien:
　　On dit qu'on est inconsolable;
　　On le dit, mais il n'en est rien,
　　Comme on verra par cette fable,
　　Ou plutôt par la vérité.
　　L'époux d'une jeune beauté
Partait pour l'autre monde. A ses côtés sa femme
Lui criait: «Attends-moi, je te suis; et mon âme,
Aussi bien que la tienne, est prête à s'envoler.»
　　Le mari fait seul le voyage.
La belle avait un père, homme prudent et sage:
　　Il laissa le torrent couler.
　　A la fin, pour la consoler:
«Ma fille, lui dit-il, c'est trop verser de larmes:
Qu'a besoin le défunt que vous noyiez vos charmes?
Puisqu'il est des vivants, ne songez plus aux morts.

　　Je ne dis pas que tout à l'heure
　　Une condition meilleure
　　Change en des noces ces transports;
Mais après certain temps souffrez qu'on vous propose
Un époux beau, bien fait, jeune, et tout autre chose
　　Que le défunt.—Ah! dit-elle aussitôt,
　　Un cloître est l'époux qu'il me faut.»
Le père lui laissa digérer sa disgrâce.
　　Un mois de la sorte se passe.
L'autre mois on l'emploie à changer tous les jours
Quelque chose à l'habit, au linge, à la coiffure.
　　Le deuil enfin sert de parure,
　　En attendant d'autres atours.
　　Toute la bande des amours
Revient au colombier; les jeux, les ris, la danse,
　　Ont aussi leur tour à la fin.
　　On se plonge soir et matin

Between a woman who has been widowed for a year
and a woman who has been widowed for a day
there's a great difference: you'd never believe
it was the same person.
One of them causes people to avoid her, the other has a thousand
allurements.
The former abandons herself to sighs, true or false;
it's always the same tone and identical conversation:
they say they're inconsolable;
they say so, but it isn't the case,
as you will see from this fable,
or rather, from reality.
The husband of a young beauty
was setting out for the next world. At his side his wife
was shouting to him: "Wait for me, I'm following you; and my soul,
just like yours, is ready to take wing."
The husband took the trip alone.
The beauty had a father, a prudent and wise man:
he let the torrent flow.
Finally, to console her,
he said: "Daughter, by now you're shedding too many tears:
What good will it do the deceased if you drown your charms?
Since there are living men, don't think about the dead ones any
more.
I'm not saying that all at once
a better state of mind
should change these outbursts into a wedding celebration;
but after a certain time allow people to recommend to you
a husband who's handsome, well built, young and just the opposite
of a dead man." "Oh!" she replied immediately,
"a convent is the husband I need."
Her father let her get used to her misfortune.
In that way a month went by.
The second month was employed in making daily changes
of some kind in her outer wear, lingerie and hairdo.
Finally her mourning became ornamental,
while she was waiting for other kinds of finery.
The whole troop of cupids
returned to the dovecote: games, laughter and dance
finally had their turn, too.
Evening and morning she immersed herself

Dans la fontaine de Jouvence.
Le père ne craint plus ce défunt tant chéri;
Mais, comme il ne parlait de rien à notre belle:
    «Où donc est le jeune mari
    Que vous m'avez promis?» dit-elle.

## Épilogue

Bornons ici cette carrière.
Les longs ouvrages me font peur.
Loin d'épuiser une matière,
On n'en doit prendre que la fleur.
Il s'en va temps que je reprenne
Un peu de forces et d'haleine
Pour fournir à d'autres projets.
Amour, ce tyran de ma vie,
Veut que je change de sujets:
Il faut contenter son envie.
Retournons à Psyché: Damon, vous m'exhortez
A peindre ses malheurs et ses félicités:
    J'y consens; peut-être ma veine
    En sa faveur s'échauffera.
Heureux si ce travail est la dernière peine
    Que son époux me causera!

## A *Madame de Montespan*

L'apologue est un don qui vient des immortels,
    Ou si c'est un présent des hommes,
Quiconque nous l'a fait mérite des autels.
    Nous devons tous tant que nous sommes
    Ériger en divinité

in the fountain of youth.
Her father was no longer afraid of that very dear departed;
but, since he wasn't mentioning anything to our beauty:
     "So where is the young husband
     you promised me?" she said.


## Epilogue [to Books I–VI]

     Let us set a limit here to this course of ours.
     Long pieces of writing frighten me.
     Far from exhausting a subject,
     one should only skim the cream from it.
     It's nearly time for me to recoup
     a little strength and breath
     with which to undertake other projects.
     Love, that tyrant of my life,
     wants me to change topics:
     his desire must be satisfied.
Let's go back to Psyche:[32] Damon, you urge me
to depict her unhappiness and her bliss:
     I consent; perhaps my inspiration
     will be kindled on her behalf.
How happy I'll be if this labor is the last suffering
     her husband causes me!


## To Madame de Montespan[33]

The fable is a gift that comes from the immortals,
     or, if it is a present from human beings,
whoever bestowed it on us deserves to be worshipped.
     Every one of us ought
     to deify

---

[32] La Fontaine's novel in prose and verse, *Les amours de Psyché et de Cupidon,* published in 1669, the year after the publication of Books I–VI of the *Fables.* In the story,
Cupid (or Love) is Psyche's husband. It is not known whom the poet is here addressing
under the poetical name of Damon.

[33] The king's beautiful and intelligent mistress, whose poetic pseudonym was Olympe
(Olympia). The present poem is the dedication to Books VII–XI of the *Fables.*

Le sage par qui fut ce bel art inventé.
C'est proprement un charme: il rend l'âme attentive,
  Ou plutôt il la tient captive,
  Nous attachant à des récits
Qui mènent à son gré les cœurs et les esprits.
O vous qui l'imitez, Olympe, si ma Muse
A quelquefois pris place à la table des dieux,
Sur ces dons aujourd'hui daignez porter les yeux,
Favorisez les jeux où mon esprit s'amuse.

Le temps qui détruit tout, respectant votre appui,
Me laissera franchir les ans dans cet ouvrage:
Tout auteur qui voudra vivre encore après lui
  Doit s'acquérir votre suffrage.
C'est de vous que mes vers attendent tout leur prix:
  Il n'est beauté dans nos écrits
Dont vous ne connaissiez jusques aux moindres traces.
Eh! qui connaît que vous les beautés et les grâces?
Paroles et regards, tout est charme dans vous.
  Ma muse en un sujet si doux
  Voudrait s'étendre davantage;
Mais il faut réserver à d'autres cet emploi,
  Et d'un plus grand maître que moi
  Votre louange est le partage.
Olympe, c'est assez qu'à mon dernier ouvrage
Votre nom serve un jour de rempart et d'abri.
Protégez désormais le livre favori
Par qui j'ose espérer une seconde vie:
  Sous vos seuls auspices, ces vers
  Seront jugés malgré l'envie
  Dignes des yeux de l'univers.
Je ne mérite pas une faveur si grande:
  La fable en son nom la demande.
Vous savez quel crédit ce mensonge a sur nous.
S'il procure à mes vers le bonheur de vous plaire,
Je croirai lui devoir un temple pour salaire;
Mais je ne veux bâtir des temples que pour vous.

the sage by whom this beautiful art was invented.
It's literally a magic spell: it makes our soul attentive
    or, rather, holds it captive,
    charming us by narratives
that lead our hearts and minds anywhere the poet wishes.
O Olympia, you who are so like the fable in that way, if my muse
has sometimes been granted a seat at the table of the gods,
deign to set your eyes on these gifts today,
lend your favor to the pastimes with which my mind idly occupies
                                        itself.
Time, which destroys everything, will respect your patronage
and will let me go down through the years by means of this book:
any author who wishes to continue living after his own day
    must obtain your approbation.
It is from you that my verses await their full valuation:
    there is no beauty in our writings
which you are not aware of down to the least detail.
Ah! Who other than you knows beauties and graces?
Words and glances, everything in you is spellbinding.
    On such a sweet theme
    my muse would like to expatiate further;
but that role must be reserved for others,
    and your praises must fall to the lot
    of a greater master than myself.
Olympia, it suffices that one day your name
will serve as a bulwark and shelter to my latest work.
Henceforth protect the favored book
through which I dare to hope for a second life:
    under your auspices alone, these verses,
    in spite of envy, will be judged
    worthy of the eyes of the universe.
I do not personally deserve such great favor:
    the fable requests it in its own name.
You know what influence this kind of fiction has over us.
If it procures for my verses the happiness of pleasing you,
I shall believe I owe it a temple as a reward;
but I wish to build temples for you alone.

## Les animaux malades de la peste

Un mal qui répand la terreur,
Mal que le ciel en sa fureur
Inventa pour punir les crimes de la terre,
La peste (puisqu'il faut l'appeler par son nom),
Capable d'enrichir en un jour l'Achéron,
        Faisait aux animaux la guerre.
Ils ne mouraient pas tous, mais tous étaient frappés.
        On n'en voyait point d'occupés
A chercher le soutien d'une mourante vie;
        Nul mets n'excitait leur envie.
        Ni loups ni renards n'épiaient
        La douce et l'innocente proie.
        Les tourterelles se fuyaient;
        Plus d'amour, partant plus de joie.
Le lion tint conseil, et dit: «Mes chers amis,
        Je crois que le ciel a permis
        Pour nos péchés cette infortune.
        Que le plus coupable de nous
Se sacrifie aux traits du céleste courroux;
Peut-être il obtiendra la guérison commune.
L'histoire nous apprend qu'en de tels accidents
        On fait de pareils dévouements.
Ne nous flattons donc point, voyons sans indulgence

        L'état de notre conscience.
Pour moi, satisfaisant mes appétits gloutons,
        J'ai dévoré force moutons.
        Que m'avaient-ils fait? Nulle offense.
Même il m'est arrivé quelquefois de manger
                Le berger.
Je me dévouerai donc, s'il le faut; mais je pense
Qu'il est bon que chacun s'accuse ainsi que moi:
Car on doit souhaiter selon toute justice

# The Plague-Stricken Animals

A misfortune that spreads terror,
a misfortune that heaven in its anger
invented to punish the crimes of the earth,
the plague (since it is necessary to call it by its name),
capable of enriching Acheron[34] in a single day,
was waging war against the animals.
They weren't all dying, but all were stricken.
None of them were to be seen occupied
in seeking sustenance for a life that was slipping away;
no food aroused their appetite.
Neither wolves nor foxes were spying upon
a gentle and innocent prey.
The turtle-doves shunned each other;
no more love, and thus no more joy.
The lion held a council, and said: "My dear friends,
I think that heaven has permitted
this catastrophe because of our sins.
Let the guiltiest one among us
sacrifice himself to the arrows of heavenly wrath;
perhaps he will obtain the cure of all.
History teaches us that in such circumstances
sacrifices of the kind are made.[35]
Therefore let us not flatter ourselves, let us observe without
indulgence
the state of our conscience.
As for me, to satisfy my greedy appetites,
I have devoured a great many sheep.
What had they done to me? No harm at all.
At times I have even happened to eat
the shepherd.
Thus I will sacrifice myself, if necessary; but I think
it right for each one to accuse himself as I have done:
because, in all justice, it is to be wished

---

[34] The world of the dead.

[35] The ancient Roman concept of *devotio,* an individual's yielding of his life to the gods to obtain divine favor for the community.

Que le plus coupable périsse.
–Sire, dit le renard, vous êtes trop bon roi;
Vos scrupules font voir trop de délicatesse;
Eh bien! manger moutons, canaille, sotte espèce,
Est-ce un péché? Non, non: vous leur fîtes, Seigneur,
    En les croquant beaucoup d'honneur;
    Et quant au berger, l'on peut dire
    Qu'il était digne de tous maux,
Étant de ces gens-là qui sur les animaux
    Se font un chimérique empire.»
Ainsi dit le renard, et flatteurs d'applaudir.
    On n'osa trop approfondir
Du tigre, ni de l'ours, ni des autres puissances,
    Les moins pardonnables offenses.
Tous les gens querelleurs, jusqu'aux simples mâtins,
Au dire de chacun étaient de petits saints.
L'âne vint à son tour et dit: «J'ai souvenance
    Qu'en un pré de moines passant,
La faim, l'occasion, l'herbe tendre, et, je pense,
    Quelque diable aussi me poussant,
Je tondis de ce pré la largeur de ma langue.
Je n'en avais nul droit, puisqu'il faut parler net.»
A ces mots on cria haro sur le baudet.
Un loup quelque peu clerc prouva par sa harangue
Qu'il fallait dévouer ce maudit animal,
Ce pelé, ce galeux, d'où venait tout leur mal.
Sa peccadille fut jugée un cas pendable.
Manger l'herbe d'autrui! quel crime abominable!
    Rien que la mort n'était capable
D'expier son forfait: on le lui fit bien voir.
Selon que vous serez puissant ou misérable,
Les jugements de cour vous rendront blanc ou noir.

that the guiltiest one of all perishes.
"Sire," said the fox, "you are too generous a king;
your scruples manifest too much sensitivity;
Come now! To eat sheep, such riffraff, a stupid bunch,
is that a sin? No, no. Your Majesty, by munching them,
      honored them extremely;
      and, as for the shepherd, one might say
      that he was deserving of every misfortune,
being of that folk which creates in its mind
      a fanciful superiority over the animals."
Thus spoke the fox, and the flatterers applauded.
      No one dared delve too deeply
into even the least pardonable offenses
      of the tiger, bear or the other potentates.
All the troublemaking species, down to the common mastiffs,
were little saints in everyone's opinion.
The donkey came in his turn and said: "I recollect
      that, when I was passing through a monastery meadow,
my hunger, the opportunity, the fresh grass and, I think,
      some devil, too, all egging me on,
I cropped a section of that meadow as wide as my tongue.
I had no right to do so, since I must confess plainly."
At these words they raised a hue and cry against the donkey.
A wolf who was somewhat of a scholar proved in a harangue
that it was necessary to sacrifice that accursed animal,
that mangy, scurvy fellow from whom all their misfortune sprang.
His peccadillo was judged to be a hanging case.
To eat someone else's grass! What an abominable crime!
      Only death was sufficient
to expiate his misdeed: and they let him see they meant it.
According to whether you are powerful or lowly,
the judgments of the royal court will paint you white or black.

# Les souhaits

Il est au Mogol des follets
Qui font office de valets,
Tiennent la maison propre, ont soin de l'équipage,
Et quelquefois du jardinage.
Si vous touchez à leur ouvrage,
Vous gâtez tout. Un d'eux près du Gange autrefois

Cultivait le jardin d'un assez bon bourgeois.
Il travaillait sans bruit, avec beaucoup d'adresse,
Aimait le maître et la maîtresse,
Et le jardin surtout. Dieu sait si les zéphyrs,
Peuple ami du démon, l'assistaient dans sa tâche.
Le follet de sa part travaillant sans relâche
Comblait ses hôtes de plaisirs.
Pour plus de marques de son zèle
Chez ces gens pour toujours il se fût arrêté,
Nonobstant la légèreté
A ses pareils si naturelle;
Mais ses confrères les esprits
Firent tant que le chef de cette république,
Par caprice ou par politique,
Le changea bientôt de logis.
Ordre lui vient d'aller au fond de la Norvège
Prendre le soin d'une maison
En tout temps couverte de neige;
Et d'Indou qu'il était on vous le fait Lapon.
Avant que de partir, l'esprit dit à ses hôtes:
«On m'oblige de vous quitter:
Je ne sais pas pour quelles fautes;
Mais enfin il le faut, je ne puis arrêter
Qu'un temps fort court, un mois, peut-être une semaine.
Employez-la; formez trois souhaits, car je puis
Rendre trois souhaits accomplis:
Trois sans plus.» Souhaiter, ce n'est pas une peine

# *The Wishes*

In the empire of the Grand Moghul[36] there are sprites
who play the part of servants,
keeping one's home clean, taking care of household chores,
and sometimes of the garden as well.
If you meddle with their work,
you spoil everything. Once upon a time, one of them, near the
Ganges,
was cultivating the garden of a quite well-to-do citizen.
He worked noiselessly and very skillfully;
he loved the man and lady of the house,
and especially the garden. God knows the west winds,
a folk friendly to the brownie, assisted him in his task!
For his part, the sprite, working without letup,
heaped joy upon his hosts.
As a further sign of his devotion,
he would have stayed with those people for good
despite the inconstancy
so natural to his kind;
but his fellow spirits
brought it about that the ruler of their state,
either capriciously or for reasons of politics,
soon made him change residence.
He received orders to proceed to the remotest part of Norway
to assume the care of a house
that was permanently covered with snow;
and from the Hindu he was, behold him transformed into a Lapp.
Before departing, the spirit said to his hosts:
"I am compelled to leave you,
for what faults I don't know,
but I must; I can only linger
a very short while, a month, perhaps a week.
Make use of that week; think of three wishes, for I am able
to grant three wishes,
three and no more." To make wishes is not a bother

---

36 Northern India.

Étrange et nouvelle aux humains.
Ceux-ci pour premier vœu demandent l'abondance,
  Et l'abondance à pleines mains
  Verse en leurs coffres la finance,
En leurs greniers le blé, dans leurs caves les vins;
Tout en crève. Comment ranger cette chevance?
Quels registres, quels soins, quel temps il leur fallut!
Tous deux sont empêchés si jamais on le fut.
  Les voleurs contre eux complotèrent,
  Les grands seigneurs leur empruntèrent,
Le prince les taxa. Voilà les pauvres gens
  Malheureux par trop de fortune.
«Otez-nous de ces biens l'affluence importune,
Dirent-ils l'un et l'autre; heureux les indigents!
La pauvreté vaut mieux qu'une telle richesse.
Retirez-vous, trésors, fuyez; et toi, déesse,
Mère du bon esprit, compagne du repos,
O médiocrité, reviens vite.» A ces mots,
La médiocrité revient; on lui fait place;
  Avec elle ils rentrent en grâce,
Au bout de deux souhaits étant aussi chanceux
  Qu'ils étaient, et que sont tous ceux
Qui souhaitent toujours et perdent en chimères
Le temps qu'ils feraient mieux de mettre à leurs affaires.
  Le follet en rit avec eux.
  Pour profiter de sa largesse,
Quand il voulut partir et qu'il fut sur le point,
  Ils demandèrent la sagesse:
  C'est un trésor qui n'embarrasse point.


## La cour du lion

Sa Majesté lionne un jour voulut connaître
De quelles nations le Ciel l'avait fait maître.
  Il manda donc par députés
  Ses vassaux de toute nature,
  Envoyant de tous les côtés
  Une circulaire écriture,
  Avec son sceau. L'écrit portait

that is strange or new to human beings.
These two as their first wish asked for wealth,
and with full hands wealth
poured cash into their coffers,
wheat into their granaries, wines into their cellars;
everything was bursting. How could they organize this property?
What ledgers, what pains, what time it took them!
Both of them were entangled if anyone ever was.
Thieves plotted against them,
great lords borrowed from them,
the ruler taxed them. And so the poor people
were unhappy through an excess of fortune.
"Remove the troubling abundance of these possessions from us,"
one and the other said; "happy are the indigent!
Poverty is preferable to riches like these.
Depart, treasures, flee; and you, goddess,
mother of good spirits, companion of repose,
Moderation, return quickly." At these words,
Moderation returned; they made room for her;
they reingratiated themselves with her,
remaining, after two wishes, no luckier
than they had been before, just as all those are
who are always wishing and who waste in daydreams
the time that they'd do better to spend on their concerns.
The sprite laughed over it along with them.
In order to take advantage of his generosity,
when he decided to leave and the very last moment had come,
they asked for wisdom:
that is a treasure which doesn't create inconvenience.

## The Court of King Lion

One day his leonine Majesty wished to learn
of which nations Heaven had made him master.
Thus through delegates he summoned
his vassals of all kinds,
sending everywhere
a circular letter
with his seal. The message stated

Qu'un mois durant le roi tiendrait
Cour plénière, dont l'ouverture
Devait être un fort grand festin,
Suivi des tours de Fagotin.
Par ce trait de magnificence
Le prince à ses sujets étalait sa puissance.
En son Louvre il les invita.
Quel Louvre! un vrai charnier, dont l'odeur se porta

D'abord au nez des gens. L'ours boucha sa narine:
Il se fût bien passé de faire cette mine.

Sa grimace déplut. Le monarque irrité
L'envoya chez Pluton faire le dégoûté.
Le singe approuva fort cette sévérité,
Et, flatteur excessif, il loua la colère
Et la griffe du prince, et l'antre, et cette odeur:
Il n'était ambre, il n'était fleur,
Qui ne fût ail au prix. Sa sotte flatterie
Eut un mauvais succès, et fut encor punie.
Ce monseigneur du Lion-là
Fut parent de Caligula.
Le renard étant proche: «Or çà, lui dit le sire,
Que sens-tu? dis-le moi. Parle sans déguiser.»
L'autre aussitôt de s'excuser,
Alléguant un grand rhume: il ne pouvait que dire
Sans odorat; bref il s'en tire.
Ceci vous sert d'enseignement:
Ne soyez à la cour, si vous voulez y plaire,
Ni fade adulateur, ni parleur trop sincère;
Et tâchez quelquefois de répondre en Normand.

that for a month the king would hold
plenary court, the opening of which
was to be a very great feast,
followed by a show of Fagotin's[37] tricks.
By this stroke of magnificence
the ruler was displaying his might to his subjects.
He invited them to his Louvre.[38]
What a Louvre!—a regular charnel house, the stench of which
was wafted
at once to the guests' nostrils. The bear held his nose:
it would have been much better for him to have omitted that
gesture.
His grimace did not please. The vexed monarch
sent him off to play the squeamish one in the realm of Pluto.[39]
The monkey heartily approved of that harsh measure,
and, overdoing his flattery, praised the wrath
and the claws of the ruler, as well as his lair and that smell:
there was no ambergris, there was no flower
which wasn't garlic by comparison. His foolish flattery
went over badly, and was punished in its turn.
That lord lion
was a relative of Caligula.[40]
The fox being nearby, the king said to him: "Now,
what do *you* smell? Tell me. Speak without dissembling."
The fox immediately begged pardon,
claiming he had a bad cold: he wasn't able to reply
without a sense of smell; in short, he got away with it.
This is a lesson to you:
At court, if you wish to please there, don't be
either an insipid flatterer or too sincere a speaker;
and try sometimes to reply like a man from Normandy.[41]

---

[37] A trained monkey popular at the time.
[38] Royal palace—not yet a museum.
[39] God of the underworld.
[40] Cruel, unstable Roman emperor (reigned 37–44).
[41] That is, shrewdly and craftily, "like a Philadelphia lawyer."

## La laitière et le pot au lait

Perrette, sur sa tête ayant un pot au lait
    Bien posé sur un coussinet,
Prétendait arriver sans encombre à la ville.
Légère et court vêtue, elle allait à grands pas,
Ayant mis ce jour-là pour être plus agile
    Cotillon simple, et souliers plats.
    Notre laitière ainsi troussée
    Comptait déjà dans sa pensée
Tout le prix de son lait, en employait l'argent,

Achetait un cent d'œufs, faisait triple couvée;
La chose allait à bien par son soin diligent.
    «Il m'est, disait-elle, facile
D'élever des poulets autour de ma maison:
    Le renard sera bien habile,
S'il ne m'en laisse assez pour avoir un cochon.
Le porc à s'engraisser coûtera peu de son;
Il était, quand je l'eus, de grosseur raisonnable;
J'aurai, le revendant, de l'argent bel et bon.
Et qui m'empêchera de mettre en notre étable,
Vu le prix dont il est, une vache et son veau,
Que je verrai sauter au milieu du troupeau?
Perrette là-dessus saute aussi, transportée.
Le lait tombe: adieu veau, vache, cochon, couvée.
La dame de ces biens, quittant d'un œil marri
    Sa fortune ainsi répandue,
    Va s'excuser à son mari,
    En grand danger d'être battue.
    Le récit en farce en fut fait:
    On l'appela *le Pot au lait*.

    Quel esprit ne bat la campagne?
    Qui ne fait châteaux en Espagne?
Picrochole, Pyrrhus, la laitière, enfin tous,

# The Milkmaid and the Jug of Milk

Perrette, carrying on her head a jug of milk
    carefully placed on a pad,
expected to arrive in town without a mishap.
Light of foot and short of skirt, she was taking long steps,
having dressed that day, to be more nimble,
    in a simple petticoat and low-heeled shoes.
    Our milkmaid, thus turned out,
    was already calculating in her mind
the full price of her milk, was already investing the money she'd get
                for it,
was buying a hundred eggs and having them hatched in three clutches;
the plan was working out well thanks to her diligent care.
    She was saying: "It's easy for me
to raise chickens around my house:
    the fox will have to be very crafty
if he doesn't leave me enough to buy a pig with.
To fatten the hog will cost only a little bran;
when I bought him, he was of a decent size;
when I sell him, I'll have a nice amount of money.
And who'll stop me from putting in our shed,
seeing the price we get for him, a cow and her calf,
which I'll see jumping in the midst of the herd?"
At that point Perrette, carried away, jumps, too.
The milk falls: goodbye to calf, cow, pig, brood of chicks.
The mistress of these possessions, leaving behind with saddened eyes
    her fortune all spilled out in this way,
    goes off to apologize to her husband,
    in great danger of being beaten.
    The event was used as the plot of a farce:
    it was called *The Jug of Milk*.

    Whose mind doesn't go wandering?
    Who doesn't build castles in Spain?
Picrochole,[42] Pyrrhus,[43] the milkmaid—in short, everybody,

---

[42] A character in Rabelais, bent on vast conquest.

[43] He of the "Pyrrhic victory": a king of Epirus who invaded Italy in 280 B.C. in vain hopes of conquering Rome.

Autant les sages que les fous?
Chacun songe en veillant, il n'est rien de plus doux;
Une flatteuse erreur emporte alors nos âmes:
 Tout le bien du monde est à nous,
 Tous les honneurs, toutes les femmes.
Quand je suis seul, je fais au plus brave un défi:
Je m'écarte, je vais détrôner le sophi;
 On m'élit roi, mon peuple m'aime;
Les diadèmes vont sur ma tête pleuvant.
Quelque accident fait-il que je rentre en moi-même,
 Je suis Gros-Jean comme devant.


## Le curé et le mort

 Un mort s'en allait tristement
 S'emparer de son dernier gîte;
 Un curé s'en allait gaîment
 Enterrer ce mort au plus vite.
Notre défunt était en carrosse porté,
 Bien et dûment empaqueté,
Et vêtu d'une robe, hélas! qu'on nomme bière,
 Robe d'hiver, robe d'été,
 Que les morts ne dépouillent guère.
 Le pasteur était à côté,
 Et récitait à l'ordinaire
 Maintes dévotes oraisons,
 Et des psaumes et des leçons,
 Et des versets, et des répons:
 «Monsieur le mort, laissez-nous faire,
On vous en donnera de toutes les façons;
 Il ne s'agit que du salaire.»
Messire Jean Chouart couvait des yeux son mort,

Comme si l'on eût dû lui ravir ce trésor,
 Et des regards semblait lui dire:
 «Monsieur le mort, j'aurai de vous
 Tant en argent, et tant en cire,

the wise as well as the foolish?
Everyone daydreams, there's nothing sweeter;
a flattering delusion carries away our souls at such times:
    all the wealth in the world is ours,
    all honors, all women.
When I'm alone, I issue a challenge to the bravest man:
I stray far off, I'm off to dethrone the Shah of Persia;
    I'm chosen king, my people love me;
crowns come raining down on my head.
Some incident makes me come back to reality,
    and I'm John the clodhopper just as I was before.


# The Parish Priest and the Dead Man

A dead man was sadly setting out
    to lay claim to his last resting place;
    a parish priest was cheerfully setting out
    to bury that dead man as quickly as possible.
The deceased was transported in a coach,
    well and duly wrapped up,
and dressed in a garment that, alas, is called a coffin,
    a garment for winter, a garment for summer,
    which the dead rarely take off.
    The shepherd of souls was alongside him
    and was reciting in customary fashion
    many a pious prayer,
    as well as psalms and lessons
    and scriptural verses and responses:
    "My dear dead man, let us do our job,
we'll supply you with every kind of attention;
    all we care about is the fee."
His reverence Jean Chouart[44] couldn't tear his eyes away from his
                                                    dead man,
as if someone were going to steal that treasure from him,
    and he seemed to say to him by the look in his eyes:
    "My dear dead man, I shall receive on your account
    this much in money, and this much in candle wax,

---

44 The name is from Rabelais.

Et tant en autres menus coûts.»
Il fondait là-dessus l'achat d'une feuillette
    Du meilleur vin des environs;
    Certaine nièce assez propette
    Et sa chambrière Pâquette
    Devaient avoir des cotillons.
    Sur cette agréable pensée
    Un heurt survient, adieu le char.
    Voilà messire Jean Chouart
Qui du choc de son mort a la tête cassée:
Le paroissien en plomb entraîne son pasteur,
    Notre curé suit son seigneur;
    Tous deux s'en vont de compagnie.
    Proprement toute notre vie
Est le curé Chouart qui sur son mort comptait,
    Et la fable du *Pot au lait.*


# Les deux coqs

Deux coqs vivaient en paix; une poule survint,
    Et voilà la guerre allumée.
Amour, tu perdis Troie; et c'est de toi que vint
    Cette querelle envenimée
Où du sang des dieux même on vit le Xanthe teint.

Longtemps entre nos coqs le combat se maintint.
Le bruit s'en répandit par tout le voisinage.
La gent qui porte crête au spectacle accourut.
    Plus d'une Hélène au beau plumage
Fut le prix du vainqueur; le vaincu disparut.
Il alla se cacher au fond de sa retraite,
    Pleura sa gloire et ses amours,
Ses amours, qu'un rival tout fier de sa défaite
Possédait à ses yeux. Il voyait tous les jours
Cet objet rallumer sa haine et son courage.

and this much in other small charges."
He was counting on that for the purchase of a quarter cask
      of the best wine in the vicinity;
      a certain quite elegant niece
      and his chambermaid Pâquette
      were to get new petticoats.
      At that pleasant thought
      there came a jolt, and goodbye coach.
      There was his reverence Jean Chouart
with his head cracked by a collision with his dead man:
the lead-encased parishioner carries along his shepherd,
      our priest follows his lord;
      both depart in company.[45]
      Truth to tell, our whole life
is the priest Chouart who was counting on this dead man,
      and the fable of "The Jug of Milk."

## The Two Roosters

Two roosters lived in peace; a hen came along,
      and behold, war broke out.
Love, you ruined Troy; and it was from you that there arose
      that embittered dispute
in which the Xanthus[46] was seen tinged with the blood of the gods
                        themselves.
The combat between our two roosters was long continued.
The report of it spread through the entire vicinity.
The crest-bearing folk ran up to watch the show.
      More than one fine-feathered Helen
was the prize of the victor; the loser disappeared.
He went off to hide in the farthest corner of his retreat,
      lamenting his glory and his sweetheart,
his sweetheart, whom a rival, very proud over defeating him,
now possessed before his very eyes. Every day he beheld
that sight, which rekindled his hatred and his ardor.

---

[45] This actually occurred at the funeral of the Comte de Boufflers in 1672.

[46] Another name for the Scamander, the river near Troy. The Greeks were fighting
for the return of Helen of Troy.

Il aiguisait son bec, battait l'air et ses flancs,

> Et, s'exerçant contre les vents,
> S'armait d'une jalouse rage.
Il n'en eut pas besoin. Son vainqueur sur les toits
  S'alla percher, et chanter sa victoire.
>   Un vautour entendit sa voix:
>   Adieu les amours et la gloire.
Tout cet orgueil périt sous l'ongle du vautour.
>   Enfin, par un fatal retour,
>   Son rival autour de la poule
>   S'en revint faire le coquet:
>   Je laisse à penser quel caquet,
>   Car il eut des femmes en foule.
La Fortune se plaît à faire de ces coups;
Tout vainqueur insolent à sa perte travaille.
Défions-nous du sort, et prenons garde à nous
>   Après le gain d'une bataille.

## Les devineresses

C'est souvent du hasard que naît l'opinion,
Et c'est l'opinion qui fait toujours la vogue.
>   Je pourrais fonder ce prologue
Sur gens de tous états; tout est prévention,
Cabale, entêtement, point ou peu de justice:
C'est un torrent; qu'y faire? Il faut qu'il ait son cours:
>   Cela fut et sera toujours.
Une femme à Paris faisait la pythonisse.
On l'allait consulter sur chaque événement:
Perdait-on un chiffon, avait-on un amant,
Un mari vivant trop, au gré de son épouse,
Une mère fâcheuse, une femme jalouse,
>   Chez la devineuse on courait,

He would sharpen his beak, he would beat the air and his sides
                                                with his wings,
    and, training with the wind as an opponent,
    he worked himself up into a jealous fury.
He had no need of it. His conqueror went to perch
  on the rooftops, where he sang of his victory.
    A vulture heard his voice:
    farewell to love and glory.
All that pride perished beneath the vulture's talons.
    Finally, through one of fate's turnabouts,
    his rival came back to play the coxcomb
    in the hen's presence:
    I leave you to imagine what cackling there was,
    because he had a crowd of wives.
Fortune enjoys playing tricks like that;
every insolent conqueror contributes to his own destruction.
Let us be distrustful of fate, and watch out for ourselves
    after we win a battle.


## The Fortune Tellers

Public opinion often springs from a chance accident,
and it's public opinion that always creates a vogue.
    I could base this preamble
on people in any profession; everything depends on bias,
intrigue or obstinacy, there's no justice or very little:
it's a raging torrent; what's to be done? It has to run its course:
    things have always been that way and always will be.
A woman in Paris had set up as a seer.[47]
People went to consult her about every occurrence:
if they lost a bit of ribbon, it they had a lover,
a husband who was living too long for his spouse's liking,
a troublesome mother, a jealous wife,
    they would run to the fortune teller,

---

[47] The term in the French text, which would be "pythonissa" in English transliteration, and the term "Sibyl" used a few lines later, were two ancient Greek designations for divinely gifted prophetesses. In La Fontaine's day, witchcraft was also implied in these appellations. Recent poisoning cases in which highly placed persons were implicated may also have been on the poet's mind.

Pour se faire annoncer ce que l'on désirait.
    Son fait consistait en adresse;
Quelques termes de l'art, beaucoup de hardiesse,
Du hasard quelquefois, tout cela concourait:
Tout cela bien souvent faisait crier miracle.

Enfin quoique ignorante à vingt et trois carats,
    Elle passait pour un oracle.
L'oracle était logé dedans un galetas.
    Là cette femme emplit sa bourse,
    Et sans avoir d'autre ressource,
Gagne de quoi donner un rang à son mari.
Elle achète un office, une maison aussi.
    Voilà le galetas rempli
D'une nouvelle hôtesse, à qui toute la ville,
Femmes, filles, valets, gros messieurs, tout enfin
Allait comme autrefois demander son destin:
Le galetas devint l'antre de la Sibylle.
L'autre femelle avait achalandé ce lieu.
Cette dernière femme eut beau faire, eut beau dire:
«Moi devine! on se moque. Eh! Messieurs, sais-je lire?
Je n'ai jamais appris que ma croix de par Dieu.»
Point de raison; fallut deviner et prédire,
    Mettre à part force bons ducats,
Et gagner malgré soi plus que deux avocats.
Le meuble et l'équipage aidaient fort à la chose:
Quatre sièges boiteux, un manche de balai;
Tout sentait son sabbat et sa métamorphose.
    Quand cette femme aurait dit vrai
    Dans une chambre tapissée,
On s'en serait moqué: la vogue était passée
   Au galetas; il avait le crédit.
    L'autre femme se morfondit.
    L'enseigne fait la chalandise.
J'ai vu dans le Palais une robe mal mise
    Gagner gros: les gens l'avaient prise
    Pour maître tel, qui traînait après soi
   Force écoutants. Demandez-moi pourquoi.

to have her tell them what they wanted to hear.
    Her strong point lay in her cleverness;
a few professional expressions, a lot of boldness,
sometimes a lucky chance, all of that contributed:
all of that very often led people to declare that a miracle had
                                    occurred.
Finally, although ninety-five per cent an ignoramus,
    she was considered an oracle.
This oracle resided in a garret.
    There that woman filled her purse
    and, without any other source of income,
earned enough to buy an official rank for her husband.
She bought his position and a house as well.
    Now the garret was occupied
by a new hostess, to whom the whole town,
women, girls, servants, bigwigs—in short, everybody—
went to inquire about their destiny just as formerly:
the garret became the Sibyl's cave.
The other female had attracted steady custom to that spot.
Despite all that this new woman did, despite her saying:
"I, a fortune teller! You're joking. Ah! Gentlemen, can I even read?
All I've ever learned is my alphabet,"[48]
reason could not prevail; she had to prophesy, predict
    and lay aside a big heap of good ducats,
and, in spite of herself, she earned more than two lawyers.
The furniture and ambiance aided greatly in the matter:
four unsteady chairs, a broomstick;
everything reeked of witches' sabbaths and changes of shape.
    If that woman had made correct predictions
    in a tapestried chamber,
they would have laughed at her; fashion had now accepted
   the garret; the garret was what influenced people.
    The other woman was left out in the cold.
    The shop sign brings in the customers.
At the law courts I've seen someone draped carelessly in a judicial robe
    making a lot of money: people had taken him
    for Lawyer So-and-so, who was being accompanied by
a horde of lawyers without a brief. Ask me why.

---

[48] Alphabet primers began with a cross called *croix de par-Dieu.*

# Le chat, la belette, et le petit lapin

Du palais d'un jeune lapin
Dame belette un beau matin
S'empara: c'est une rusée.
Le maître étant absent, ce lui fut chose aisée.
Elle porta chez lui ses pénates un jour
Qu'il était allé faire à l'Aurore sa cour
Parmi le thym et la rosée.
Après qu'il eut brouté, trotté, fait tous ses tours,

Janot Lapin retourne aux souterrains séjours.
La belette avait mis le nez à la fenêtre.
«O dieux hospitaliers, que vois-je ici paraître?»
Dit l'animal chassé du paternel logis.
O là! Madame la belette,
Que l'on déloge sans trompette,
Ou je vais avertir tous les rats du pays.»
La dame au nez pointu répondit que la terre
Était au premier occupant.
C'était un beau sujet de guerre
Qu'un logis où lui-même il n'entrait qu'en rampant!
«Et quand ce serait un royaume,
Je voudrais bien savoir, dit-elle, quelle loi
En a pour toujours fait l'octroi
A Jean, fils ou neveu de Pierre ou de Guillaume,
Plutôt qu'à Paul, plutôt qu'à moi.»
Jean Lapin allégua la coutume et l'usage.
«Ce sont, dit-il, leurs lois qui m'ont de ce logis
Rendu maître et seigneur, et qui, de père en fils,
L'ont de Pierre à Simon, puis à moi Jean transmis.
Le premier occupant, est-ce une loi plus sage?
–Or bien, sans crier davantage,
Rapportons-nous, dit-elle, à Raminagrobis.»

# The Cat, the Weasel and the Little Rabbit

A young rabbit's palace
was seized and occupied one fine morning
by Madame Weasel: she's a shrewd one.
The owner being away, it was easy for her.
She transferred her household to his home one day
when he had gone out to pay court to the dawn
 amid the thyme and dew.
After he had nibbled grass, trotted around and done all his usual
                 stints,
Johnny Rabbit returned to his underground residence.
The weasel was looking out the window.
"O gods of hospitality, what is this I see before me?"
said the animal who had been driven from the residence of his fathers.
 "Hey, there! Madame Weasel,
 move out quickly and quietly,
or I'll go and inform all the rats in the countryside."
The lady with the pointed nose replied that land
 belonged to the first comer.
 What a fine object to fight over,
a house which even he could only enter by crawling!
 "And even if it were a kingdom,
I'd like to know," she said, "what law
 conceded it in perpetuity
to John, son or nephew of Peter or William,
 rather than to Paul, rather than to me."
John Rabbit cited custom and common practice as arguments.
"It is their laws," he said, "which have made me
lord and master of this house, and which, from father to son,
have handed it down from Peter to Simon, then to me, John.
The first comer! Is that a wiser law?"
 "All right, then, without any more shouting,"
she said, "let's refer the case to Raminagrobis."[49]

---

[49] This name; the name Grippeminaud below (a combination of *gripper*, "to seize craftily with claws," and *minauder*, "to put on falsely ingratiating airs"); the rare word *chattemite* (literally, "gentle she-cat") and the concept of a magistrate (bearer of a fur-trimmed robe) as a furry cat (*chat fourré*) are all borrowings from Rabelais.

C'était un chat vivant comme un dévot ermite,
     Un chat faisant la chattemite,
Un saint homme de chat, bien fourré, gros et gras,
     Arbitre expert sur tous les cas.
     Jean Lapin pour juge l'agrée.
     Les voilà tous deux arrivés
     Devant sa majesté fourrée.
Grippeminaud leur dit: «Mes enfants, approchez,
Approchez; je suis sourd; les ans en sont la cause.»
L'un et l'autre approcha, ne craignant nulle chose.
Aussitôt qu'à portée il vit les contestants,
     Grippeminaud le bon apôtre,
Jetant des deux côtés la griffe en même temps,
Mit les plaideurs d'accord en croquant l'un et l'autre.


Ceci ressemble fort aux débats qu'ont parfois
Les petits souverains se rapportant aux rois.


## La mort et le mourant

     La mort ne surprend point le sage:
     Il est toujours prêt à partir,
     S'étant su lui-même avertir
Du temps où l'on se doit résoudre à ce passage.
     Ce temps, hélas! embrasse tous les temps:
Qu'on le partage en jours, en heures, en moments,
     Il n'en est point qu'il ne comprenne
Dans le fatal tribut; tous sont de son domaine;
Et le premier instant où les enfants des rois
     Ouvrent les yeux à la lumière
     Est celui qui vient quelquefois
     Fermer pour toujours leur paupière.
     Défendez-vous par la grandeur,
Alléguez la beauté, la vertu, la jeunesse,
     La mort ravit tout sans pudeur.
Un jour le monde entier accroîtra sa richesse.
     Il n'est rien de moins ignoré,
     Et puisqu'il faut que je le die,
     Rien où l'on soit moins préparé.
Un mourant qui comptait plus de cent ans de vie

This was a cat who lived the life of a pious hermit,
    a cat who played the part of a humble flatterer,
a saintly fellow of a cat, very furry, big and fat,
      an expert arbitrator of all legal cases.
      John Rabbit accepted him as a judge.
      Both parties had now come
      before his furry majesty.
Grippeminaud said to them: "Come nearer, my children,
come nearer; I am deaf; my age is to blame for that."
Both of them drew nearer, fearing nothing.
As soon as he saw the litigants within reach,
      Grippeminaud, the sanctimonious hypocrite,
lashing out with his claws on both sides at once,
brought the opponents together again by gobbling up one and the
                                      other.

This bears a great resemblance to the quarrels that petty rulers
sometimes get into when they refer their affairs to powerful kings.


# Death and the Dying Man

      Death doesn't take the wise man by surprise:
      he is always ready to depart,
        having been capable of warning himself
about the moment when a man must face up to this change of state.
      Alas! That moment comprises all moments:
whether it's divided into days, hours or minutes,
      there's no subdivision that it fails to include
when it claims its fatal tribute; all men fall under its jurisdiction;
and the first instant in which the children of kings
      open their eyes to the light
      is the same one that sometimes
      closes their eyelids forever.
      Defend yourself by stating your high rank,
cite as arguments your beauty, virtue, youth,
      death snatches everything away shamelessly.
One day the whole world will be added to its riches.
      There is no fact that is better known,
      and since I must say it,
      none for which people are worse prepared.
A dying man who had been alive more than a hundred years

Se plaignait à la Mort que précipitamment
Elle le contraignait de partir tout à l'heure,
  Sans qu'il eût fait son testament,
Sans l'avertir au moins. «Est-il juste qu'on meure
Au pied levé? dit-il; attendez quelque peu.
Ma femme ne veut pas que je parte sans elle;
Il me reste à pourvoir un arrière-neveu;
Souffrez qu'à mon logis j'ajoute encore une aile.
Que vous êtes pressante, ô déesse cruelle!
–Vieillard, lui dit la Mort, je ne t'ai point surpris.
Tu te plains sans raison de mon impatience.
Eh! n'as-tu pas cent ans? Trouve-moi dans Paris
Deux mortels aussi vieux, trouve-m'en dix en France.
Je devais, ce dis-tu, te donner quelque avis
  Qui te disposât à la chose:
 J'aurais trouvé ton testament tout fait,
Ton petit-fils pourvu, ton bâtiment parfait.
Ne te donna-t-on pas des avis quand la cause
  Du marcher et du mouvement,
  Quand les esprits, le sentiment,
Quand tout faillit en toi? Plus de goût, plus d'ouïe;

Toute chose pour toi semble être évanouie;
Pour toi l'astre du jour prend des soins superflus.
Tu regrettes des biens qui ne te touchent plus.
  Je t'ai fait voir tes camarades
  Ou morts, ou mourants, ou malades.
Qu'est-ce que tout cela, qu'un avertissement?
  Allons, vieillard, et sans réplique;
  Il n'importe à la république
  Que tu fasses ton testament.»
La Mort avait raison. Je voudrais qu'à cet âge
On sortît de la vie ainsi que d'un banquet,
Remerciant son hôte, et qu'on fît son paquet:
Car de combien peut-on retarder le voyage?
Tu murmures, vieillard; vois ces jeunes mourir,
  Vois-les marcher, vois-les courir
A des morts, il est vrai, glorieuses et belles,
Mais sûres cependant, et quelquefois cruelles.
J'ai beau te le crier: mon zèle est indiscret:
Le plus semblable aux morts meurt le plus à regret.

was complaining to Death that, all of a sudden,
it was forcing him to depart immediately,
    without his having made his will,
without at least giving him any warning. "Is it fair for someone to die
on the spur of the moment?" he asked; "wait a little bit.
My wife doesn't want me to depart without her;
I still have to set up one of my great-grandsons in life;
allow me to add another wing to my house.
How you rush people, O cruel goddess!"
"Old man," Death said to him, "I didn't take you by surprise.
It's unreasonable for you to complain about my impatience.
Tell me, aren't you a hundred? Find me in Paris
two mortals that old, find me ten in France.
You say I should have given you some notice
    that would prepare your mind for the event:
    then I'd have found your will all made out,
your grandson established, your construction finished.
Weren't you given any notices when the wellspring
    of walking and moving,
        when your animal spirits, your sensations,
when everything in you started to fail? No more sense of taste or
                                            hearing;
for you everything seems to have disappeared;
for you the star of the day wastes its efforts.
You regret the loss of properties that no longer affect you.
    I've shown you your comrades
    either dead, or dying, or ill.
What is all that if it isn't a warning?
    Come along, old man, and without backtalk;
    it's of no import to the state
    whether you make your will or not."
Death was right. I'd like to see people at that age
leave life as if leaving a banquet,
thanking their host and gathering their belongings:
because how long can the trip be postponed?
You grumble, old man; look at these young men dying,
    look at them marching off, look at them running
toward a death that is glorious and beautiful, it's true,
but nevertheless certain, and sometimes cruel.
It's in vain that I shout this to you; my ardor is misplaced:
the man who most resembles the dead dies the most unwillingly.

# Le savetier et le financier

Un savetier chantait du matin jusqu'au soir:
　　C'était merveilles de le voir,
Merveilles de l'ouïr; il faisait des passages,
　　Plus content qu'aucun des sept sages.
Son voisin au contraire, étant tout cousu d'or,
　　Chantait peu, dormait moins encor.
　　C'était un homme de finance.
Si sur le point du jour parfois il sommeillait,
Le savetier alors en chantant l'éveillait,
　　Et le financier se plaignait
　　Que les soins de la Providence
N'eussent pas au marché fait vendre le dormir
　　Comme le manger et le boire.
　　En son hôtel il fait venir
Le chanteur, et lui dit: «Or çà, sire Grégoire,
Que gagnez-vous par an?–Par an? Ma foi, Monsieur,
　　Dit avec un ton de rieur
Le gaillard savetier, ce n'est point ma manière
De compter de la sorte, et je n'entasse guère
　Un jour sur l'autre: il suffit qu'à la fin
　　J'attrape le bout de l'année.
　　Chaque jour amène son pain.
–Eh bien! que gagnez-vous, dites-moi, par journée?
–Tantôt plus, tantôt moins: le mal est que toujours
(Et sans cela nos gains seraient assez honnêtes),
Le mal est que dans l'an s'entremêlent des jours
　　Qu'il faut chômer: on nous ruine en fêtes.
L'une fait tort à l'autre, et monsieur le curé
De quelque nouveau saint charge toujours son prône.»
Le financier, riant de sa naïveté,
Lui dit: «Je vous veux mettre aujourd'hui sur le trône.
Prenez ces cent écus: gardez-les avec soin,
　　Pour vous en servir au besoin.»
Le savetier crut voir tout l'argent que la terre
　　Avait depuis plus de cent ans
　　Produit pour l'usage des gens.

## The Cobbler and the Financier

A cobbler used to sing from morning to evening;
    it was wonderful to see him,
wonderful to hear him; he would perform cadenzas,
    happier than any of the seven sages.
His neighbor, on the other hand, who was rolling in money,
    sang very little, slept even less;
    he was a man of finance.
If, at daybreak, he sometimes dozed a bit,
then the cobbler would awaken him by singing;
    and the financier complained
    that the plans of Providence
had not arranged for sleep to be sold in the marketplace
    like food and drink.
    He summoned the singer
to his mansion, and said to him: "Look here, Master Gregory,
what do you earn per year?" "Per year? My goodness, sir,"
    said the merry Cobbler
with laughter in his voice, "I don't generally
count my earnings that way; and I don't pile up
  one day's receipts on another's; it's enough if finally
    I make ends meet when the year is over;
    every day brings in some bread."
"Well then, tell me, what do you earn per day?"
"Sometimes more, sometimes less: the trouble is that always
(and otherwise our income would be quite respectable),
the trouble is that during the year days are mixed in
  when we have to sit idle: they ruin us with holidays.
One holiday drives out the other, and the priest
is always burdening his sermon with some new saint."
The financier, laughing at his simplicity,
said to him: "Today I shall place you on the throne.
Take this hundred crowns; guard it with care
    so you can use it when necessary."
The Cobbler thought he saw all the money that the earth
    had, for over a hundred years,
    produced for the use of man.

Il retourne chez lui; dans sa cave il enserre
    L'argent et sa joie à la fois.
Plus de chant; il perdit la voix
Du moment qu'il gagna ce qui cause nos peines.
    Le sommeil quitta son logis,
    Il eut pour hôtes les soucis,
    Les soupçons, les alarmes vaines.
Tout le jour il avait l'œil au guet; et la nuit,
    Si quelque chat faisait du bruit,
Le chat prenait l'argent. A la fin le pauvre homme
S'en courut chez celui qu'il ne réveillait plus.
«Rendez-moi, lui dit-il, mes chansons et mon somme,
    Et reprenez vos cent écus.»

## Le lion, le loup, et le renard

Un lion décrépit, goutteux, n'en pouvant plus,
Voulait que l'on trouvât remède à la vieillesse.
Alléguer l'impossible aux rois, c'est un abus.
    Celui-ci parmi chaque espèce
Manda des médecins; il en est de tous arts.
Médecins au lion viennent de toutes parts;
De tous côtés lui vient des donneurs de recettes.
    Dans les visites qui sont faites,
Le renard se dispense, et se tient clos et coi.
Le loup en fait sa cour, daube au coucher du roi

Son camarade absent: le prince tout à l'heure
Veut qu'on aille enfumer renard dans sa demeure,
Qu'on le fasse venir. Il vient, est présenté,
Et, sachant que le loup lui faisait cette affaire:
«Je crains, Sire, dit-il, qu'un rapport peu sincère
    Ne m'ait à mépris imputé
    D'avoir différé cet hommage;
    Mais j'étais en pèlerinage,
Et m'acquittais d'un vœu fait pour votre santé.
    Même j'ai vu dans mon voyage
Gens experts et savants, leur ai dit la langueur
Dont Votre Majesté craint à bon droit la suite:

He returned home; in his cellar he locked up
    the money, and his joy at the same time.
    No more singing: he lost his voice
the moment he acquired the cause of our woes.
    Sleep abandoned his dwelling;
    he had for guests worries,
    suspicions, false alarms;
all day he kept a sharp lookout; and at night
    if some cat made noise,
the cat was taking the money. Finally the poor man
ran to the home of the one he no longer awakened:
"Give me back," he said, "my songs and my sleep,
    and take back your hundred crowns."

# The Lion, the Wolf and the Fox

A decrepit, gout-ridden lion, devoid of all vigor,
wanted some cure to be found for old age.
To assert to kings that their wishes are impossible is an error.
    This king summoned doctors
belonging to every animal species; there are doctors in all specialties.
Physicians came to the lion from everywhere;
from all sides he receives writers of prescriptions.
    From the visits made to the lion
the fox absents himself, and remains quiet and secluded.
The wolf takes this opportunity to ingratiate himself; at the king's
                            bedtime ceremony
he denigrates his absent colleague: the ruler immediately
orders men to go and smoke the fox out of his hole
and make him come. He comes, he is presented,
and, knowing that the wolf created this situation for him,
he says: "I fear, Sire, that a rather untruthful report
    has charged me with contempt
    for having delayed this homage;
    but I was on a pilgrimage,
and was fulfilling a vow I had made for your health.
    In fact, on my journey I went to see
experts and scholars, and told them about the weakness
whose consequences Your Majesty has every right to fear:

Vous ne manquez que de chaleur;
Le long âge en vous l'a détruite.
D'un loup écorché vif appliquez-vous la peau
Toute chaude et toute fumante;
Le secret sans doute en est beau
Pour la nature défaillante.
Messire loup vous servira,
S'il vous plaît, de robe de chambre.»
Le roi goûte cet avis-là:
On écorche, on taille, on démembre
Messire loup. Le monarque en soupa,
Et de sa peau s'enveloppa.

Messieurs les courtisans, cessez de vous détruire:
Faites, si vous pouvez, votre cour sans vous nuire.
Le mal se rend chez vous au quadruple du bien.
Les daubeurs ont leur tour d'une ou d'autre manière:
Vous êtes dans une carrière
Où l'on ne se pardonne rien.

## Le pouvoir des fables

### A Monsieur de Barillon

La qualité d'ambassadeur
Peut-elle s'abaisser à des contes vulgaires?
Vous puis-je offrir mes vers et leurs grâces légères?
S'ils osent quelquefois prendre un air de grandeur,
Seront-ils point traités par vous de téméraires?
Vous avez bien d'autres affaires
A démêler que les débats
Du lapin et de la belette.
Lisez-les, ne les lisez pas;
Mais empêchez qu'on ne nous mette
Toute l'Europe sur les bras.
Que de mille endroits de la terre
Il nous vienne des ennemis,

all you're lacking is heat;
your great age has destroyed it in you.
Wrap yourself in the skin of a wolf flayed alive,
    while it's still hot and smoking;
    its hidden properties are no doubt beneficial
    to flagging natural functions.
    Doctor Wolf, if you please,
    will serve as a dressing gown."
    The king likes that advice:
    they flay, cut up and dismember
  Doctor Wolf. The monarch supped on him
    and wrapped himself in his skin.

Courtiers, cease destroying one another:
if you can, ingratiate yourselves without harming each other.
In your milieu evil is returned at a rate four times greater than good.
Backbiters get their punishment in one manner or another:
    you're engaged in a career
    in which no one ever forgives or is forgiven.

# *The Power of Fables*

## To Monsieur de Barillon[50]

    Can the rank of ambassador
stoop to hearing everyday stories?
May I offer you my verses and their unweighty graces?
If they sometimes venture to assume an air of grandeur,
won't you call them foolhardy?
    You have many other matters
    to resolve than the squabbles
    of the rabbit and the weasel.
    Read them, don't read them:
    but prevent us from becoming encumbered
    with all of Europe.
    If from a thousand places on earth
    enemies rush upon us,

---

[50] More properly spelled Barrillon; French ambassador to England.

J'y consens; mais que l'Angleterre
Veuille que nos deux rois se lassent d'être amis,
    J'ai peine à digérer la chose.
N'est-il point encor temps que Louis se repose?
Quel autre Hercule enfin ne se trouverait las
De combattre cette hydre? et faut-il qu'elle oppose
Une nouvelle tête aux efforts de son bras?
    Si votre esprit plein de souplesse,
    Par éloquence et par adresse,
Peut adoucir les cœurs et détourner ce coup,
Je vous sacrifierai cent moutons: c'est beaucoup
    Pour un habitant du Parnasse.
    Cependant faites-moi la grâce
    De prendre en don ce peu d'encens.
    Prenez en gré mes vœux ardents,
Et le récit en vers qu'ici je vous dédie.
Son sujet vous convient; je n'en dirai pas plus:
    Sur les éloges que l'envie
    Doit avouer qui vous sont dus,
    Vous ne voulez pas qu'on appuie.

Dans Athène autrefois, peuple vain et léger,
Un orateur, voyant sa patrie en danger,
Courut à la tribune, et d'un art tyrannique
Voulant forcer les cœurs dans une république,
Il parla fortement sur le commun salut.
On ne l'écoutait pas: l'orateur recourut
    A ces figures violentes
Qui savent exciter les âmes les plus lentes.
Il fit parler les morts, tonna, dit ce qu'il put.

Le vent emporta tout; personne ne s'émut.
    L'animal aux têtes frivoles,
Étant fait à ces traits, ne daignait l'écouter.

that's all right with me; but if England
decides that our two kings should tire of being friends,[51]
    that's a matter hard for me to stomach.
Isn't it time by now for Louis to have some rest?
What other Hercules wouldn't find himself weary at last
of fighting that hydra? And must it present
a new head to confront the efforts of his arm?[52]
    If your mind, full of resourcefulness,
      through eloquence and through cleverness,
can soften hearts and turn aside this blow,
I shall sacrifice a hundred sheep to you: that's a lot
    for an inhabitant of Parnassus.[53]
    Meanwhile grant me the favor
    of accepting this small amount of incense as a gift.
    Deign to accept my sincere good wishes
and the verse narrative that I here dedicate to you.
Its subject suits you; I'll say no more about it:
    you do not like people to dwell
    on the praises that even envy
    must admit are due to you.

Once, in Athens, a frivolous and flighty city,
an orator, seeing his homeland in danger,
dashed to the rostrum and, wishing to bend people's minds
with the tyranny of art in a republic,
he spoke forcefully about public safety.
He wasn't listened to: the orator had recourse
    to those violent images
which are able to inflame the most sluggish minds.
He put words in the mouth of dead men, he thundered, he said
              all he could.
All was gone with the wind; no one was stirred.
    The many-headed, trivial-minded mob,
being accustomed to those sallies, didn't deign to listen to him.

---

[51] In 1678, the British Parliament wanted King Charles II (who was heavily subsidized by Louis XIV) to declare war on France as part of the European coalition against that aggressor.

[52] One of Hercules' labors was fighting the hydra, each of whose many heads grew back every time it was cut off.

[53] The mountain of the muses.

Tous regardaient ailleurs: il en vit s'arrêter

A des combats d'enfants, et point à ses paroles.
Que fit le harangueur? Il prit un autre tour.
«Cérès, commença-t-il, faisait voyage un jour
    Avec l'anguille et l'hirondelle;
Un fleuve les arrête, et l'anguille en nageant,
    Comme l'hirondelle en volant,
Le traversa bientôt.» L'assemblée à l'instant,
Cria tout d'une voix: «Et Cérès, que fit-elle?
    – Ce qu'elle fit? Un prompt courroux
    L'anima d'abord contre vous.
Quoi! de contes d'enfants son peuple s'embarrasse!
    Et du péril qui le menace
Lui seul entre les Grecs il néglige l'effet!
Que ne demandez-vous ce que Philippe fait?»
    A ce reproche l'assemblée,
    Par l'apologue réveillée,
    Se donne entière à l'orateur:
    Un trait de fable en eut l'honneur.
Nous sommes tous d'Athène en ce point, et moi-même,
Au moment que je fais cette moralité,
    Si *Peau d'âne* m'était conté,
    J'y prendrais un plaisir extrême.
Le monde est vieux, dit-on, je le crois; cependant
Il le faut amuser encor comme un enfant.

Everyone was looking in a different direction; he saw some of them
                                         intent
on fights between children, and not at all on his words.
What did the speaker do? He tried another tack.
"Ceres,"[54] he began, "was traveling one day
    with the eel and the swallow;
they were halted by a river, and the eel by swimming
    and the swallow by flying
soon crossed it." The assembly, that instant,
cried out with one voice: "And Ceres, what did she do?"
    "What she did? A prompt anger
    against you seized upon her at once.
What, her city wastes its time on children's stories
    and, alone among the Greeks,
disregards the effects of the danger that threatens it?
Why don't you ask what Philip[55] is doing?"
    At this reproach the assembly,
    brought to its senses by the fable,
    lent its ears wholeheartedly to the orator:
    a flash of fable was to be thanked for that.
In this regard, we're all from Athens, and I myself,
at the very moment I point this moral,
    would take extreme delight
    if someone recited "Donkey Skin"[56] to me.
The world is old, people say, and I believe it; all the same
it still needs to be entertained like a child.

---

[54] In Greek, Demeter, goddess of grain, who had a shrine near Athens; thus, "her city," eight lines later.

[55] This mention of Philip of Macedon (father of Alexander the Great), who was threatening to conquer the Greek city-states, suggests that the orator is his famous opponent Demosthenes (second half of the fourth century B.C.), although he was not the orator meant in the original Aesop fable on which this La Fontaine fable is based.

[56] A nursery tale retold and published later in the century by Charles Perrault.

## L'ours et l'amateur des jardins

Certain ours montagnard, ours à demi léché,
Confiné par le sort dans un bois solitaire,
Nouveau Bellérophon, vivait seul et caché.
Il fût devenu fou: la raison d'ordinaire
N'habite pas longtemps chez les gens séquestrés.
Il est bon de parler, et meilleur de se taire;
Mais tous deux sont mauvais alors qu'ils sont outrés.
    Nul animal n'avait affaire
    Dans les lieux que l'ours habitait,
    Si bien que tout ours qu'il était,
Il vint à s'ennuyer de cette triste vie.
Pendant qu'il se livrait à la mélancolie,
    Non loin de là certain vieillard
    S'ennuyait aussi de sa part.
Il aimait les jardins, était prêtre de Flore;
    Il l'était de Pomone encore.
Ces deux emplois sont beaux; mais je voudrais parmi
    Quelque doux et discret ami:
Les jardins parlent peu, si ce n'est dans mon livre;
    De façon que, lassé de vivre
Avec des gens muets, notre homme un beau matin
Va chercher compagnie, et se met en campagne.
    L'ours porté d'un même dessein
    Venait de quitter sa montagne.
    Tous deux par un cas surprenant
    Se rencontrent en un tournant.
L'homme eut peur: mais comment esquiver? et que faire?

Se tirer en Gascon d'une semblable affaire
Est le mieux. Il sut donc dissimuler sa peur.
    L'ours très mauvais complimenteur

# The Bear and the Garden Enthusiast

A certain mountain bear, an only half-licked bear,[57]
pent up by fate within a lonely forest,
like a new Bellerophon,[58] lived alone and secluded.
He would have gone crazy: usually reason
does not long dwell in people cut off from society.
It's a good thing to talk, and a better one to be silent;
but both are bad when carried to extremes.
    No animal had any business
    in the places where the bear resided,
    so that, bearlike as he was,
he came to be bored by that dreary life.
While he was indulging in melancholy,
    not far from there a certain old man
    was also experiencing boredom himself.
He loved gardens, he was a priest of Flora,
    and of Pomona as well.[59]
These two pursuits are lovely; but in the midst of them I'd like
    some gentle-mannered, discreet friend:
gardens don't talk very much, except in my own book;
    so that, tired of living
with mute folk, one fine morning our man
went out to seek company, and took the field.
    The bear, prompted by a similar plan,
    had just left his mountain.
    By a surprising coincidence they both
    met each other at a bend in the road.
The man got scared: but how could he get away? What was he
                              to do?
To get oneself out of such a fix like a Gascon[60]
is the best thing. Thus he managed to disguise his fear.
    The bear, who wasn't much on etiquette,

---

[57] That is, a roughneck, ignorant of social niceties; refers to the belief that new-born bear cubs had to be shaped by their mother's tongue.

[58] From ancient Greek legend, a recluse hated by the gods.

[59] Flora was the ancient Roman goddess of flowers; Pomona, of fruit trees.

[60] Through bravado, or by maintaining one's composure.

Lui dit: «Viens-t'en me voir.» L'autre reprit: «Seigneur,
Vous voyez mon logis; si vous me vouliez faire
Tant d'honneur que d'y prendre un champêtre repas:
J'ai des fruits, j'ai du lait. Ce n'est peut-être pas
De Nosseigneurs les ours le manger ordinaire;
Mais j'offre ce que j'ai.» L'ours l'accepte; et d'aller.
Les voilà bons amis avant que d'arriver.
Arrivés, les voilà se trouvant bien ensemble;
  Et, bien qu'on soit, à ce qu'il semble,
  Beaucoup mieux seul qu'avec des sots,
Comme l'ours en un jour ne disait pas deux mots,
L'homme pouvait sans bruit vaquer à son ouvrage.
L'ours allait à la chasse, apportait du gibier,
  Faisait son principal métier
D'être bon émoucheur, écartait du visage
De son ami dormant ce parasite ailé
  Que nous avons mouche appelé.
Un jour que le vieillard dormait d'un profond somme,
Sur le bout de son nez une allant se placer
Mit l'ours au désespoir; il eut beau la chasser.
«Je t'attraperai bien, dit-il. Et voici comme.»
Aussitôt fait que dit: le fidèle émoucheur
Vous empoigne un pavé, le lance avec roideur,
Casse la tête à l'homme en écrasant la mouche,
Et non moins bon archer que mauvais raisonneur,
Roide mort étendu sur la place il le couche.

Rien n'est si dangereux qu'un ignorant ami;
  Mieux vaudrait un sage ennemi.

said to him: "Come see me, pal." The other replied: "Sir,
you see my abode; if you wished to honor me
by partaking of a rustic meal there:
I have fruit, I have milk. Perhaps that isn't
the normal diet of ursine gentlemen;
but I offer what I have." The bear accepted; and off they went.
They were already good friends before they arrived.
Once arrived, they got along well together;
      and even though, apparently,
      people are much better off alone than with fools for company,
since the bear didn't speak two words in the course of a day,
the man had plenty of free time for his work without any fuss.
The bear would go out hunting, he'd bring back game,
      but he made it his chief occupation
to be a good fly-chaser, driving away from the face
of his sleeping friend that winged parasite
      to which we have given the name of fly.
One day when the old man was in a deep sleep,
one of them, settling on the tip of his nose,
drove the bear to despair; nothing he did could chase it away.
"I'll get you for sure," he said, "and here's how."
No sooner said than done: the faithful fly-chaser
picked up a paving stone, hurled it at top velocity,
and split the man's skull while crushing the fly;
and, no less good at marksmanship than he was bad at reasoning,
he stretched him out on the ground stiff as a board.

Nothing is as dangerous as an ignorant friend;
      you'd be better off with a wise enemy.

## Les deux amis

Deux vrais amis vivaient au Monomotapa:
L'un ne possédait rien qui n'appartînt à l'autre.

    Les amis de ce pays-là
    Valent bien, dit-on, ceux du nôtre.
Une nuit que chacun s'occupait au sommeil,
Et mettait à profit l'absence du soleil,
Un de nos deux amis sort du lit en alarme;
Il court chez son intime, éveille les valets:
Morphée avait touché le seuil de ce palais.
L'ami couché s'étonne, il prend sa bourse, il s'arme;
Vient trouver l'autre, et dit: «Il vous arrive peu
De courir quand on dort; vous me paraissiez homme

A mieux user du temps destiné pour le somme.
N'auriez-vous point perdu tout votre argent au jeu?
En voici. S'il vous est venu quelque querelle,
J'ai mon épée, allons. Vous ennuyez-vous point
De coucher toujours seul? Une esclave assez belle
Était à mes côtés: voulez-vous qu'on l'appelle?
– Non, dit l'ami, ce n'est ni l'un ni l'autre point:
    Je vous rends grâce de ce zèle.
Vous m'êtes en dormant un peu triste apparu;
J'ai craint qu'il ne fût vrai, je suis vite accouru.
    Ce maudit songe en est la cause.»
Qui d'eux aimait le mieux? que t'en semble, lecteur?
Cette difficulté vaut bien qu'on la propose.
Qu'un ami véritable est une douce chose!
Il cherche vos besoins au fond de votre cœur;
    Il vous épargne la pudeur
    De les lui découvrir vous-même.
    Un songe, un rien, tout lui fait peur
    Quand il s'agit de ce qu'il aime.

# *The Two Friends*

Two true friends lived in Monomotapa:[61]
There was nothing that one of them owned that didn't belong to the
                                                                    other.
    Friends in that country
      are just as good as those in ours, people say.
One night when each of them was occupied in slumber,
and was taking advantage of the absence of sunlight,
one of our two friends leaped out of bed in alarm;
he ran to the home of his bosom friend and awakened the servants:
Morpheus[62] had crossed the threshold of that palace.
The friend in bed was amazed; he took his purse, he armed himself,
went to greet the other man, and said: "It's very unusual for you
to be running about at the time people sleep; you seem to me to be
                                                                    a man
who'd make a better use of the time set aside for slumber.
Could it be that you've lost all your money gambling?
Here is some. If you've gotten into some dispute,
my sword is at your service; let's go. Perhaps you're bored
by always sleeping alone? A very pretty slave girl
was by my side: do you want her to be called over?"
"No," said the friend, "it isn't any of those things:
    I thank you for your warm response.
While I slept you appeared to me, looking a little sad;
I was afraid it might be true, and I ran over quickly to help.
    That damned dream was the cause of this."
Which of them loved the other more? What do you think, reader?
This problem is one well worth posing.
What a sweet thing it is to have a genuine friend!
He reads the bottom of your heart to see what you have need of;
    he spares you the immodesty
    of revealing it to him yourself.
    A dream, a trifle, everything frightens him
    when it concerns the one he loves.

---

[61] A native kingdom in what is now Zimbabwe that lasted from the fifteenth through the eighteenth centuries; by La Fontaine's day, however, it was a Portuguese dependency.
[62] God of sleep.

# Les obsèques de la lionne

La femme du lion mourut:
Aussitôt chacun accourut
Pour s'acquitter envers le prince
De certains compliments de consolation,
    Qui sont surcroît d'affliction.
    Il fit avertir sa province
    Que les obsèques se feraient
Un tel jour, en tel lieu: ses prévôts y seraient
    Pour régler la cérémonie
    Et pour placer la compagnie.
    Jugez si chacun s'y trouva.
    Le prince aux cris s'abandonna,
    Et tout son antre en résonna.
    Les lions n'ont point d'autre temple.
    On entendit à son exemple
Rugir en leurs patois messieurs les courtisans.
Je définis la cour un pays où les gens,
Tristes, gais, prêts à tout, à tout indifférents,
Sont ce qu'il plaît au prince, ou, s'ils ne peuvent l'être,
    Tâchent au moins de le paraître,
Peuple caméléon, peuple singe du maître:
On dirait qu'un esprit anime mille corps;
C'est bien là que les gens sont de simples ressorts.
    Pour revenir à notre affaire,
Le cerf ne pleura point; comment eût-il pu faire?
Cette mort le vengeait; la reine avait jadis
    Étranglé sa femme et son fils.
Bref il ne pleura point. Un flatteur l'alla dire,
    Et soutint qu'il l'avait vu rire.
La colère du roi, comme dit Salomon,
Est terrible, et surtout celle du roi lion;
Mais le cerf n'avait pas accoutumé de lire.
Le monarque lui dit: «Chétif hôte des bois,

# The Funeral of the Lioness

The lion's wife died:
immediately everyone hastened over
in order to do their duty to the ruler
by spouting those formulas of consolation
which only add to one's sorrow.
He had notice given to his province
that the funeral would be held
on a certain day, in a certain place: his marshals would be there
to regulate the ceremony
and show the guests to their places.
Just imagine whether everyone showed up.
The ruler abandoned himself to cries of grief,
with which his whole den resounded.
Lions have no other house of worship.
Following his example could be heard
the courtiers roaring in their own local dialects.
I define the court as a country whose inhabitants,
sad, merry, ready for anything, indifferent to everything,
are whatever the ruler wants them to be, or, if they can't be that,
at least try to seem so,
a chameleon folk, a folk that apes its master:
you would think that a single mind moves a thousand bodies;
it's there if anywhere that people are merely mechanical.
To get back to our story,
the deer refused to weep; how could he have?
That death avenged him; in the past the queen had
throttled his wife and his son.
In short, he wouldn't weep. A flatterer went to report this,
even alleging that he'd seen him laugh.
The king's wrath, as Solomon says,[63]
is awesome, and especially that of the lion king;
but the deer wasn't in the habit of reading.
The monarch said to him: "Wretched forest dweller,

---

[63] Proverbs 16:14: "The wrath of a king is as messengers of death." The book of
Proverbs in the Bible is traditionally attributed to King Solomon.

Tu ris, tu ne suis pas ces gémissantes voix.
Nous n'appliquerons point sur tes membres profanes
   Nos sacrés ongles; venez, loups,
   Vengez la reine, immolez tous
   Ce traître à ses augustes mânes.»
Le cerf reprit alors: «Sire, le temps de pleurs
Est passé; la douleur est ici superflue.
Votre digne moitié, couchée entre des fleurs,
   Tout près d'ici m'est apparue,
   Et je l'ai d'abord reconnue.
«Ami, m'a-t-elle dit, garde que ce convoi,
«Quand je vais chez les dieux, ne t'oblige à des larmes.
«Aux champs Élysiens j'ai goûté mille charmes,
«Conversant avec ceux qui sont saints comme moi.
«Laisse agir quelque temps le désespoir du roi.
«J'y prends plaisir.» A peine on eut ouï la chose
Qu'on se mit à crier: «Miracle! apothéose!»
Le cerf eut un présent, bien loin d'être puni.
   Amusez les rois par des songes,
Flattez-les, payez-les d'agréables mensonges,
Quelque indignation dont leur cœur soit rempli,
Ils goberont l'appât, vous serez leur ami.

## L'âne et le chien

Il se faut entr'aider; c'est la loi de nature.
   L'âne un jour pourtant s'en moqua,
   Et ne sais comme il y manqua;
   Car il est bonne créature.
Il allait par pays accompagné du chien,
   Gravement, sans songer à rien,
   Tous deux suivis d'un commun maître.
Ce maître s'endormit: l'âne se mit à paître.
   Il était alors dans un pré,
   Dont l'herbe était fort à son gré.
Point de chardons pourtant; il s'en passa pour l'heure:

you laugh, you do not imitate these moaning voices.
We shall not attack your profane limbs
    with our sacred claws; come, wolves,
    avenge the queen, all of you sacrifice
    this traitor to her noble shade."
Then the deer replied: "Sire, the time for tears
has passed; sorrow is no longer wanted here.
Your worthy consort, laid out among flowers,
    appeared to me in a vision quite nearby,
    and I recognized her at once.
'Friend,' she said to me, 'make sure that that cortège,
when I go to join the gods, does not cause you to shed tears.
In the Elysian Fields[64] I have tasted a thousand pleasures,
conversing with those who are as saintly as I.
Let the king's despair run its course for a while.
It gives me pleasure.' " Scarcely had that tale been heard
when the cry arose: "Miracle! Apotheosis!"
The deer, far from being punished, received a gift.
    Deceive kings with dreams,
flatter them, gratify them with pleasing lies;
no matter what indignation fills their heart,
they'll swallow the bait and you'll be their friend.


## The Donkey and the Dog

People must help one another; it's a law of nature.
    Nevertheless one day the donkey scoffed at it,
    and violated it, I don't know why;
    because he's a good creature.
He was walking through the countryside accompanied by the dog,
    with a serious air, with nothing on his mind,
    and they were followed by the man who owned both of them.
That owner fell asleep: the donkey started to graze.
    At that time he was in a meadow
    in which he liked the grass extremely well.
And yet there were no thistles; for the moment he did without
                               them:

---

[64] The abode of the happy, blameless souls in the underworld.

Il ne faut pas toujours être si délicat;
    Et faute de servir ce plat
    Rarement un festin demeure.
    Notre baudet s'en sut enfin
Passer pour cette fois. Le chien mourant de faim
Lui dit: «Cher compagnon, baisse-toi, je te prie;
Je prendrai mon dîné dans le panier au pain.»
Point de réponse, mot: le roussin d'Arcadie
    Craignit qu'en perdant un moment
    Il ne perdît un coup de dent.
    Il fit longtemps la sourde oreille.
Enfin il répondit: «Ami, je te conseille
D'attendre que ton maître ait fini son sommeil,
Car il te donnera sans faute à son réveil
    Ta portion accoutumée.
    Il ne saurait tarder beaucoup.»
    Sur ces entrefaites un loup
Sort du bois, et s'en vient; autre bête affamée.

L'âne appelle aussitôt le chien à son secours.
Le chien ne bouge, et dit: «Ami, je te conseille
De fuir en attendant que ton maître s'éveille:
Il ne saurait tarder; détale vite, et cours.
Que si ce loup t'atteint, casse-lui la mâchoire.
On t'a ferré de neuf; et si tu me veux croire,
Tu l'étendras tout plat.» Pendant ce beau discours,
Seigneur loup étrangla le baudet sans remède.
    Je conclus qu'il faut qu'on s'entr'aide.


# *L'avantage de la science*

    Entre deux bourgeois d'une ville
    S'émut jadis un différend.
    L'un était pauvre, mais habile;
    L'autre riche, mais ignorant.

one can't always be so demanding;
    and a banquet is rarely canceled
    for lack of that particular dish.
    In short, our donkey managed
to do without it that time. The dog, dying of hunger,
said to him: "Dear companion, bend down, I beg of you;
I'll take my dinner out of the bread basket."
No answer, not a word: the "Arcadian pony"[65]
    was afraid that if he wasted a minute
    he'd lose a mouthful.
    For a long time he turned a deaf ear.
Finally he replied: "Friend, I advise you
to wait until your master has finished his nap,
because when he wakes up he's sure to give you
    your usual helping.
    It shouldn't be much longer."
    As this was going on, a wolf
emerged from the forest and approached them: yet another famished
                                     animal.

The donkey immediately called to the dog for help.
The dog, who didn't budge, said: "Friend, I advise you
to run away until your master wakes up:
it shouldn't be long; move out quickly and run.
And if this wolf catches up with you, break his jaw.
You've got brand-new horseshoes; and, if you take my word for it,
you'll lay him out cold." During this elegant speech,
Sir Wolf throttled the donkey till he was beyond medical aid.
    My conclusion is that people need to help one another.


## The Advantage of Knowledge

    Between two citizens of a town
    a quarrel once arose.
    One was poor but clever;
    the other, rich but ignorant.

---

[65] Arcady in ancient Greece was noted for the donkeys raised there; thus, "Arcadian pony" = "donkey." An English equivalent (rarely found nowadays) is "Jerusalem pony" (because Jesus rode a donkey when entering Jerusalem).

Celui-ci sur son concurrent
Voulait emporter l'avantage,
Prétendait que tout homme sage
Était tenu de l'honorer.
C'était tout homme sot: car pourquoi révérer
Des biens dépourvus de mérite?
La raison m'en semble petite.
«Mon ami, disait-il souvent
         Au savant,
Vous vous croyez considérable;
Mais, dites-moi, tenez-vous table?
Que sert à vos pareils de lire incessamment?
Ils sont toujours logés à la troisième chambre,
Vêtus au mois de juin comme au mois de décembre,
Ayant pour tout laquais leur ombre seulement.
     La république a bien affaire
     De gens qui ne dépensent rien!
     Je ne sais d'homme nécessaire
Que celui dont le luxe épand beaucoup de bien.
Nous en usons, Dieu sait: notre plaisir occupe
L'artisan, le vendeur, celui qui fait la jupe,
Et celle qui la porte, et vous, qui dédiez

     A messieurs les gens de finance
     De méchants livres bien payés.»
     Ces mots remplis d'impertinence
     Eurent le sort qu'ils méritaient.
L'homme lettré se tut, il avait trop à dire.
La guerre le vengea, bien mieux qu'une satire.
Mars détruisit le lieu que nos gens habitaient.
     L'un et l'autre quitta sa ville:
     L'ignorant resta sans asile;
     Il reçut partout des mépris;
L'autre reçut partout quelque faveur nouvelle.
     Cela décida leur querelle.
Laissez dire les sots; le savoir a son prix.

The latter, wishing to gain the advantage
over his rival,
claimed that every wise man
was obliged to honor him.
In reality, it was every foolish man: for why respect
wealth devoid of merit?
I don't see much reason for it.
"My friend," he would often say
to the scholar,
"you consider yourself noteworthy;
but tell me, do you maintain a table for entertaining?
What good does it do the likes of you to read all the time?
They always live in a garret,
dressed in June the same way as in December,
having nothing but their own shadow as their only lackey.
The state really has a need
of people who don't spend anything!
The only man I deem necessary
is one whose luxury spending spreads around a lot of income.
We use our wealth, heaven knows: our pleasure gives business to
the artisan, the vendor, the man who makes skirts
and the woman who wears them; and also to you people, who
dedicate
to the respectable financiers
miserable books for which you're well paid."
These words full of absurdity
had the fate they deserved.
The educated man remained silent; he had too much to say.
The war avenged him, much better than a satire would have.
Mars[66] destroyed the place where our heroes lived.
Both of them left their hometown:
the ignoramus remained without a refuge;
he was met everywhere with contempt;
the other was met everywhere with some new mark of regard.
That settled their dispute.
Let fools talk; knowledge has its worth.

---

[66] God of war.

# Les deux pigeons

Deux pigeons s'aimaient d'amour tendre.
L'un d'eux s'ennuyant au logis
Fut assez fou pour entreprendre
Un voyage en lointain pays.
L'autre lui dit: «Qu'allez-vous faire?
Voulez-vous quitter votre frère?
L'absence est le plus grand des maux:
Non pas pour vous, cruel. Au moins que les travaux,
Les dangers, les soins du voyage,
Changent un peu votre courage.
Encor si la saison s'avançait davantage!
Attendez les zéphyrs. Qui vous presse? Un corbeau
Tout à l'heure annonçait malheur à quelque oiseau.
Je ne songerai plus que rencontre funeste,
Que faucons, que réseaux. «Hélas! dirai-je, il pleut:
«Mon frère a-t-il tout ce qu'il veut,
«Bon soupé, bon gîte, et le reste?»
Ce discours ébranla le cœur
De notre imprudent voyageur;
Mais le désir de voir et l'humeur inquiète
L'emportèrent enfin. Il dit: «Ne pleurez point:
Trois jours au plus rendront mon âme satisfaite;
Je reviendrai dans peu conter de point en point
Mes aventures à mon frère.
Je le désennuierai: quiconque ne voit guère
N'a guère à dire aussi. Mon voyage dépeint
Vous sera d'un plaisir extrême.
Je dirai: «J'étais là; telle chose m'avint»;
Vous y croirez être vous-même.»
A ces mots en pleurant ils se dirent adieu.
Le voyageur s'éloigne; et voilà qu'un nuage
L'oblige de chercher retraite en quelque lieu.
Un seul arbre s'offrit, tel encor que l'orage
Maltraita le pigeon en dépit du feuillage.
L'air devenu serein, il part tout morfondu,
Sèche du mieux qu'il peut son corps chargé de pluie,
Dans un champ à l'écart voit du blé répandu,

# *The Two Pigeons*

Two pigeons loved each other deeply.
One of them, growing bored at home,
was mad enough to undertake
a journey to a far-off land.
The other said to him: "What are you going to do?
Do you want to leave your brother?
Absence is the greatest of calamities:
not for you, cruel one. At least I hope that the trouble involved,
    the dangers and the cares attendant on the journey
    will modify your resolve to some extent.
If only it were later in the springtime!
Wait for the warm west wind. What's your rush? A raven
just now announced a catastrophe for some bird.
All my dreams from now on will be of disastrous mishaps,
falcons, nets. 'Alas!' I shall say, 'it's raining:
    does my brother have everything he needs,
    a good supper, a good lodging and all the rest?' "
    This speech saddened the heart
    of our imprudent traveler;
but the desire to see things and his restless nature
finally won the day. He said: "Don't cry:
three days at most will satisfy my mind;
I'll come back before long and tell my adventures
    to my brother in every detail.
I'll relieve him from his boredom; whoever sees little of the world
has little to say, as well. The depiction of my journey
    will give you extreme pleasure.
I'll say: 'I was there; such and such a thing happened to me';
    you'll think you were there yourself."
After these words they said goodbye tearfully.
The traveler had gone some distance, when a cloud
compelled him to seek shelter somewhere.
Only one tree was available, and of such a sort that the storm
did harm to the pigeon in spite of the foliage.
The sky cleared up, he set out again chilled through;
he dried his rain-soaked body to the best of his ability;
in an out-of-the-way field he saw some strewn wheat,

Voit un pigeon auprès: cela lui donne envie;
Il y vole, il est pris: ce blé couvrait d'un lacs
　　Les menteurs et traîtres appas.
Le lacs était usé; si bien que de son aile,
De ses pieds, de son bec, l'oiseau le rompt enfin.
Quelque plume y périt; et le pis du destin

Fut qu'un certain vautour à la serre cruelle
Vit notre malheureux qui, traînant la ficelle
Et les morceaux du lacs qui l'avait attrapé,
　　Semblait un forçat échappé.
Le vautour s'en allait le lier, quand des nues
Fond à son tour un aigle aux ailes étendues.
Le pigeon profita du conflit des voleurs,
S'envola, s'abattit auprès d'une masure,
　　Crut pour ce coup que ses malheurs
　　Finiraient par cette aventure;
Mais un fripon d'enfant (cet âge est sans pitié)
Prit sa fronde, et du coup tua plus d'à moitié
　　La volatile malheureuse,
　Qui, maudissant sa curiosité,
　　Traînant l'aile, et tirant le pié,
　　Demi-morte et demi-boiteuse,
　　Droit au logis s'en retourna.
　　Que bien que mal elle arriva,
　　Sans autre aventure fâcheuse.
Voilà nos gens rejoints; et je laisse à juger
De combien de plaisirs ils payèrent leurs peines.
Amants, heureux amants, voulez-vous voyager?
　　Que ce soit aux rives prochaines;
Soyez-vous l'un à l'autre un monde toujours beau,
　　Toujours divers, toujours nouveau;
Tenez-vous lieu de tout, comptez pour rien le reste.
J'ai quelquefois aimé; je n'aurais pas alors
　　Contre le Louvre et ses trésors,
Contre le firmament et sa voûte céleste,
　　Changé les bois, changé les lieux
Honorés par les pas, éclairés par les yeux
　　De l'aimable et jeune bergère

and saw a pigeon near it: that aroused his appetite;
he flew there and was caught: that wheat was covering
    the lying and treacherous allurement of a snare.
The snare was old and worn; and so, with his wings,
feet and beak, the bird finally tore it.
He lost a few feathers in doing so; but the worst that fate had to
                                                offer
was that a certain vulture with cruel talons
saw our unfortunate friend, who, dragging behind him the cord
and pieces of the snare in which he had been caught,
    looked like an escaped convict.
The vulture was on its way to seize him, when out of the clouds
an eagle, in its turn, swooped down with outstretched wings.
The pigeon took advantage of the fight between the highwaymen,
flew away and alighted near a hovel,
    thinking for the moment his misfortunes
    would be limited to that adventure;
but a rascally boy (that age knows no pity)
took his slingshot and with the blow more than half-killed
    the unhappy fowl,
  who, cursing his curiosity,
    with trailing wing and dragging foot,
    half-dead and half-lame,
    returned straight home.
    Somehow or other he got there,
    without any other troublesome incidents.
Now our friends were reunited; and I leave it to you to imagine
with how many pleasures they made up for their sorrows.
Lovers, happy lovers, do you want to travel?
    Let it be to nearby shores;
be one to the other a world that's always beautiful,
    always varied, always new;
consider that you contain everything, count all the rest as naught.
I have loved in the past; at that time I wouldn't have
    taken the Louvre[67] and its treasures,
the firmament and its celestial vault,
    in exchange for the woods, in exchange for the places
honored by the feet and brightened by the eyes
    of the lovable young shepherdess

---

[67] The royal palace in Paris.

Pour qui sous le fils de Cythère
Je servis engagé par mes premiers serments.

Hélas! quand reviendront de semblables moments?
Faut-il que tant d'objets si doux et si charmants
Me laissent vivre au gré de mon âme inquiète?
Ah! si mon cœur osait encor se renflammer!
Ne sentirai-je plus de charme qui m'arrête?
       Ai-je passé le temps d'aimer?


## Le gland et la citrouille

Dieu fait bien ce qu'il fait. Sans en chercher la preuve
En tout cet univers, et l'aller parcourant,
       Dans les citrouilles je la treuve.
       Un villageois, considérant
Combien ce fruit est gros, et sa tige menue:
«A quoi songeait, dit-il, l'auteur de tout cela?
Il a bien mal placé cette citrouille-là.
       Hé parbleu! je l'aurais pendue
       A l'un des chênes que voilà.
       C'eût été justement l'affaire;
       Tel fruit, tel arbre, pour bien faire.
C'est dommage, Garo, que tu n'es point entré
Au conseil de celui que prêche ton curé;
Tout en eût été mieux: car pourquoi par exemple
Le gland, qui n'est pas gros comme mon petit doigt,
       Ne pend-il pas en cet endroit?
       Dieu s'est mépris: plus je contemple
Ces fruits ainsi placés, plus il semble à Garo
       Que l'on a fait un quiproquo.»
Cette réflexion embarrassant notre homme:
«On ne dort point, dit-il, quand on a tant d'esprit.»
Sous un chêne aussitôt il va prendre son somme.
Un gland tombe: le nez du dormeur en pâtit.
Il s'éveille; et portant la main sur son visage,

for whose sake I served under the son of Cytherea,[68]
having enlisted in his regiment through my very first plighting of
love.

Alas! When will moments like those come back?
With so many sweet and charming women before me,
must I go on living at the beck and call of my restless mind?
Oh, if my heart could still venture to catch fire again!
Will I no longer fall under any spell that will halt my steps?
Have my loving days gone by for good?

## The Acorn and the Pumpkin

What God does, He does well. Without seeking proofs for this
all over the universe, and scouring all through it,
I find the proof in pumpkins.
A rural villager, considering
how large that fruit is, and how thin its stalk,
said: "What could the Creator of all this have been thinking of?
He's put that pumpkin in the wrong place.
Say! I'd have hung it
on one of those oak trees over there.
That would've been a proper arrangement;
'like fruit, like tree,' and things would've been right.
It's too bad, Garo,[69] that you weren't on
the advisory board of the Fellow your priest preaches about;
everything would have been better: because, for example, why
doesn't the acorn, which isn't as big as my little finger,
hang here where the pumpkin is?
God made a mistake; the more I observe
the placement of these fruits, the more it seems to Garo
that things have been incorrectly switched around."
These reflections confusing our hero,
he said: "Who can get enough sleep when his mind is so active?"
Immediately he goes to take a nap beneath an oak.
An acorn falls: the sleeper's nose is struck by it.
He awakens; and, putting his hand to his face,

---

68 Venus, goddess of love. Her son is Cupid, or Love.
69 Garo is the name of the peasant, who is talking to himself.

Il trouve encor le gland pris au poil du menton.
Son nez meurtri le force à changer de langage:
«Oh! oh! dit-il, je saigne! Et que serait-ce donc
S'il fût tombé de l'arbre une masse plus lourde,
  Et que ce gland eût été gourde?
Dieu ne l'a pas voulu: sans doute il eut raison;
  J'en vois bien à présent la cause.»
  En louant Dieu de toute chose,
  Garo retourne à la maison.


## L'huître et les plaideurs

Un jour deux pèlerins sur le sable rencontrent
Une huître que le flot y venait d'apporter:
Ils l'avalent des yeux, du doigt ils se la montrent;

A l'égard de la dent, il fallut contester.
L'un se baissait déjà pour amasser la proie;
L'autre le pousse, et dit: «Il est bon de savoir
  Qui de nous en aura la joie.
Celui qui le premier a pu l'apercevoir
En sera le gobeur; l'autre le verra faire.

  – Si par là l'on juge l'affaire,
Reprit son compagnon, j'ai l'œil bon, Dieu merci.
  – Je ne l'ai pas mauvais aussi,
Dit l'autre, et je l'ai vue avant vous, sur ma vie.
– Eh bien! vous l'avez vue, et moi je l'ai sentie.»
  Pendant tout ce bel incident,
Perrin Dandin arrive: ils le prennent pour juge.
Perrin fort gravement ouvre l'huître, et la gruge,
  Nos deux messieurs le regardant.
Ce repas fait, il dit d'un ton de président:

«Tenez, la cour vous donne à chacun une écaille,
Sans dépens, et qu'en paix chacun chez soi s'en aille.»

he finds the acorn still stuck in the hair on his chin.
The bruise on his nose forces him to speak in different terms;
"Oh! Oh!" he says, "I'm bleeding! Then, how would it be
if a heavier mass had fallen from the tree,
    and if that acorn had been a gourd?
God didn't want it so: surely, He was right;
    now I clearly see His reasons for it."
    Praising God for all things,
    Garo goes back home.

## The Oyster and the Litigants

One day two pilgrims found on the sand
an oyster that the ocean had just washed up there:
they swallowed it with their eyes, they pointed it out to one another
                              with their fingers;
as for what their teeth would do, that was a matter of dispute.
One of them was already stooping down to pick up his booty;
the other shoved him aside, saying: "It would be good to determine
    which of us will have the joy of it.
The one who was able to notice it first
will be the one to gulp it down; the other will stand by and watch
                              him."
    "If that's the way the matter is to be judged,"
his companion replied, "I have good eyes, thank God."
    "Mine aren't bad, either,"
said the other, "and I saw it before you, I'd stake my life on it."
"Very well! You saw it, and *I* smelled it."
    During these lovely proceedings
Perrin Dandin[70] arrived: they chose him as an arbitrator.
With immense gravity, Perrin opened the oyster and swallowed it,
    while our two gentlemen were watching.
When that meal was over, he said, in the manner of a presiding
                              judge:
"Take this, the court awards each of you one valve of the shell,
without requiring costs; both of you can now go home in peace."

---

[70] The name of a comic judge in Rabelais and in Racine's play *Les plaideurs*.

Mettez ce qu'il en coûte à plaider aujourd'hui;
Comptez ce qu'il en reste à beaucoup de familles;
Vous verrez que Perrin tire l'argent à lui,
Et ne laisse aux plaideurs que le sac et les quilles.

## Le chat et le renard

Le chat et le renard, comme beaux petits saints,
    S'en allaient en pèlerinage.
C'étaient deux vrais tartufs, deux archipatelins,
Deux francs patte-pelus, qui des frais du voyage,
Croquant mainte volaille, escroquant maint fromage,
    S'indemnisaient à qui mieux mieux.
Le chemin était long, et partant ennuyeux,
    Pour l'accourcir ils disputèrent.
    La dispute est d'un grand secours;
    Sans elle on dormirait toujours.
    Nos pèlerins s'égosillèrent.
Ayant bien disputé l'on parla du prochain.
    Le renard au chat dit enfin:
    «Tu prétends être fort habile:
En sais-tu tant que moi? J'ai cent ruses au sac.
–Non, dit l'autre; je n'ai qu'un tour dans mon bissac,
    Mais je soutiens qu'il en vaut mille.»
Eux de recommencer la dispute à l'envi.
Sur le que si, que non, tous deux étant ainsi,
    Une meute apaisa la noise.
Le chat dit au renard: «Fouille en ton sac, ami:
    Cherche en ta cervelle matoise
Un stratagème sûr. Pour moi, voici le mien.»
A ces mots sur un arbre il grimpa bel et bien.
    L'autre fit cent tours inutiles,
Entra dans cent terriers, mit cent fois en défaut
    Tous les confrères de Brifaut.

Consider what it costs to go to law today;
count up what's left over for many a family;
you'll see that Perrin attracts the money to himself,
and leaves the litigants only the ninepins and their carrying bag.[71]


# The Cat and the Fox

The cat and the fox, like fine little saints,
    were off on a pilgrimage.
They were two real hypocrites, two arch-humbugs,[72]
two out-and-out sneaks, who by munching many a chicken
and filching many a cheese, vied with each other
    in repaying themselves for their travel expenses.
The way was long, and so they were bored;
    to make it shorter, they argued.
    Arguing is very helpful;
    without it people would go on sleeping.
    Our pilgrims shouted themselves hoarse.
After plenty of arguing, they discussed their fellow creatures.
    Finally the fox said to the cat:
    "You claim to be very clever:
do you know as much as I do? I have a hundred ruses up my sleeve."
"No," said the other; "I have only one trick in my shoulder-bag,
    but I maintain that it's worth a thousand."
They started arguing again, each trying to outdo the other.
While they were engaged in ifs and buts, both being made that way,
    the sound of a pack of hounds silenced their squabbling.
The cat said to the fox: "Look up your sleeve, friend:
    rack your crafty brain
for a surefire stratagem. As for me, here's mine."
Saying that, he climbed up a tree, and that was that.
    The other tried a hundred useless tricks,
entered a hundred holes, a hundred times he threw
    all of Brifaut's[73] colleagues off the scent.

---

[71] That is, he leaves them the objects by means of which they wished to settle a wager, but takes away the stakes they were playing for.

[72] The French terms refer to characters in two plays, Moliere's *Tartuffe* and the fifteenth-century farce about the lawyer Patelin.

[73] Name of a hound ("glutton").

Partout il tenta des asiles,
    Et ce fut partout sans succès:
La fumée y pourvut ainsi que les bassets.
Au sortir d'un terrier, deux chiens aux pieds agiles
    L'étranglèrent du premier bond.
Le trop d'expédients peut gâter une affaire;
On perd du temps au choix, on tente, on veut tout faire.

    N'en ayons qu'un, mais qu'il soit bon.


# Le singe et le chat

Bertrand avec Raton, l'un singe, et l'autre chat,
Commensaux d'un logis, avaient un commun maître.
D'animaux malfaisants c'était un très bon plat;
Ils n'y craignaient tous deux aucun, quel qu'il pût être.
Trouvait-on quelque chose au logis de gâté?
L'on ne s'en prenait point aux gens du voisinage.
Bertrand dérobait tout; Raton de son côté
Était moins attentif aux souris qu'au fromage.
Un jour, au coin du feu nos deux maîtres fripons
    Regardaient rôtir des marrons.
Les escroquer était une très bonne affaire:
Nos galants y voyaient double profit à faire,
Leur bien premièrement, et puis le mal d'autrui.
Bertrand dit à Raton: «Frère, il faut aujourd'hui
    Que tu fasses un coup de maître.
Tire-moi ces marrons. Si Dieu m'avait fait naître
    Propre à tirer marrons du feu,
    Certes marrons verraient beau jeu.»
Aussitôt fait que dit: Raton avec sa patte,
    D'une manière délicate,
Écarte un peu la cendre, et retire les doigts,
    Puis les reporte à plusieurs fois;
Tire un marron, puis deux, et puis trois en escroque,
    Et cependant Bertrand les croque.

He sought refuge everywhere,
and everywhere unsuccessfully:
smoke[74] saw to that, as well as the basset hounds.[75]
As he emerged from a hole, two dogs with agile feet
throttled him at their first bound.
Too many devices may ruin an enterprise;
you lose time choosing between them; you act tentatively; you want
to try everything.
Let's have only one, but make it a good one.

# The Monkey and the Cat

Bertrand and Raton, one a monkey and the other a cat,
were messmates in one home and were both owned by one man.
They were a first-rate duo of malicious animals;
neither one was afraid of anybody there, whoever it might be.
Was something in the house found damaged?
Other people in the vicinity were never blamed.
Bertrand stole everything; for his part, Raton
paid less attention to the mice than to the cheese.
One day, at the fireside, our two expert rascals
were watching chestnuts roasting.
To filch them was a very tempting matter:
our rogues saw a double profit to be made,
first of all a benefit to themselves, secondly harm done to others.
Bertrand said to Raton: "Brother, today you must
perform a master stroke.
Pull out those chestnuts for me. If God had created me
with the power to pull chestnuts from the fire,
certain chestnuts wouldn't know what hit them."
No sooner said than done: Raton with his paw,
in dainty fashion,
shoved aside the ashes a bit and withdrew his toes,
then put them forward again several times;
he pulled out one chestnut, then two, then stole three,
and in the meanwhile Bertrand ate them.

---

[74] Used to smoke the fox out of his earth.
[75] Specially bred for entering foxes' earths.

Une servante vient: adieu mes gens; Raton
    N'était pas content, ce dit-on.
Aussi ne le sont pas la plupart de ces princes
    Qui flattés d'un pareil emploi,
    Vont s'échauder en des provinces
    Pour le profit de quelque roi.


## Discours à Madame de la Sablière

Iris, je vous louerais, il n'est que trop aisé;
Mais vous avez cent fois notre encens refusé,
En cela peu semblable au reste des mortelles,
Qui veulent tous les jours des louanges nouvelles.
Pas une ne s'endort à ce bruit si flatteur.
Je ne les blâme point, je souffre cette humeur:
Elle est commune aux dieux, aux monarques, aux belles.
Ce breuvage vanté par le peuple rimeur,
Le nectar que l'on sert au maître du tonnerre,
Et dont nous enivrons tous les dieux de la terre,
C'est la louange, Iris. Vous ne la goûtez point;
D'autres propos chez vous récompensent ce point,
    Propos, agréables commerces,
Où le hasard fournit cent matières diverses,
    Jusque-là qu'en votre entretien
La bagatelle a part: le monde n'en croit rien.
    Laissons le monde et sa croyance:
    La bagatelle, la science,
Les chimères, le rien, tout est bon. Je soutiens
    Qu'il faut de tout aux entretiens:
    C'est un parterre où Flore épand ses biens;

A maid came by; farewell to my heroes; Raton
    was displeased, people say.
Equally displeased are most of those petty rulers
    who, flattered by being made use of that way,
    go off to get scalded in some province
    for the profit of some powerful king.


# *Discourse to Madame de la Sablière*[76]

Iris, I would praise you, it's all too easy;
but a hundred times you have declined our incense,
in that regard being quite unlike all other mortal women,
who wish for new praises daily.
Not one of them dozes off on hearing such a flattering sound.
I don't blame them a bit, I tolerate that frame of mind:
it is shared by gods, monarchs and beautiful women.
That beverage vaunted by the tribe of rhymers,
the nectar that is served to the master of the thunder,[77]
and which all we gods of the earth get drunk on,
it is praise, Iris. You have no taste for it;
other kinds of talk compensate you for the lack of it,
    talk, agreeable social intercourse,
in which chance supplies a hundred varied themes,
    to the extent that in your conversation
even witty trifles have their share: society won't believe it.
    Let's leave society and its beliefs aside:
    witty trifles, scholarly subjects,
fantasies, a mere nothing—they're all good. I maintain
    that conversations need a little of everything:
    they are a flower bed in which Flora[78] exhibits her wealth;

---

[76] See the Introduction for more about this patroness (poetic pseudonym: Iris, goddess of the rainbow), to whom the poet dedicated two brilliant *discours*. In this one he refutes a theory proposed by René Descartes (1596–1650), which was especially repugnant to him: that animals do not possess an intelligence of the same type as man's, but are merely mechanisms totally controlled by instincts. The counter-theory enunciated by La Fontaine toward the end of the poem is derived from the philosophy of Descartes's chief rival, Pierre Gassendi (1592–1655).

[77] Jupiter, king of the gods.
[78] Goddess of flowers.

Sur différentes fleurs l'abeille s'y repose,
    Et fait du miel de toute chose.
Ce fondement posé, ne trouvez pas mauvais
Qu'en ces fables aussi j'entremêle des traits
      De certaine philosophie
      Subtile, engageante et hardie.
On l'appelle nouvelle. En avez-vous ou non
      Ouï parler? Ils disent donc
      Que la bête est une machine;
Qu'en elle tout se fait sans choix et par ressorts:
Nul sentiment, point d'âme, en elle tout est corps.
      Telle est la montre qui chemine,
A pas toujours égaux, aveugle et sans dessein.
      Ouvrez-la, lisez dans son sein;
Mainte roue y tient lieu de tout l'esprit du monde;
      La première y meut la seconde,
Une troisième suit, elle sonne à la fin.
Au dire de ces gens, la bête est toute telle:
      L'objet la frappe en un endroit;
      Ce lieu frappé s'en va tout droit,
Selon nous, au voisin en porter la nouvelle;
Le sens de proche en proche aussitôt la reçoit.

L'impression se fait, mais comment se fait-elle?
      Selon eux, par nécessité,
      Sans passion, sans volonté:
      L'animal se sent agité
    De mouvements que le vulgaire appelle
Tristesse, joie, amour, plaisir, douleur cruelle,
      Ou quelque autre de ces états.
Mais ce n'est point cela; ne vous y trompez pas.
Qu'est-ce donc? Une montre. Et nous? C'est autre chose.
Voici de la façon que Descartes l'expose;

Descartes, ce mortel dont on eût fait un dieu
    Chez les païens, et qui tient le milieu
Entre l'homme et l'esprit, comme entre l'huître et l'homme
Le tient tel de nos gens, franche bête de somme;
Voici, dis-je, comment raisonne cet auteur.
Sur tous les animaux, enfants du Créateur,
J'ai le don de penser, et je sais que je pense.

the bee alights on a variety of flowers there
    and makes honey out of each one.
On this basis, please do not take it amiss
if in these fables, too, I introduce some elements
    of a certain philosophy
    that is subtle, alluring and bold.
It's called new. Have you or haven't you
    heard people speak about it? Well, then, they say
    that animals are machines;
that all their activities are performed without volition and mechanically:
no feelings, no soul, they are just material bodies.
    They are like a timepiece that keeps going,
with constantly regular motion, blind and devoid of intentions.
    Open it up, study its inside;
within it, many a cogwheel takes the place of all earthly intelligence;
    the first wheel moves the second,
a third follows, and finally the timepiece rings.
To hear these people talk, an animal is exactly like that:
    a perceived object impinges on it at some spot;
    that affected spot proceeds at once,
according to the general view, to report the news to its neighbor;
from step to step the animal's sensory center soon receives the
                          message.
An imprint is made, but how is it made?
    According to them, this happens by necessity,
    without emotion, without will power;
    the animals feels itself stirred
  by impulses that the common man calls
sadness, joy, love, pleasure, cruel pain,
    or some other of these conditions.
But that's not really the case; don't be deceived by it.
What is the animal, then? A timepiece. And what are we?
                      Something else.
Here is how Descartes expounds the matter;
Descartes, that mortal who would have been made a god
  if he had lived among the pagans; Descartes, who falls between
mortal man and pure spirit, just as some people among us,
out-and-out beasts of burden, fall between the oyster and man;
here, I say, is how that author reasons.
Alone among all animals, children of the Creator,
I have the gift of thought, and I know that I think.

Or vous savez, Iris, de certaine science,
    Que, quand la bête penserait,
    La bête ne réfléchirait
    Sur l'objet, ni sur sa pensée.
Descartes va plus loin, et soutient nettement
    Qu'elle ne pense nullement.
    Vous n'êtes point embarrassée
De le croire, ni moi. Cependant quand au bois
    Le bruit des cors, celui des voix,
N'a donné nul relâche à la fuyante proie,
    Qu'en vain elle a mis ses efforts
    A confondre et brouiller la voie,
L'animal chargé d'ans, vieux cerf, et de dix cors,
En suppose un plus jeune, et l'oblige par force
A présenter aux chiens une nouvelle amorce.
Que de raisonnements pour conserver ses jours!
Le retour sur ses pas, les malices, les tours,
    Et le change, et cent stratagèmes
Dignes des plus grands chefs, dignes d'un meilleur sort!
    On le déchire après sa mort:
    Ce sont tous ses honneurs suprêmes.

    Quand la perdrix
    Voit ses petits
En danger, et n'ayant qu'une plume nouvelle,
Qui ne peut fuir encor par les airs le trépas,
Elle fait la blessée, et va traînant de l'aile,
Attirant le chasseur et le chien sur ses pas,
Détourne le danger, sauve ainsi sa famille,
Et puis quand le chasseur croit que son chien la pille,
Elle lui dit adieu, prend sa volée, et rit
De l'homme, qui confus des yeux en vain la suit.

    Non loin du Nord il est un monde
    Où l'on sait que les habitants
    Vivent ainsi qu'aux premiers temps
    Dans une ignorance profonde:
Je parle des humains; car quant aux animaux,
    Ils y construisent des travaux,
Qui des torrents grossis arrêtent le ravage,
Et font communiquer l'un et l'autre rivage.
L'édifice résiste, et dure en son entier;

Now, you know, Iris, of a certainty,
    that, if animals could think,
    they would not reflect
    about the object of their thought or about the thought itself.
Descartes goes further, and clearly maintains
    that they don't think at all.
    It doesn't trouble you
to believe this, nor does it me. And yet, when, in the woods,
    the sound of the horns and the sound of voices
has given no respite to the fleeing quarry,
    when it has made every effort, in vain,
    to confuse and deceive those on its track,
the animal laden with years, an old stag, a five-pronger,
puts a younger one in his place, and compels it by force
to offer a new allurement to the hounds.
How much reasoning he uses to save his life!
The retracing of his steps, cunning ploys, tricks,
    throwing the dogs off his scent, and a hundred stratagems
worthy of the greatest generals, worthy of a better fate!
    He is torn apart after his death:
    those are his only final honors.

        When the partridge
        sees her young
in danger, knowing that they have only a juvenal plumage
with which they cannot avoid death by flying away,
she pretends to be wounded and runs about trailing her wing,
drawing the hunter and the hound after her;
she averts the danger and thus saves her family,
and then, when the hunter thinks his hound is about to seize her,
she bids him farewell, takes flight and laughs
at the man who, embarrassed and helpless, watches her go.

        Not far from the North Pole there is a population
        whose inhabitants are known
        to live, just as in primitive times,
        in profound ignorance:
I am speaking of the human beings; for, as regards the animals,
    they erect constructions there
which arrest the ravages of the swollen torrents,
and join one river bank to the other.
The structure is resistant, and remains whole;

Après un lit de bois, est un lit de mortier.
Chaque castor agit; commune en est la tâche;
Le vieux y fait marcher le jeune sans relâche.
Maint maître d'œuvre y court, et tient haut le bâton.
 La république de Platon
 Ne serait rien que l'apprentie
 De cette famille amphibie.
Ils savent en hiver élever leurs maisons,
 Passent les étangs sur des ponts,
 Fruit de leur art, savant ouvrage;
 Et nos pareils ont beau le voir,
 Jusqu'à présent tout leur savoir
 Est de passer l'onde à la nage.

Que ces castors ne soient qu'un corps vide d'esprit,
Jamais on ne pourra m'obliger à le croire;
Mais voici beaucoup plus: écoutez ce récit,
 Que je tiens d'un roi plein de gloire.
Le défenseur du Nord vous sera mon garant;
Je vais citer un prince aimé de la victoire;
Son nom seul est un mur à l'empire ottoman;
C'est le roi polonais; jamais un roi ne ment.
 Il dit donc que sur sa frontière
Des animaux entre eux ont guerre de tout temps:
Le sang qui se transmet des pères aux enfants
 En renouvelle la matière.
Ces animaux, dit-il, sont germains du renard.
 Jamais la guerre avec tant d'art
 Ne s'est faite parmi les hommes,
 Non pas même au siècle où nous sommes.
Corps de garde avancé, vedettes, espions,
Embuscades, partis, et mille inventions
D'une pernicieuse et maudite science,
 Fille du Styx et mère des héros,
 Exercent de ces animaux
 Le bon sens et l'expérience.

after a layer of wood there comes a layer of mortar.
Every beaver is active; the task is shared by all;
the old ones make the young ones work without letup.
Many a foreman runs about, giving orders with firm authority.
    Plato's republic,
      by comparison, is only an apprentice stage
      of this amphibious society.
In winter they know how to build their homes,
    they cross over ponds on bridges,
      products of their skill, scientific artifacts;
      and our fellow men learn nothing by watching them;
      up to now, all they know how to do
      is to swim across the water.

No one will ever compel me to believe
that these beavers are bodies devoid of mind;
but here is a much more cogent example: listen to this narrative,
    which was told to me by a king[79] full of glory.
The defender of the north will be my guarantor;
I am going to name a ruler beloved of victory;
his name alone is a rampart against the Ottoman Empire;
I mean the king of Poland; a king never lies.
    Well, then, he says that on his borders
certain animals constantly wage war with one another:
the blood transmitted from fathers to sons
    keeps the feud fresh.
These animals, he says, are cousins to the fox.
    Never has war been waged
    by men with such art,
      not even in the century in which we live.
Advance guards, scouts, spies,
ambushes, patrols and a thousand inventions
of a pernicious, accursed branch of learning,
    offspring of the Styx[80] and mother of heroes,
      exercise the common sense and experience
      of those animals.

---

[79] Jan Sobieski, who won a victory over the Turks in 1673. Possibly the poet did not hear this directly from the king but from a French diplomat who attended his patroness' salon.

[80] River in the underworld.

Pour chanter leurs combats, l'Achéron nous devrait
    Rendre Homère. Ah! s'il le rendait,
Et qu'il rendît aussi le rival d'Épicure!
Que dirait ce dernier sur ces exemples-ci?
Ce que j'ai déjà dit, qu'aux bêtes la nature
Peut par les seuls ressorts opérer tout ceci;
    Que la mémoire est corporelle,
Et que, pour en venir aux exemples divers,
    Que j'ai mis en jour dans ces vers,
    L'animal n'a besoin que d'elle.
L'objet, lorsqu'il revient, va dans son magasin

    Chercher par le même chemin
    L'image auparavant tracée,
Qui sur les mêmes pas revient pareillement,
    Sans le secours de la pensée,
    Causer un même événement.
    Nous agissons tout autrement.
    La volonté nous détermine,
Non l'objet ni l'instinct. Je parle, je chemine;
    Je sens en moi certain agent;
    Tout obéit dans ma machine
    A ce principe intelligent.
Il est distinct du corps, se conçoit nettement,
    Se conçoit mieux que le corps même:
De tous nos mouvements, c'est l'arbitre suprême.
    Mais comment le corps l'entend-il?
    C'est là le point: je vois l'outil
Obéir à la main; mais la main, qui la guide?
Eh! qui guide les cieux, et leur course rapide?
Quelque ange est attaché peut-être à ces grands corps.
Un esprit vit en nous, et meut tous nos ressorts:
L'impression se fait. Le moyen, je l'ignore.
On ne l'apprend qu'au sein de la Divinité;
Et s'il faut en parler avec sincérité,
    Descartes l'ignorait encore.
Nous et lui là-dessus nous sommes tous égaux.

To sing of their battles, Acheron[81] would have to
    give us back Homer. Oh, if it only would,
and if it would also give back the rival of Epicurus![82]
What would that last-mentioned man say about these examples?
The same as I've already reported, that in animals nature
can perform all these operations purely mechanically;
    that memory is a material object,
and that—to discuss the various examples
    I have brought to light in these verses—
animals need nothing else than that material memory.
The perceived object, when reflected back, goes into the animal's
                                storehouse,
    following the same path, to seek out
    the image previously imprinted,
which likewise retraces the same steps,
    without the aid of thought,
    and brings about the same response.
    We human beings behave quite otherwise.
    Our actions are determined by our will,
not by the exterior object or instinct. I talk, I walk;
    I feel a certain active force inside me;
    everything in my constitution obeys
    that intelligent principle.
It is separate from the body, it is clearly conceived,
    in fact it is conceived more clearly than the body itself:
it is the final arbiter of all our movements.
    But how does the body perceive it?
    That's the point: I see the tool
obeying the hand; but who guides the hand?
Ah! Who guides the heavens, and their rapid motion?
Perhaps some angel is attached to those great heavenly bodies.
A spirit lives in us, and moves all our mechanisms:
sensory impressions are accomplished. But how, I know not.
We can only learn this in the bosom of the Deity;
and, if the truth about it is to be spoken,
    even Descartes did not yet know the answer.
On that subject we and he are all equals.

---

  [81] The underworld, or afterlife.

  [82] That is, Descartes, opponent of Gassendi; the latter renewed the atomic theory of
the Greek philosopher Epicurus (341–270 B.C.).

Ce que je sais, Iris, c'est qu'en ces animaux
    Dont je viens de citer l'exemple,
Cet esprit n'agit pas, l'homme seul est son temple.
Aussi faut-il donner à l'animal un point
    Que la plante après tout n'a point.
    Cependant la plante respire:
Mais que répondra-t-on à ce que je vais dire?


## Les deux rats, le renard, et l'œuf

Deux rats cherchaient leur vie, ils trouvèrent un œuf.
Le dîné suffisait à gens de cette espèce!
Il n'était pas besoin qu'ils trouvassent un bœuf.
    Pleins d'appétit et d'allégresse,
Ils allaient de leur œuf manger chacun sa part,
Quand un quidam parut. C'était maître renard;
    Rencontre incommode et fâcheuse.
Car comment sauver l'œuf? Le bien empaqueter,
Puis des pieds de devant ensemble le porter,
    Ou le rouler, ou le traîner,
C'était chose impossible autant que hasardeuse.
    Nécessité l'ingénieuse
    Leur fournit une invention.
Comme ils pouvaient gagner leur habitation,
L'écornifleur étant à demi-quart de lieue,
L'un se mit sur le dos, prit l'œuf entre ses bras,

Puis malgré quelques heurts, et quelques mauvais pas,
    L'autre le traîna par la queue.
Qu'on m'aille soutenir, après un tel récit,
    Que les bêtes n'ont point d'esprit.


    Pour moi, si j'en étais le maître,
Je leur en donnerais aussi bien qu'aux enfants.
Ceux-ci pensent-ils pas dès leurs plus jeunes ans?
Quelqu'un peut donc penser ne se pouvant connaître.
    Par un exemple tout égal,
    J'attribuerais à l'animal
Non point une raison selon notre manière,

What I do know, Iris, is that, in those animals
    which I have just cited as examples,
that spirit does not operate; man alone is its temple.
Thus, animals must be granted a merit
    that plants, after all, do not possess.
    and yet plants breathe:
but what answer will be given to what I am about to say?


## *The Two Rats, the Fox and the Egg*

Two rats were seeking sustenance; they found an egg.
That was dinner enough for folk of that type!
It wasn't necessary for them to find an ox.
    Full of appetite and cheerfulness,
each one was going to eat his share of their egg
when they caught sight of another fellow. It was Master Fox;
    an inconvenient, troublesome encounter.
For, how could they save the egg? To wrap it up carefully,
then carry it together in their forepaws,
    or to roll it, or to drag it,
was just as out of the question as it was dangerous.
    Ingenious necessity
    provided them with an invention.
Since they were able to reach their home,
the scrounger still being an eighth of a league distant,
one of them lay down on his back and took the egg between his
                              paws;
then, despite a few jolts and a few stumbles,
    the other one dragged him away by the tail.
After a story like that, let them come to me and declare
    that animals have no intelligence.


    As for me, if I were to decide the matter,
I'd grant them intelligence just as I grant it to children.
Don't children think even in their youngest years?
Therefore, someone can think while still unable to know himself.
    Using a quite similar reasoning,
    I would attribute to animals
not a rationality of our order,

Mais beaucoup plus aussi qu'un aveugle ressort:
Je subtiliserais un morceau de matière,
Que l'on ne pourrait plus concevoir sans effort,
Quintessence d'atome, extrait de la lumière,
Je ne sais quoi plus vif et plus mobile encor
Que le feu: car enfin, si le bois fait la flamme,
La flamme en s'épurant peut-elle pas de l'âme
Nous donner quelque idée, et sort-il pas de l'or
Des entrailles du plomb? Je rendrais mon ouvrage
Capable de sentir, juger, rien davantage,
      Et juger imparfaitement,
Sans qu'un singe jamais fît le moindre argument.


      A l'égard de nous autres hommes,
Je ferais notre lot infiniment plus fort:
      Nous aurions un double trésor;
L'un cette âme pareille en tous tant que nous sommes,

      Sages, fous, enfants, idiots,
Hôtes de l'univers sous le nom d'animaux;
L'autre encore une autre âme, entre nous et les anges
      Commune en un certain degré;
      Et ce trésor à part créé
Suivrait parmi les airs les célestes phalanges,
Entrerait dans un point sans en être pressé,
Ne finirait jamais quoique ayant commencé,
      Choses réelles quoique étranges.
      Tant que l'enfance durerait,
Cette fille du Ciel en nous ne paraîtrait
      Qu'une tendre et faible lumière;
L'organe étant plus fort, la raison percerait
      Les ténèbres de la matière,
      Qui toujours envelopperait
      L'autre âme, imparfaite et grossière.

and yet much more than a blind mechanism:
I would posit a very fine particle of matter,
which couldn't be conceived of without an effort,
a quintessence of atom, an extract of light,
something or other even more lively and mobile
than fire: because, finally, if wood creates flame,
cannot flame, becoming further refined, give us some idea
of the soul, and isn't gold produced
from the heart of lead? I'd make my creature
able to feel and judge, no more than that,
          and to judge imperfectly,
not allowing a monkey ever to indulge in the slightest rational
                                        argument.

          As for us human beings,
I'd make our lot an infinitely greater one:
          we would have a double treasure;
one of which would be that soul which is the same in every one
                                        of us,
          whether wise men, fools, children or idiots,
all guests of the universe under the name of animals;
while the other would be yet another soul, shared to a certain extent
          by us and the angels;
          and this treasure, separately created,
would follow the celestial troops through the sky,
would be gathered into a point without being compressed,
would never end although it began,
          things that are real though strange.
          As long as childhood lasted,
that daughter of Heaven within us would appear
          only as a tender, feeble light;
when our bodies were stronger, reason would pierce
          the darkness of matter,
          which would always envelop
          the other soul, since that one is imperfect and coarse.

# La tortue et les deux canards

Une tortue était, à la tête légère,
Qui lasse de son trou voulut voir le pays.
Volontiers on fait cas d'une terre étrangère;
Volontiers gens boiteux haïssent le logis.
    Deux canards à qui la commère
    Communiqua ce beau dessein
Lui dirent qu'ils avaient de quoi la satisfaire:
    «Voyez-vous ce large chemin?
Nous vous voiturerons par l'air en Amérique,
    Vous verrez mainte république,
Maint royaume, maint peuple, et vous profiterez
Des différentes mœurs que vous remarquerez.
Ulysse en fit autant.» On ne s'attendait guère
    De voir Ulysse en cette affaire.
La tortue écouta la proposition.
Marché fait, les oiseaux forgent une machine
    Pour transporter la pèlerine.
Dans la gueule en travers on lui passe un bâton.
«Serrez bien, dirent-ils; gardez de lâcher prise»;
Puis chaque canard prend ce bâton par un bout.
La tortue enlevée, on s'étonne partout
    De voir aller en cette guise
    L'animal lent et sa maison,
Justement au milieu de l'un et l'autre oison.
«Miracle! criait-on. Venez voir dans les nues
    Passer la reine des tortues.
–La reine! Vraiment oui. Je la suis en effet;
Ne vous en moquez point.» Elle eût beaucoup mieux fait
De passer son chemin sans dire aucune chose:
Car lâchant le bâton en desserrant les dents,
Elle tombe, elle crève aux pieds des regardants.
Son indiscrétion de sa perte fut cause.

# The Tortoise and the Two Ducks

There was a light-headed tortoise
Who, tired of her hole, wished to travel.
People are wont to make much of foreign countries,
the lame are wont to hate their home.
    Two ducks to whom the goodwife
    communicated this fine plan
told her they had a means to satisfy her:
    "Do you see this wide pathway?
We will transport you through the air to America;
    you'll see many a country,
many a kingdom, many a nation, and you'll profit
by the different customs you'll observe.
Ulysses[83] did the same." One hardly expected
    to see Ulysses mixed up in this.
The tortoise listened to the proposal.
Once agreed on, the birds created a device
    for carrying the pilgrim.
They put a stick in her mouth crossways.
"Bite down hard," they said; "be sure not to let go";
then each duck took hold of one end of that stick.
When the tortoise was in the air, folk everywhere were amazed
    to see that slow animal and her house
    traveling in that fashion,
exactly halfway between one and the other duck.[84]
"A miracle!" was the cry. "Come and see the queen
    of tortoises going by in the clouds."
"The queen! It's really true. I am one, indeed;
don't laugh about it." She would have done much better
to go her way without saying anything:
because, letting go of the stick when unclenching her teeth,
she fell and split apart at the feet of the onlookers.
Her lack of discernment was the cause of her destruction.

---

[83] When wandering for ten years after the fall of Troy.
[84] Literally "gosling."

Imprudence, babil, et sotte vanité,
    Et vaine curiosité,
    Ont ensemble étroit parentage;
    Ce sont enfants tous d'un lignage.


# Le berger et le roi

Deux démons à leur gré partagent notre vie,
Et de son patrimoine ont chassé la raison.
Je ne vois point de cœur qui ne leur sacrifie.
Si vous me demandez leur état et leur nom,
J'appelle l'un Amour, et l'autre Ambition.
Cette dernière étend le plus loin son empire;
    Car même elle entre dans l'amour.
Je le ferais bien voir; mais mon but est de dire
Comme un roi fit venir un berger à sa cour.
Le conte est du bon temps, non du siècle où nous sommes.
Ce roi vit un troupeau qui couvrait tous les champs,
Bien broutant, en bon corps, rapportant tous les ans,
Grâce aux soins du berger, de très notables sommes.
Le berger plut au roi par ces soins diligents.
«Tu mérites, dit-il, d'être pasteur de gens;
Laisse là tes moutons, viens conduire des hommes.
    Je te fais juge souverain.»
Voilà notre berger la balance à la main.
Quoiqu'il n'eût guère vu d'autres gens qu'un ermite,
Son troupeau, ses mâtins, le loup, et puis c'est tout,
Il avait du bon sens; le reste vient ensuite.
    Bref il en vint fort bien à bout.
L'ermite son voisin accourut pour lui dire:
«Veillé-je, et n'est-ce point un songe que je vois?
Vous favori! vous grand! Défiez-vous des rois:
Leur faveur est glissante, on s'y trompe; et le pire,
C'est qu'il en coûte cher; de pareilles erreurs
Ne produisent jamais que d'illustres malheurs.
Vous ne connaissez pas l'attrait qui vous engage.
Je vous parle en ami. Craignez tout.» L'autre rit,

    Et notre ermite poursuivit:

Carelessness, talkativeness, foolish vanity
    and vain curiosity
    are all closely related;
    they're all children of one family.

## The Shepherd and the King

Two spirits divide our life between them just as they please,
and have driven reason from her ancestral home.
I can see no heart that does not offer sacrifice to them.
If you ask me their nature and their name,
I call one Love and the other Ambition.
The latter enjoys the more extensive dominions,
    because it even enters into the state of love.
I would gladly show this; but my goal is to tell
how a king summoned a shepherd to his court.
The story dates from the good old days, not from the age we live in.
That king saw a flock covering all the fields,
happily grazing, in good condition and, thanks to the shepherd's care,
bringing in very respectable profits every year.
The king liked the shepherd for that diligent care.
He said: "You deserve to be a shepherd of people;
leave your sheep, and come and lead men.
    I make you chief justice."
Now our shepherd held the scales of the law in his hands.
Even though he had hardly seen any other people than a hermit,
his flock, his sheepdogs, the wolf, and that's all,
he had common sense; all the rest follows.
    In short, he managed things very successfully.
His neighbor the hermit came to say to him:
"Am I awake? Is this not a dream I'm seeing?
You a favorite! You a grandee! Don't trust kings:
their favor is slippery, it's deceptive; and, worst of all,
it costs one dear; errors like this
never result in anything but signal disasters.
You aren't aware of the attraction that is alluring you.
I'm speaking to you as a friend. Fear everything." The other man
                               laughed,
    and our hermit continued:

«Voyez combien déjà la cour vous rend peu sage.
Je crois voir cet aveugle, à qui dans un voyage
  Un serpent engourdi de froid
Vint s'offrir sous la main: il le prit pour un fouet.
Le sien s'était perdu, tombant de sa ceinture.
Il rendait grâce au Ciel de l'heureuse aventure,
Quand un passant cria: «Que tenez-vous? ô dieux!
«Jetez cet animal traître et pernicieux,
«Ce serpent.–C'est un fouet.–C'est un serpent, vous dis-je.
«A me tant tourmenter quel intérêt m'oblige?
«Prétendez-vous garder ce trésor?–Pourquoi non?
«Mon fouet était usé; j'en retrouve un fort bon;
  «Vous n'en parlez que par envie.»
  L'aveugle enfin ne le crut pas;
  Il en perdit bientôt la vie.
L'animal dégourdi piqua son homme au bras.
  Quant à vous, j'ose vous prédire
Qu'il vous arrivera quelque chose de pire.
–Eh! que me saurait-il arriver que la mort?
–Mille dégoûts viendront», dit le prophète ermite.

Il en vint en effet; l'ermite n'eut pas tort.
Mainte peste de cour fit tant, par maint ressort,
Que la candeur du juge, ainsi que son mérite,
Furent suspects au prince. On cabale, on suscite
Accusateurs et gens grevés par ses arrêts.
«De nos biens, dirent-ils, il s'est fait un palais.»
Le prince voulut voir ces richesses immenses;
Il ne trouva partout que médiocrité,
Louanges du désert et de la pauvreté;
  C'étaient là ses magnificences.
«Son fait, dit-on, consiste en des pierres de prix.
Un grand coffre en est plein, fermé de dix serrures.»
Lui-même ouvrit ce coffre, et rendit bien surpris
  Tous les machineurs d'impostures.
Le coffre étant ouvert, on y vit des lambeaux,
  L'habit d'un gardeur de troupeaux,
Petit chapeau, jupon, panetière, houlette,
  Et, je pense, aussi sa musette.
«Doux trésors, ce dit-il, chers gages qui jamais
N'attirâtes sur vous l'envie et le mensonge,

"See how the court is already draining your wisdom from you.
I seem to be seeing that blind man who, when traveling,
      found within hand's reach
a snake numb with cold: he thought it was a whip.
His own had gotten lost, falling out of his belt.
He was thanking Heaven for the fortunate occurrence
when a passer-by called: 'What are you holding? O gods!
Throw away that treacherous, malicious animal,
that snake!' 'It's a whip.' 'It's a snake, I tell you.
What interest compels me to torment myself so much?
Do you expect to keep that treasure?' 'Why not?
My whip was old and worn; I've found another, very good one;
      you are only speaking out of envy.'
      In short, the blinded man didn't believe it;
      soon he lost his life on that account.
The animal, emerging from its torpor, bit the man in the arm.
      As for you, I venture to predict to you
that something worse will happen to you."
"Oh! What could happen to me but death?"
"A thousand unpleasant things are in store," said the prophetic
                                             hermit.
And they *were* in store; the hermit wasn't wrong.
Many a plaguy courtier, through many a ploy,
brought it about that the judge's honesty, as well as his merit,
became suspect to the ruler. They intrigued, they suborned
accusers and people who had been injured by his judgments.
They said, "He's built himself a palace with our money."
The ruler demanded to see those immense riches;
everywhere he found only a moderate life style,
indications that the judge prized the wilderness and poverty;
      that was his magnificent mode of life.
Then they said: "His wealth is all invested in precious stones.
He has a big chest full of them, fastened with ten locks."
He himself opened that chest, affording a great surprise
      to all the fabricators of falsehoods.
When the chest was open, it was seen to contain ragged clothing,
      the outfit of a man who keeps watch over flocks,
a small hat, a smock, a scrip, a crook
      and, I believe, his bagpipe, too.
"Dear treasures," he said, "beloved reminders that never
drew envy or lies down upon you,

Je vous reprends; sortons de ces riches palais
    Comme l'on sortirait d'un songe.
Sire, pardonnez-moi cette exclamation.
J'avais prévu ma chute en montant sur le faîte.
Je m'y suis trop complu; mais qui n'a dans la tête

    Un petit grain d'ambition?»


## *Discours à Monsieur le duc de la Rochefoucauld*

Je me suis souvent dit, voyant de quelle sorte
    L'homme agit, et qu'il se comporte
En mille occasions comme les animaux:
Le roi de ces gens-là n'a pas moins de défauts
    Que ses sujets, et la nature
    A mis dans chaque créature
Quelque grain d'une masse où puisent les esprits:
J'entends les esprits-corps, et pétris de matière.
    Je vais prouver ce que je dis.
A l'heure de l'affût, soit lorsque la lumière
Précipite ses traits dans l'humide séjour,
Soit lorsque le soleil rentre dans sa carrière,
Et que, n'étant plus nuit, il n'est pas encor jour,
Au bord de quelque bois sur un arbre je grimpe;
Et nouveau Jupiter, du haut de cet Olympe,
    Je foudroie à discrétion
    Un lapin qui n'y pensait guère.
Je vois fuir aussitôt toute la nation
    Des lapins qui sur la bruyère,
    L'œil éveillé, l'oreille au guet,
S'égayaient et de thym parfumaient leur banquet.
    Le bruit du coup fait que la bande
    S'en va chercher sa sûreté
    Dans la souterraine cité;
Mais le danger s'oublie, et cette peur si grande
S'évanouit bientôt. Je revois les lapins

I take you up again; let us leave behind these rich palaces
    as one would leave behind a dream.
Sire, forgive me for this outburst.
I had foreseen my fall while climbing to the heights.
I took too much pleasure in my new life, but who doesn't have in
                               his head
    some little grain of ambition?"

# *Discourse to the Duke de La Rochefoucauld*[85]

I have often said to myself, seeing in what way
    man acts, and how he behaves
like the animals on a thousand occasions:
man, the king of those folk, doesn't have fewer faults
    than his subjects, and nature
    has put into every creature
some grain of a substance from which the intelligence draws:
I mean the material intelligence, which is mingled with matter.[86]
    I shall prove what I say.
At the hour of stalking game, either when the sun
is plunging its beams into its ocean abode in the west,
or when it is returning to its daily course
and, though no longer night, it is not yet day,
I climb a tree at the edge of some wood;
and, a new Jupiter, from the height of that Olympus,
    at discretion I blast with my lightning
    a rabbit who was hardly thinking about it.
Immediately I see fleeing the entire nation
    of rabbits who, on the heath,
    their eyes alert, their ears raised to listen,
had been making merry and flavoring their banquet with thyme.
    The noise of the shot makes the band
    go off to seek safety
    in their underground town;
but danger is forgotten, and that fear, great as it was,
soon wears off. I see the rabbits again

---

[85] The famous author (1613–1680) of the *Maximes*, *Mémoires* and other works.
[86] See the end of the "Discours à Madame de la Sablière."

Plus gais qu'auparavant revenir sous mes mains.
Ne reconnaît-on pas en cela les humains?
    Dispersés par quelque orage,
    A peine ils touchent le port
    Qu'ils vont hasarder encor
    Même vent, même naufrage.
    Vrais lapins on les revoit
    Sous les mains de la Fortune.
Joignons à cet exemple une chose commune.
Quand des chiens étrangers passent par quelque endroit
    Qui n'est pas de leur détroit,
    Je laisse à penser quelle fête.
    Les chiens du lieu n'ayants en tête
Qu'un intérêt de gueule, à cris, à coups de dents,
    Vous accompagnent ces passants
    Jusqu'aux confins du territoire.
Un intérêt de biens, de grandeur, et de gloire,
Aux gouverneurs d'États, à certains courtisans,
A gens de tous métiers en fait tout autant faire.
    On nous voit tous, pour l'ordinaire,
Piller le survenant, nous jeter sur sa peau.
La coquette et l'auteur sont de ce caractère;
    Malheur à l'écrivain nouveau.
Le moins de gens qu'on peut à l'entour du gâteau,
    C'est le droit du jeu, c'est l'affaire.
Cent exemples pourraient appuyer mon discours;
    Mais les ouvrages les plus courts
Sont toujours les meilleurs. En cela j'ai pour guide
Tous les maîtres de l'art, et tiens qu'il faut laisser
Dans les plus beaux sujets quelque chose à penser:
    Ainsi ce discours doit cesser.
Vous qui m'avez donné ce qu'il a de solide,
Et dont la modestie égale la grandeur,
Qui ne pûtes jamais écouter sans pudeur
    La louange la plus permise,
    La plus juste et la mieux acquise,
Vous enfin dont à peine ai-je encore obtenu
Que votre nom reçût ici quelques hommages,
Du temps et des censeurs défendant mes ouvrages,
Comme un nom qui des ans et des peuples connu,
Fait honneur à la France, en grands noms plus féconde

returning within my reach even merrier than before.
Couldn't you recognize human beings in that story?
    Scattered by some storm,
    no sooner do they reach port
    than they go off again to risk
    the same wind, the same shipwreck.
    You can see them again, real rabbits,
    in the hands of Fortune.
Let's add to that example an everyday experience.
When strange dogs pass by some spot
    that isn't in their own district,
    you can just imagine the hubbub.
    The local dogs, having nothing on their mind
but the interests of their gullet, with barks, with bites,
    accompany those passers-by
    all the way to the edge of their territory.
The interests of wealth, grandeur and glory
make the rulers of states, certain courtiers
and people of all professions do just the same.
    We can all be seen, as a rule,
attacking the newcomer, pouncing onto his hide.
Coquettes and writers are of that nature;
    woe to any new author!
Keep as few people as possible from sharing the pie,
    that's the rule of the game, that's the order of business.
I could bolster my argument with a hundred examples;
    but the shortest pieces of writing
are always the best. In that I have as my guide
all the masters of the art, and I hold that in the finest themes
something should be left to the reader's imagination;
    therefore this discourse must come to an end.
You who have furnished me with whatever solidity it has,
you whose modesty is equal to your greatness,
you who could never listen without embarrassment
    to even the most permissible praise,
    the most justified and the best deserved;
in short, you from whom I received permission only with difficulty
to render some slight homage to your name here—
your name, which will protect my works against time and critics,
being one that, known to all nations through the years,
does honor to France, which is richer in great names

     Qu'aucun climat de l'univers,
Permettez-moi du moins d'apprendre à tout le monde
Que vous m'avez donné le sujet de ces vers.

# Le songe d'un habitant du Mogol

Jadis certain Mogol vit en songe un vizir
Aux champs Élysiens possesseur d'un plaisir
Aussi pur qu'infini, tant en prix qu'en durée;
Le même songeur vit en une autre contrée
     Un ermite entouré de feux,
Qui touchait de pitié même les malheureux.
Le cas parut étrange, et contre l'ordinaire;
Minos en ces deux morts semblait s'être mépris.
Le dormeur s'éveilla, tant il en fut surpris.
Dans ce songe pourtant soupçonnant du mystère,
     Il se fit expliquer l'affaire.
L'interprète lui dit: «Ne vous étonnez point,
Votre songe a du sens, et si j'ai sur ce point
     Acquis tant soit peu d'habitude,
C'est un avis des dieux. Pendant l'humain séjour,
Ce vizir quelquefois cherchait la solitude;
Cet ermite aux vizirs allait faire sa cour.»

Si j'osais ajouter au mot de l'interprète,
J'inspirerais ici l'amour de la retraite:
Elle offre à ses amants des biens sans embarras,
Biens purs, présents du Ciel, qui naissent sous les pas.
Solitude où je trouve une douceur secrète,
Lieux que j'aimai toujours, ne pourrai-je jamais,
Loin du monde et du bruit goûter l'ombre et le frais?
O qui m'arrêtera sous vos sombres asiles?
Quand pourront les neuf Sœurs, loin des cours et des villes,

than any other region in the universe —
at least allow me to inform all the world
that you gave me the theme for these verses.


## The Dream of an Inhabitant of the Moghul Empire

Once a certain Moghul[87] subject saw in a dream a vizier[88]
in the Elysian Fields[89] who possessed a pleasure
as pure as it was infinite, in value as well as duration;
the same dreamer saw, in another region,
      a hermit surrounded by flames,
whose suffering moved even the other unfortunates to pity.
The case seemed strange and contrary to expectations;
Minos[90] seemed to have made an error about those two dead men.
The sleeper awoke, so surprised was he by what he had seen.
Nevertheless, suspecting there was some mystery in that dream,
      he had the matter explained to him.
The dream interpreter told him: "Don't be amazed,
your dream has a meaning, and if in these affairs
      I have any experience at all,
it's a warning from the gods. During his sojourn on earth,
that vizier from time to time sought out solitude;
that hermit used to go and ingratiate himself with viziers."

If I dared to add anything to the interpreter's words,
I would here inspire people with the love of the lonely hideaway;
it offers its lovers treasures that are free of cares,
pure treasures, gifts from Heaven, that spring up beneath their feet.
Solitude, in which I find a secret sweetness,
places I always loved, will I never be able
to enjoy your shadow and coolness far from the world and its noise?
Oh, who will allow me to tarry in your shady refuge?
When will the nine sisters,[91] far from courts and cities,

---

[87] Islamic empire in Northern India.
[88] A chief minister, whose duties make him live in the midst of society.
[89] Home of blessed souls in the underworld.
[90] Judge of the dead, who assigns them to bliss or woe.
[91] The muses.

M'occuper tout entier, et m'apprendre des cieux
Les divers mouvements inconnus à nos yeux,
Les noms et les vertus de ces clartés errantes,
Par qui sont nos destins et nos mœurs différentes?
Que si je ne suis né pour de si grands projets,
Du moins que les ruisseaux m'offrent de doux objets!
Que je peigne en mes vers quelque rive fleurie!
La Parque à filets d'or n'ourdira point ma vie;
Je ne dormirai point sous de riches lambris.
Mais voit-on que le somme en perde de son prix?
En est-il moins profond, et moins plein de délices?
Je lui voue au désert de nouveaux sacrifices.
Quand le moment viendra d'aller trouver les morts,
J'aurai vécu sans soins, et mourrai sans remords.

## Le paysan du Danube

Il ne faut point juger des gens sur l'apparence.
Le conseil en est bon; mais il n'est pas nouveau:
        Jadis l'erreur du souriceau
Me servit à prouver le discours que j'avance.
        J'ai pour le fonder à présent
Le bon Socrate, Ésope, et certain paysan
Des rives du Danube, homme dont Marc-Aurèle
        Nous fait un portrait fort fidèle.
On connaît les premiers; quant à l'autre, voici
        Le personnage en raccourci.
Son menton nourrissait une barbe touffue,
        Toute sa personne velue
Représentait un ours, mais un ours mal léché.
Sous un sourcil épais il avait l'œil caché,
Le regard de travers, nez tortu, grosse lèvre,
        Portait sayon de poil de chèvre,
        Et ceinture de joncs marins.

occupy all my time and teach me the various motions
of the heavens that are unknown to our eyes,
the names and powers of those wandering stars
which make our destinies and behavior so different?
And if I wasn't born for mighty schemes,
at least let the brooks offer me pleasant sights!
Let me depict in my verses some flowery bank!
The Fates won't weave gold threads into the fabric of my life;
I won't sleep beneath richly coffered ceilings.
But has anyone seen sleep lose its value on that account?
Is it less deep and less full of delights?
I vow new sacrifices to it in the wilderness.
When the moment comes to go and join the dead,
I shall have lived without care, and I shall die without regret.

## *The Peasant of the Danube*

People should not be judged by their appearance.
This is good advice, but it isn't new:
   in the past the young mouse's mistake
gave me an example for proving the thesis I put forward.
   As a basis for it now I have
worthy Socrates, Aesop[92] and a certain peasant
from the banks of the Danube, a man of whom Marcus Aurelius[93]
   gives us a very faithful portrait.
The first two are well known; as for the third, here is
   the character in a summary description.
His chin nourished a bushy beard,
   his whole hairy body
was like a bear's—a rough, cross-grained bear's.
His eyes were hidden under dense eyebrows;
he had a scowling look in them, a twisted nose, thick lips;
   he wore a goatskin tunic
   and a belt of furze.

---

92 Both were said to be very ugly, but wise.

93 A Roman emperor (reigned 161–180) who fought campaigns along the Danube; this anecdote was attributed to him by the Spanish writer Antonio de Guevara (ca. 1480–1548).

Cet homme ainsi bâti fut député des villes
Que lave le Danube: il n'était point d'asiles
　　　Où l'avarice des Romains
Ne pénétrât alors, et ne portât les mains.
Le député vint donc, et fit cette harangue:
«Romains, et vous, Sénat, assis pour m'écouter,
Je supplie avant tout les dieux de m'assister:
Veuillent les Immortels, conducteurs de ma langue,
Que je ne dise rien qui doive être repris!
Sans leur aide, il ne peut entrer dans les esprits
　　　Que tout mal et toute injustice:
Faute d'y recourir, on viole leurs lois,
Témoin nous, que punit la romaine avarice;

Rome est par nos forfaits, plus que par ses exploits,
　　　L'instrument de notre supplice.
Craignez, Romains, craignez que le Ciel quelque jour
Ne transporte chez vous les pleurs et la misère,
Et mettant en nos mains par un juste retour
Les armes dont se sert sa vengeance sévère,
　　　Il ne vous fasse en sa colère
　　　Nos esclaves à votre tour.
Et pourquoi sommes-nous les vôtres? qu'on me die
En quoi vous valez mieux que cent peuples divers?
Quel droit vous a rendus maîtres de l'univers?
Pourquoi venir troubler une innocente vie?
Nous cultivions en paix d'heureux champs, et nos mains
Étaient propres aux arts ainsi qu'au labourage:
　　　Qu'avez-vous appris aux Germains?
　　　Ils ont l'adresse et le courage;
　　　S'ils avaient eu l'avidité,
　　　Comme vous, et la violence,
Peut-être en votre place ils auraient la puissance,
Et sauraient en user sans inhumanité.
Celle que vos préteurs ont sur nous exercée
　　　N'entre qu'à peine en la pensée.
　　　La majesté de vos autels
　　　Elle-même en est offensée:
　　　Car sachez que les Immortels
Ont les regards sur nous. Grâces à vos exemples,

With such an appearance, this man was a delegate from the cities
washed by the Danube: there was no refuge
    into which the greed of the Romans
did not extend and stretch out its hands at that time.
Thus, the delegate came and made this oration:
"Romans and you, senators, seated here to listen to me,
before all else I beseech the gods to assist me:
may it be the wish of the Immortals who guide my tongue
that I say nothing deserving of reproach!
Without their aid, the only thing that can enter one's mind
    is every kind of evil and injustice:
for lack of seeking it, one violates their laws;
let my people be a witness to that, now being punished by Roman
                         greed;
through our misdeeds more than through its own exploits, Rome is
    the instrument of our suffering.
Be afraid, Romans, be afraid lest Heaven some day
transfer to your land those tears and that misery,
and, by a fair turnabout, placing in our hands
the weapons used by its severe vengeance,
    make you in its wrath
    our slaves in your turn.
And why are we yours? Someone tell me
wherein you are better than a hundred different nations.
What right has made you masters of the world?
Why did you come to disturb our innocent life?
We were tilling fertile fields in peace, and our hands
were as apt for the arts as for plowing:
    what have you taught the Germanic tribes?
    They have skill and courage;
    if they had had avidity,
    like you, and violence,
perhaps they would have the power instead of you,
and would know how to use it without inhumanity.
The power that your colonial governors have exercised over us
    is barely imaginable.
    The very majesty of your altars
    is offended by it:
    for know that the Immortals
have their eye on us men. Thanks to your examples,

Ils n'ont devant les yeux que des objets d'horreur,
      De mépris d'eux, et de leurs temples,
D'avarice qui va jusques à la fureur.
Rien ne suffit aux gens qui nous viennent de Rome;
      La terre, et le travail de l'homme
Font pour les assouvir des efforts superflus.
      Retirez-les: on ne veut plus
      Cultiver pour eux les campagnes;
Nous quittons les cités, nous fuyons aux montagnes,
      Nous laissons nos chères compagnes;
Nous ne conversons plus qu'avec des ours affreux,
Découragés de mettre au jour des malheureux,
Et de peupler pour Rome un pays qu'elle opprime.
      Quant à nos enfants déjà nés,
Nous souhaitons de voir leurs jours bientôt bornés:
Vos préteurs au malheur nous font joindre le crime.
      Retirez-les, ils ne nous apprendront
      Que la mollesse et que le vice;
      Les Germains comme eux deviendront
      Gens de rapine et d'avarice.
C'est tout ce que j'ai vu dans Rome à mon abord:
      N'a-t-on point de présent à faire?
Point de pourpre à donner? c'est en vain qu'on espère
Quelque refuge aux lois; encor leur ministère
A-t-il mille longueurs. Ce discours un peu fort
      Doit commencer à vous déplaire.
      Je finis. Punissez de mort
      Une plainte un peu trop sincère.»
A ces mots, il se couche, et chacun étonné
Admire le grand cœur, le bon sens, l'éloquence,
      Du sauvage ainsi prosterné.
On le créa patrice; et ce fut la vengeance
Qu'on crut qu'un tel discours méritait. On choisit
      D'autres préteurs, et par écrit
Le Sénat demanda ce qu'avait dit cet homme,
Pour servir de modèle aux parleurs à venir.
      On ne sut pas longtemps à Rome
      Cette éloquence entretenir.

all they see before them is sights of horror,
 scorn for them and their temples,
greed that reaches frenetic proportions.
Nothing satisfies the people who come to us from Rome;
 the soil and human labor
strive in vain to appease them.
  Recall them: we no longer wish
  to till our farmlands for them;
we are abandoning our towns and fleeing into the hills,
 we are leaving behind our beloved wives;
the only company we now have is that of frightful bears,
since we do not wish to give birth to children who must be unfortunate
and to populate for Rome's benefit a country that she oppresses.
  As for those children of ours already born,
we hope to see their life soon terminated;
your governors make us add crime to our misfortune.
 Recall them, all they will teach us
  is luxury and vice;
  like them, the Germans will become
  a nation of pillaging and greed.
That is all I saw in Rome on my arrival:
  'Doesn't anyone have a gift to give,
Any purple[94] to bestow?' It's in vain that one hopes
for any refuge in the laws; their procedure, too,
is plagued with a thousand delays. This rather strong speech
  must be beginning to displease you.
  I conclude it. Punish by death
  a complaint that is somewhat too frank."
Saying this, he lay down, and everyone, astonished,
admired the great heart, the good sense and the eloquence
  of the savage who thus lay prostrate.
He was made a patrician;[95] and that was the punishment
which people thought such a speech deserved. They chose
  different governors, and the Senate ordered
the words spoken by that man to be set down in writing,
to serve as a model for future speakers.
  That level of eloquence was not maintained
  very long in Rome.

---

[94] A symbol of political office.
[95] A high honorary rank; in reality, not bestowed until the fourth century A.D.

# Le vieillard et les trois jeunes hommes

Un octogénaire plantait.
«Passe encor de bâtir; mais planter à cet âge!»
Disaient trois jouvenceaux, enfants du voisinage:
Assurément il radotait.
«Car, au nom des dieux, je vous prie,
Quel fruit de ce labeur pouvez-vous recueillir?
Autant qu'un patriarche il vous faudrait vieillir.
A quoi bon charger votre vie
Des soins d'un avenir qui n'est pas fait pour vous?
Ne songez désormais qu'à vos erreurs passées:
Quittez le long espoir, et les vastes pensées;
Tout cela ne convient qu'à nous.
– Il ne convient pas à vous-mêmes,
Repartit le vieillard. Tout établissement
Vient tard et dure peu. La main des Parques blêmes
De vos jours et des miens se joue également.
Nos termes sont pareils par leur courte durée.
Qui de nous des clartés de la voûte azurée
Doit jouir le dernier? Est-il aucun moment
Qui vous puisse assurer d'un second seulement?
Mes arrière-neveux me devront cet ombrage:
Hé bien! défendez-vous au sage
De se donner des soins pour le plaisir d'autrui?
Cela même est un fruit que je goûte aujourd'hui:
J'en puis jouir demain, et quelques jours encore;
Je puis enfin compter l'aurore
Plus d'une fois sur vos tombeaux.»
Le vieillard eut raison; l'un des trois jouvenceaux
Se noya dès le port allant à l'Amérique;
L'autre afin de monter aux grandes dignités,
Dans les emplois de Mars servant la république,
Par un coup imprévu vit ses jours emportés;

# The Old Man and the Three Young Men

A man in his eighties was having trees planted.
"New construction might still be all right; but to plant at that age!"
said three striplings, neighbors' children:
     surely he was in his dotage.
     "For I ask you, in the name of the gods,
what fruit of this labor can you gather?
You'd have to grow as old as a Biblical patriarch.
     What's the use of burdening your life
with cares for a future that isn't granted to you?
From this point on, think only about your past mistakes:
give up long-range hopes and expansive thoughts;
     all that is only suitable for us."
     "It isn't suitable for *you*,"
replied the old man. "Every kind of foundation in life
comes late and doesn't last long. The hands of the pallid Fates
make sport of your life just as they do of mine.
Our terms of life are equal in their short duration.
Who among us is to be the last to enjoy
the brightness of the azure canopy? Is there any moment
that can assure you of even the very next one?
My great-grandchildren will owe this shady spot to me:
     All right! Do you forbid the wise man
to take pains for other people's pleasure?
That very pleasure is a fruit that I taste today:
I can enjoy it tomorrow, and for a few days more;
     finally, I may still be able to see the sun rise
     more than once over your graves."
The old man was right; one of the three striplings
drowned in the very harbor on his way to America;
the second, in order to attain high rank,
was serving the state in the field of Mars[96]
when he saw his life snatched away by an unforeseen blow;

---

[96] God of war.

Le troisième tomba d'un arbre
Que lui-même il voulut enter;
Et pleurés du vieillard, il grava sur leur marbre

Ce que je viens de raconter.

# *Épilogue*

C'est ainsi que ma muse, aux bords d'une onde pure,
        Traduisait en langue des dieux
        Tout ce que disent sous les cieux
Tant d'êtres empruntant la voix de la nature.
        Trucheman de peuples divers,
Je les faisais servir d'acteurs en mon ouvrage:
        Car tout parle dans l'univers;
        Il n'est rien qui n'ait son langage.
Plus éloquents chez eux qu'ils ne sont dans mes vers,
Si ceux que j'introduis me trouvent peu fidèle,
Si mon œuvre n'est pas un assez bon modèle,
        J'ai du moins ouvert le chemin:
D'autres pourront y mettre une dernière main.
Favoris des neuf Sœurs, achevez l'entreprise;
Donnez mainte leçon que j'ai sans doute omise:
Sous ces inventions il faut l'envelopper.
Mais vous n'avez que trop de quoi vous occuper:
Pendant le doux emploi de ma muse innocente,
Louis dompte l'Europe, et d'une main puissante
Il conduit à leur fin les plus nobles projets
        Qu'ait jamais formés un monarque.
Favoris des neuf Sœurs, ce sont là des sujets
        Vainqueurs du temps et de la Parque.

the third fell from a tree
    into which he wanted to insert a graft himself;
and they were mourned by the old man, who engraved on their
                                        tombstones
    the story I have just told.


# Epilogue [to Books VII–XI]

It is thus that my muse, by the banks of a clear stream,
    translated into the language of the gods[97]
    everything spoken beneath the skies
by so many beings who borrow the voice of nature.
    An interpreter of various nations,
I made them serve as actors in my book:
    for everything in the world speaks;
    there is nothing that doesn't have its form of speech.
More eloquent among themselves than they are in my verses,
if those I introduce find me insufficiently faithful,
if my work is not a good enough model,
    at least I have blazed the trail:
others will be able to add the finishing touches.
Protégés of the nine sisters,[98] complete the undertaking:
teach many a lesson that I have no doubt omitted:
the lesson must be clothed in this type of story.
But you have more than enough to busy yourself with:
during the gentle labors of my innocent muse,
Louis has been conquering Europe, and with a mighty hand
he is bringing to fruition the most noble plans
    a monarch ever formed.
Protégés of the nine sisters, there you have themes
    that will overcome time and the Fates.

---

[97] Poetry.
[98] The muses.

## Le vieux chat et la jeune souris

Une jeune souris de peu d'expérience
Crut fléchir un vieux chat, implorant sa clémence,
Et payant de raisons le Raminagrobis:
    «Laissez-moi vivre: une souris
    De ma taille et de ma dépense
    Est-elle à charge en ce logis?
    Affamerais-je, à votre avis,
    L'hôte et l'hôtesse, et tout leur monde?
    D'un grain de blé je me nourris;
    Une noix me rend toute ronde.
A présent je suis maigre; attendez quelque temps;
Réservez ce repas à messieurs vos enfants.»
Ainsi parlait au chat la souris attrapée.
    L'autre lui dit: «Tu t'es trompée.
Est-ce à moi que l'on tient de semblables discours?
Tu gagnerais autant de parler à des sourds.
Chat et vieux, pardonner? Cela n'arrive guères.
    Selon ces lois, descends là-bas,
    Meurs, et va-t'en tout de ce pas
    Haranguer les sœurs filandières.
Mes enfants trouveront assez d'autres repas.»
    Il tint parole; et, pour ma fable,
Voici le sens moral qui peut y convenir:
La jeunesse se flatte, et croit tout obtenir;
    La vieillesse est impitoyable.

# The Old Cat and the Young Mouse

A young mouse, with little experience of the world,
thought he could soften an old cat by begging him for mercy
and by putting off Raminagrobis[99] with various arguments:
  "Let me live: is a mouse
  of my size, and one that causes so little damage,
  such a burden to this household?
  In your opinion, would I starve out
  the owner and his wife, and all their family and servants?
  I nourish myself on a grain of wheat;
  a nut makes my belly round and tight.
At the moment I'm thin; wait a while;
save this meal for the young masters, your children."
Thus the mouse spoke to the cat who had caught him.
  The cat replied: "You've made a mistake.
Is it to me that such speeches should be made?
You'd gain the same benefit by speaking to the deaf.
Is a cat, and an old one, to let you off? That hardly ever happens.
  According to the laws we live by, descend to the underworld,
  die, and go off this very instant
  to make speeches to the thread-spinning sisters.[100]
My children will find plenty of other meals."
  He kept his word; and as for my fable,
here is the moral that seems to fit it:
youth deludes itself and thinks it can obtain anything;
  old age is pitiless.

---

[99] Standard literary name for a cat, used elsewhere by La Fontaine.
[100] The Fates.

# Le renard, les mouches, et le hérisson

Aux traces de son sang, un vieux hôte des bois,
    Renard fin, subtil, et matois,
Blessé par des chasseurs et tombé dans la fange,
Autrefois attira ce parasite ailé
    Que nous avons mouche appelé.
Il accusait les dieux, et trouvait fort étrange
Que le sort à tel point le voulût affliger
    Et le fît aux mouches manger.
«Quoi! se jeter sur moi, sur moi le plus habile
    De tous les hôtes des forêts?
Depuis quand les renards sont-ils un si bon mets?
Et que me sert ma queue? est-ce un poids inutile?
Va! le Ciel te confonde, animal importun.
    Que ne vis-tu sur le commun!»
    Un hérisson du voisinage,
    Dans mes vers nouveau personnage,
Voulut le délivrer de l'importunité
    Du peuple plein d'avidité.
«Je les vais de mes dards enfiler par centaines,
Voisin renard, dit-il, et terminer tes peines.
– Garde-t'en bien, dit l'autre; ami, ne le fais pas;
Laisse-les, je te prie, achever leur repas.
Ces animaux sont saouls; une troupe nouvelle
Viendrait fondre sur moi, plus âpre et plus cruelle.»
Nous ne trouvons que trop de mangeurs ici-bas:
Ceux-ci sont courtisans, ceux-là sont magistrats.
Aristote appliquait cet apologue aux hommes.
    Les exemples en sont communs,
    Surtout au pays où nous sommes.
Plus telles gens sont pleins, moins ils sont importuns.

# The Fox, the Flies and the Hedgehog

By the traces of his blood an old forest dweller,
    a shrewd, crafty, wily fox,
wounded by hunters and fallen into the mire,
once attracted that winged parasite
    to which we have given the name of fly.
He was accusing the gods, and found it very strange
that fate wished to afflict him to such a degree
    that it was having him eaten up by flies.
"What! to pounce upon me, upon me, the cleverest
    of all the dwellers in the forest?
Since when have foxes been such a tasty dish?
And what good is my tail to me? Is it a useless weight?
Go away! May Heaven confound you, bothersome animal!
    Why don't you live off the community?"[101]
    A hedgehog in the vicinity,
    a new character in my verses,
wanted to free him from the importunity
    of that folk full of greed.
"I will skewer them on my quills by the hundreds,
neighbor fox," he said, "and put an end to your suffering."
"Absolutely not," said the fox, "don't do that, friend;
I beg you, let them finish their meal.
These animals are full; a new troop
would come and settle on me, fiercer and more cruel."
Here on earth we find all too many devourers:
these are courtiers, those are magistrates.
Aristotle applied this fable to human beings.
    Examples of it are all around us,
    especially in the country we live in.
The fuller such people are, the less they pester us.

---

[101] There is an untranslatable play on words here; the line can also be translated:
"Why don't you live off common animals (not one as special as I am)?"

# Le corbeau, la gazelle, la tortue, et le rat
A MADAME DE LA SABLIÈRE

Je vous gardais un temple dans mes vers:
Il n'eût fini qu'avecque l'univers.
Déjà ma main en fondait la durée
Sur ce bel art qu'ont les dieux inventé,
Et sur le nom de la divinité
Que dans ce temple on aurait adorée.
Sur le portail j'aurais ces mots écrits:
PALAIS SACRÉ DE LA DÉESSE IRIS;
Non celle-là qu'a Junon à ses gages,
Car Junon même et le maître des dieux
Serviraient l'autre, et seraient glorieux
Du seul honneur de porter ses messages.
L'apothéose à la voûte eût paru.
Là tout l'Olympe en pompe eût été vu
Plaçant Iris sous un dais de lumière.
Les murs auraient amplement contenu
Toute sa vie, agréable matière,
Mais peu féconde en ces événements
Qui des États font les renversements.
Au fond du temple eût été son image,
Avec ses traits, son souris, ses appas,
Son art de plaire et de n'y penser pas,
Ses agréments à qui tout rend hommage.
J'aurais fait voir à ses pieds des mortels,
Et des héros, des demi-dieux encore,
Même des dieux; ce que le monde adore
Vient quelquefois parfumer ses autels.
J'eusse en ses yeux fait briller de son âme
Tous les trésors, quoique imparfaitement:

# The Raven, the Gazelle, the Tortoise and the Rat

## TO MADAME DE LA SABLIÈRE[102]

I was reserving a temple for you in my poetry:
it would only have terminated with the universe.
My hand was already basing its duration
on that beautiful art which the gods invented,
and on the name of the deity
that would have been worshipped in that temple.
Over the portal I would have written these words:
SACRED PALACE OF THE GODDESS IRIS—
not the Iris whom Juno has in her employ,
because Juno herself and the master of the gods
would serve that other one, and would be proud
of the mere honor of bearing her messages.
The scene of apotheosis would have appeared on the vault.
There all of Olympus would have been seen in pomp
placing Iris beneath a canopy of light.
The walls would have contained, in extensive scenes,
her entire life, a pleasing subject
but one not rich in those events
which cause governments to be overturned.
At the rear of the temple her statue would have stood,
with her features, her smile, her charms,
her art of giving pleasure while not even trying,
her grace, to which all pay homage.
I would have shown at her feet mortals
and heroes and also demigods,
even gods; those whom the world worships
come at times to burn incense on her altars.
I would have shown shining in her eyes all the treasures
of her soul, although inadequately:

---

[102] Patroness of the poet. Her poetic pseudonym was Iris (the rainbow; messenger of Juno, queen of the gods).

Car ce cœur vif et tendre infiniment
Pour ses amis, et non point autrement;
Car cet esprit qui né du firmament
A beauté d'homme avec grâces de femme,
Ne se peut pas comme on veut exprimer.
O vous, Iris, qui savez tout charmer,
Qui savez plaire en un degré suprême,
Vous que l'on aime à l'égal de soi-même
(Ceci soit dit sans nul soupçon d'amour;
Car c'est un mot banni de votre cour;
Laissons-le donc), agréez que ma muse
Achève un jour cette ébauche confuse.
J'en ai placé l'idée et le projet,
Pour plus de grâce, au-devant d'un sujet
Où l'amitié donne de telles marques,
Et d'un tel prix, que leur simple récit
Peut quelque temps amuser votre esprit.
Non que ceci se passe entre monarques:
Ce que chez vous nous voyons estimer
N'est pas un roi qui ne sait point aimer;
C'est un mortel qui sait mettre sa vie
Pour son ami. J'en vois peu de si bons.
Quatre animaux vivant de compagnie
Vont aux humains en donner des leçons.

La gazelle, le rat, le corbeau, la tortue,
Vivaient ensemble unis; douce société.
Le choix d'une demeure aux humains inconnue
    Assurait leur félicité.
Mais quoi! l'homme découvre enfin toutes retraites.
    Soyez au milieu des déserts,
    Au fond des eaux, au haut des airs,
Vous n'éviterez point ses embûches secrètes.
La gazelle s'allait ébattre innocemment,
    Quand un chien, maudit instrument
    Du plaisir barbare des hommes,
Vint sur l'herbe éventer les traces de ses pas.
Elle fuit, et le rat à l'heure du repas
Dit aux amis restants: «D'où vient que nous ne sommes
    Aujourd'hui que trois conviés?
La gazelle déjà nous a-t-elle oubliés?»

because that heart, alert and infinitely tender
for her friends, but not at all otherwise;
because that mind which, born in heaven,
has the beauty of a man's along with feminine graces,
cannot be expressed as fully as one could wish.
O you, Iris, you who can charm everyone,
you who can please to a supreme degree,
you whom people cherish as much as themselves
(let this be said without any hint at love,
for that is a word banished from your court;
let us therefore omit it), permit my muse
to complete this rough sketch some day.
I have made the idea and the plan of it,
for added grace, the preface to a theme
in which friendship exhibits such tokens,
and such precious ones, that the mere recitation of them
may entertain your mind for a while.
Not that these events occur among monarchs:
that which we see you value
is not a king incapable of loving;
it is a mere mortal capable of risking his life
for his friend. I see few who are so good.
Four animals living together
will teach a lesson to human beings.

The gazelle, the rat, the raven and the tortoise
were living together in harmony; a sweet association.
The choice of a dwelling unknown to human beings
        assured their happiness.
And yet, man eventually discovers every hiding place.
        Go to the midst of the wilderness,
        the bottom of the sea, high in the sky,
you won't avoid his secret ambushes.
The gazelle was setting out for an innocent gambol
        when a hound, accursed tool
        of man's barbarous pleasures,
managed to scent the traces of her steps on the grass.
She fled, and at mealtime the rat
said to the remaining friends: "How is it that we are
        only three at table today?
Has the gazelle already forgotten us?"

A ces paroles, la tortue
S'écrie, et dit: «Ah! si j'étais
Comme un corbeau d'ailes pourvue,
Tout de ce pas je m'en irais
Apprendre au moins quelle contrée,
Quel accident, tient arrêtée
Notre compagne au pied léger:
Car à l'égard du cœur il en faut mieux juger.»

      Le corbeau part à tire d'aile.
Il aperçoit de loin l'imprudente gazelle
      Prise au piège et se tourmentant.
Il retourne avertir les autres à l'instant.
Car de lui demander quand, pourquoi ni comment
      Ce malheur est tombé sur elle,
Et perdre en vains discours cet utile moment,
      Comme eût fait un maître d'école,
      Il avait trop de jugement.
      Le corbeau donc vole et revole.
      Sur son rapport, les trois amis
      Tiennent conseil. Deux sont d'avis
      De se transporter sans remise
      Aux lieux où la gazelle est prise.
«L'autre, dit le corbeau, gardera le logis.
Avec son marcher lent, quand arriverait-elle?
      Après la mort de la gazelle.»
Ces mots à peine dits, ils s'en vont secourir
      Leur chère et fidèle compagne,
      Pauvre chevrette de montagne.
      La tortue y voulut courir.
      La voilà comme eux en campagne,
Maudissant ses pieds courts avec juste raison,
Et la nécessité de porter sa maison.
Rongemaille (le rat eut à bon droit ce nom)
Coupe les nœuds du lacs: on peut penser la joie.
Le chasseur vient, et dit: «Qui m'a ravi ma proie?»
Rongemaille, à ces mots, se retire en un trou,

At these words the tortose
called out, saying: "Oh, if only I were
provided with wings like a raven,
I would set out this very instant
at least to learn what region,
what incident, is holding back
our fleet-footed companion:
for, with respect to her feelings, we must judge better of them than
that."

The raven flies away hastily.
From a distance he perceives the careless gazelle
        caught in a trap and tormenting herself.
At once he returned to inform the others.
Because to ask her when, why or how
        that misfortune befell her,
and to waste that needful moment in empty talk,
        as a schoolteacher would have done—
        he had too much good sense for that.
        Thus the raven flew there and flew back.
        After he had reported, the three friends
        held council. It was the opinion of two of them
        to travel without delay
        to the spot where the gazelle was caught.
"The other one," said the raven, "will stay home.
With her slow gait, when would she arrive?
        After the gazelle was dead."
Scarcely were these words spoken when they set out to aid
        their dear, faithful companion,
        the poor mountain deer.[103]
        The tortoise wanted to run to the spot.
        There she was in the countryside just like them,
cursing with good reason her stubby legs
and the necessity of carrying her house with her.
Rongemaille[104] (the rat bore that name, and rightly so)
cut the knots of the snare: their joy can be imagined.
The hunter came and said: "Who has stolen my quarry?"
At these words Rongemaille withdrew into a hole,

---

[103] *Chevrette* may mean a goat or a roedeer; a gazelle, of course, is neither, and is not a mountain dweller.

[104] "Mesh gnawer."

Le corbeau sur un arbre, en un bois la gazelle;
     Et le chasseur, à demi fou
     De n'en avoir nulle nouvelle,
Aperçoit la tortue, et retient son courroux.
     «D'où vient, dit-il, que je m'effraie?
Je veux qu'à mon souper celle-ci me défraie.»
Il la mit dans son sac. Elle eût payé pour tous,
Si le corbeau n'en eût averti la chevrette.
     Celle-ci, quittant sa retraite,
Contrefait la boiteuse, et vient se présenter.
     L'homme de suivre, et de jeter
Tout ce qui lui pesait, si bien que Rongemaille
Autour des nœuds du sac tant opère et travaille
     Qu'il délivre encor l'autre sœur
Sur qui s'était fondé le souper du chasseur.

Pilpay conte qu'ainsi la chose s'est passée.
Pour peu que je voulusse invoquer Apollon,
J'en ferais pour vous plaire un ouvrage aussi long
     Que l'*Iliade* ou l'*Odyssée*.
Rongemaille ferait le principal héros,
Quoique à vrai dire ici chacun soit nécessaire.
Portemaison l'infante y tient de tels propos
     Que monsieur du Corbeau va faire
Office d'espion, et puis de messager.
La gazelle a d'ailleurs l'adresse d'engager
Le chasseur à donner du temps à Rongemaille.
     Ainsi chacun en son endroit
     S'entremet, agit et travaille.
A qui donner le prix? Au cœur, si l'on m'en croit.

the raven onto a tree and the gazelle into the forest;
    and the hunter, half-crazed
    by not knowing what had become of it,
caught sight of the tortoise, and restrained his anger.
    "Why," he said, "should I be upset?
I want this animal to reimburse me by becoming my supper."
He put her in his bag. She would have paid the price for them all,
if the raven hadn't informed the gazelle of what was going on.
    The latter, leaving her hiding place,
pretended to be lame and came out to show herself.
    The man followed her, and threw off
everything that was weighing him down, so that Rongemaille
worked and toiled at the knots in the bag
    until he released his other sister as well,
on whom the hunter's supper had been predicated.

Bidpai[105] tells us that the events went that way.
If only I wanted to invoke Apollo,[106]
I would write, to please you, a poem on the subject as long
    as the Iliad or the Odyssey.
Rongemaille would be the chief hero,
although, to tell the truth, each of them is necessary.
Princess Portemaison[107] makes such a vivid speech in the story
    that Sir Raven goes off to do
duty as a scout and then as a messenger.
Furthermore, the gazelle has the presence of mind to engage
the hunter and thus give Rongemaille time.
    Thus each one in his place
    intervenes, acts and labors.
To whom should the prize be awarded? To the heart, if you listen
                                    to me.

---

[105] A legendary fable writer in India. Stories attributed to him were collected in the early centuries A.D. and spread abroad to many other countries.

[106] God of poetry.

[107] "House carrier," the tortoise.

# Le renard, le loup, et le cheval

Un renard jeune encor, quoique des plus madrés,
Vit le premier cheval qu'il eût vu de sa vie.
Il dit à certain loup, franc novice: «Accourez:
    Un animal paît dans nos prés,
Beau, grand; j'en ai la vue encor toute ravie.

–Est-il plus fort que nous? dit le loup en riant.
    Fais-moi son portrait, je te prie.
–Si j'étais quelque peintre ou quelque étudiant,
Repartit le renard, j'avancerais la joie
    Que vous aurez en le voyant.
Mais venez. Que sait-on? peut-être est-ce une proie
    Que la Fortune nous envoie.»
Ils vont; et le cheval, qu'à l'herbe on avait mis,
Assez peu curieux de semblables amis,
Fut presque sur le point d'enfiler la venelle.
«Seigneur, dit le renard, vos humbles serviteurs
Apprendraient volontiers comment on vous appelle.»
Le cheval, qui n'était dépourvu de cervelle,
Leur dit: «Lisez mon nom, vous le pouvez, Messieurs;
Mon cordonnier l'a mis autour de ma semelle.»
Le renard s'excusa sur son peu de savoir.
«Mes parents, reprit-il, ne m'ont point fait instruire;
Ils sont pauvres, et n'ont qu'un trou pour tout avoir.
Ceux du loup, gros messieurs, l'ont fait apprendre a lire.»
    Le loup, par ce discours flatté,
    S'approcha; mais sa vanité
Lui coûta quatre dents: le cheval lui desserre
Un coup; et haut le pied. Voilà mon loup par terre,
    Mal en point, sanglant et gâté.
«Frère, dit le renard, ceci nous justifie
    Ce que m'ont dit des gens d'esprit:
Cet animal vous a sur la mâchoire écrit
Que de tout inconnu le sage se méfie.»

# The Fox, the Wolf and the Horse

A fox who was still young, though one of the wiliest,
saw the first horse he'd ever seen in his life.
He said to a certain wolf, who was a raw novice: "Come!
　　There's an animal grazing in our meadows
that's beautiful and tall; my eyes are still delighted at the sight of
　　　　　　　　　　　　　　　　　　　　　　him."
"Is he stronger than we are?" said the wolf, laughing;
　　"describe him to me, please."
"If I were some painter or some student,"
replied the fox, "I would give you a foretaste of the pleasure
　　that you'll experience when you see him.
But come! who knows? Maybe he's a prey
　　that good fortune has sent our way."
They set out; and the horse, who had been turned out to grass
and was not very eager to meet new friends of that sort,
was almost on the point of escaping.
"Sir," said the fox, "your humble servants
would gladly learn your name."
The horse, who wasn't short on brains,
said to them: "Read my name; you can do that, gentlemen;
my shoemaker put it in writing around my soles."
The fox apologized for his lack of knowledge.
"My parents," he replied, "didn't have me educated;
they're poor, and a hole in the ground is all they own.
Those of the wolf, people of standing, had him taught to read."
　　The wolf, flattered by this speech,
　　came up close; but his vanity
cost him four teeth: the horse unleashed a kick
at him; then bolted away. There was the wolf on the ground,
　　in poor shape, bleeding and injured.
"Brother," said the fox, "this confirms for us
　　what clever people have told me:
that animal has written on your jaw
that the wise man is suspicious of anything unknown to him."

## Le singe

Il est un singe dans Paris
A qui l'on avait donné femme.
Singe en effet d'aucuns maris,
Il la battait: la pauvre dame
En a tant soupiré qu'enfin elle n'est plus.
Leur fils se plaint d'étrange sorte;
Il éclate en cris superflus:
Le père en rit; sa femme est morte.
Il a déjà d'autres amours
Que l'on croit qu'il battra toujours.
Il hante la taverne, et souvent il s'enivre.
N'attendez rien de bon du peuple imitateur,
Qu'il soit singe, ou qu'il fasse un livre.
La pire espèce, c'est l'auteur.


## Le philosophe scythe

Un philosophe austère, et né dans la Scythie,
Se proposant de suivre une plus douce vie,
Voyagea chez les Grecs, et vit en certains lieux
Un sage assez semblable au vieillard de Virgile,
Homme égalant les rois, homme approchant des dieux,

Et, comme ces derniers, satisfait et tranquille.
Son bonheur consistait aux beautés d'un jardin.
Le Scythe l'y trouva, qui la serpe à la main,
De ses arbres à fruits retranchait l'inutile,
Ébranchait, émondait, ôtait ceci, cela,

# The Ape

There was an ape in Paris
to whom a wife had been given.
Truly an ape of some husbands,
he used to beat her: the poor lady
sighed over it so much that finally she was no more.
Their son laments in an odd way;
he bursts out into useless cries:
the father laughs over it; his wife is dead.
he already has other sweethearts
whom it is believed he'll go on beating.
He haunts the tavern, and often gets drunk.
Don't expect anything good from imitative folk,
whether apes or writers of books.
The worst sort of all is the author.

# The Scythian Philosopher

An austere philosopher born in the land of the Scythians,[108]
resolving to live a less harsh life,
traveled to Greece, where in a certain spot he saw
a wise man much like Vergil's old man,[109]
a man the equal of kings, a man who came close to being like the
                                                          gods,
and, like the latter, contented and peaceful.
His happiness consisted of the beauties of a garden.
The Scythian found him there, his billhook in his hand,
trimming away superfluous parts of his fruit trees,
cutting branches, pruning, removing this and that,

---

[108] The Scythians were a group of nomadic Iranian tribes who settled in southern Russia and adjacent steppe regions between about 700 and 300 B.C. Although they developed a notable material culture, they were considered barbarians by the supercilious, ethnocentric Greeks, and this attitude is here carried over by the poet.

[109] In Book IV of the *Georgics*, the Roman poet Vergil (70–19 B.C.) mentions an old man who was happy as a king while living off the few vegetables he himself grew.

    Corrigeant partout la nature,
Excessive à payer ses soins avec usure.
    Le Scythe alors lui demanda
Pourquoi cette ruine. Était-il d'homme sage
De mutiler ainsi ces pauvres habitants?
«Quittez-moi votre serpe, instrument de dommage;
      Laissez agir la faux du temps:
Ils iront assez tôt border le noir rivage.
–J'ôte le superflu, dit l'autre, et, l'abattant,

    Le reste en profite d'autant.»
Le Scythe, retourné dans sa triste demeure,
Prend la serpe à son tour, coupe et taille à toute heure;
Conseille à ses voisins, prescrit à ses amis
      Un universel abatis.
Il ôte de chez lui les branches les plus belles,
Il tronque son verger contre toute raison,
      Sans observer temps ni saison,
      Lunes ni vieilles ni nouvelles.
Tout languit et tout meurt. Ce Scythe exprime bien

      Un indiscret stoïcien.
      Celui-ci retranche de l'âme
Désirs et passions, le bon et le mauvais,
      Jusqu'aux plus innocents souhaits.
Contre de telles gens, quant à moi, je réclame.
Ils ôtent à nos cœurs le principal ressort:
Ils font cesser de vivre avant que l'on soit mort.


# Le juge arbitre, l'hospitalier, et le solitaire

Trois saints, également jaloux de leur salut,
Portés d'un même esprit, tendaient à même but.
Ils s'y prirent tous trois par des routes diverses.
Tous chemins vont à Rome: ainsi nos concurrents
Crurent pouvoir choisir des sentiers différents.
L'un, touché des soucis, des longueurs, des traverses,

everywhere correcting nature,
which was repaying his cares excessively and usuriously.
    The Scythian then asked him
why this havoc. Was it the wise man's way
to mutilate those poor garden dwellers like that?
"Please put away your hook, that instrument of harm;
    let the scythe of Time operate:
they will soon enough border the dark shores."[110]
"I'm removing the excess," said the other man, "and, when I cut
                                                        it off,
    all the rest profits by it to that extent."
The Scythian, having returned to his dismal homeland,
takes up the hook in his turn, chops and cuts at all hours;
he advises for his neighbors, he prescribes to his friends,
    a universal tree-clearing.
On his own property he removes the finest branches,
he truncates his orchard contrary to all reason,
    without observing time or season,
    old or new moons.
Everything withers and everything dies. That Scythian is a good
                                                        symbol
    of an unsubtle stoic.
    The stoic lops away from his soul
desires and passions, the good and the bad,
    down to the most innocent wishes.
As for me, I protest against such people.
They deprive our hearts of their mainspring:
they make us cease living before we are dead.


# The Arbitrator, the Hospitaler and the Recluse

Three saintly men, equally desirous of salvation,
driven by the same spirit, were tending toward the same goal.
Each of the three went about it by another path.
All roads lead to Rome: thus, our competitors
thought that each could choose a different route.
One of them, saddened by the worries, delays and setbacks

---

110 Of the underworld.

Qu'en apanage on voit aux procès attachés,
S'offrit de les juger sans récompense aucune,
Peu soigneux d'établir ici-bas sa fortune.
Depuis qu'il est des lois, l'homme, pour ses péchés,
Se condamne à plaider la moitié de sa vie.
La moitié? Les trois quarts et bien souvent le tout.
Le conciliateur crut qu'il viendrait à bout
De guérir cette folle et détestable envie.
Le second de nos saints choisit les hôpitaux.
Je le loue, et le soin de soulager ces maux
Est une charité que je préfère aux autres.
Les malades d'alors, étant tels que les nôtres,
Donnaient de l'exercice au pauvre hospitalier;
Chagrins, impatients, et se plaignant sans cesse:
«Il a pour tels et tels un soin particulier;
        Ce sont ses amis; il nous laisse.»
Ces plaintes n'étaient rien au prix de l'embarras
Où se trouva réduit l'appointeur de débats.
Aucun n'était content; la sentence arbitrale
        A nul des deux ne convenait:
        Jamais le juge ne tenait
        A leur gré la balance égale.
De semblables discours rebutaient l'appointeur.
Il court aux hôpitaux, va voir leur directeur.
Tous deux ne recueillant que plainte et que murmure,
Affligés, et contraints de quitter ces emplois,
Vont confier leur peine au silence des bois.
Là sous d'âpres rochers, près d'une source pure,
Lieu respecté des vents, ignoré du soleil,
Ils trouvent l'autre saint, lui demandent conseil.
«Il faut, dit leur ami, le prendre de soi-même.
        Qui mieux que vous sait vos besoins?
Apprendre à se connaître est le premier des soins
Qu'impose à tous mortels la Majesté suprême.
Vous êtes-vous connus dans le monde habité?
L'on ne le peut qu'aux lieux pleins de tranquillité:
Chercher ailleurs ce bien est une erreur extrême.
        Troublez l'eau: vous y voyez-vous?
Agitez celle-ci. –Comment nous verrions-nous?
        La vase est un épais nuage
Qu'aux effets du cristal nous venons d'opposer.

that are inseparable concomitants of law trials,
volunteered to judge them without any recompense,
because he wasn't concerned with making his fortune here on earth.
Ever since laws have existed, man, for his sins,
condemns himself to litigation for half of his life.
Half? Three quarters, and very often all of it.
This peacemaker believed he could succeed
in curing that mad and hateful yen.
The second of our saints chose hospitals.
I praise him, and the labor of relieving those pains
is a charity I prefer to all the rest.
The patients of that day, being the same as ours,
gave the poor hospitaler plenty of worries;
cranky, impatient and complaining ceaselessly:
"He's giving special attention to So-and-so and What's-his-name;
    they're friends of his; us he neglects."
These complaints were nothing compared with the awful situation
in which the settler of disputes found himself.
No one was satisfied; his decisions as arbitrator
    didn't suit either party:
    the judge never held
    the scales of justice equitably enough for them.
Such talk disheartened the arbitrator.
He runs to the hospitals, goes to see their director.
Both of them, garnering only complaints and grumbling,
unhappy, forced to abandon those positions,
set out to confide their sorrow to the silence of the woods.
There, beneath rough rocks, near a pure spring,
a place respected by the winds and ignored by the sun,
they find the third saint and ask his advice.
Their friend says: "One must receive it from oneself.
    Who knows your needs better than you do?
To learn to know oneself is the primary task
that the supreme Majesty lays upon all mortals.
Did you know yourself when in the populous world?
A man can only do so in places full of calm:
to seek that benefit elsewhere is a grave mistake.
    Stir up the water: can you see yourself in it?
Disturb this spring." "How could we see ourselves?
    The silt forms a dense cloud
that we have just set in opposition to the effect of the crystal stream."

–Mes frères, dit le saint, laissez-la reposer,
    Vous verrez alors votre image.
Pour vous mieux contempler, demeurez au désert.»
    Ainsi parla le solitaire.
Il fut cru, l'on suivit ce conseil salutaire.
Ce n'est pas qu'un emploi ne doive être souffert.
Puisqu'on plaide, et qu'on meurt, et qu'on devient malade,
Il faut des médecins, il faut des avocats.
Ces secours, grâce à Dieu, ne nous manqueront pas:
Les honneurs et le gain, tout me le persuade.
Cependant on s'oublie en ces communs besoins.

O vous, dont le public emporte tous les soins,
    Magistrats, princes et ministres,
Vous que doivent troubler mille accidents sinistres,
Que le malheur abat, que le bonheur corrompt,
Vous ne vous voyez point, vous ne voyez personne.
Si quelque bon moment à ces pensers vous donne,
    Quelque flatteur vous interrompt.
Cette leçon sera la fin de ces ouvrages:
Puisse-t-elle être utile aux siècles à venir!
Je la présente aux rois, je la propose aux sages:
    Par où saurais-je mieux finir?

"My brothers," says the saint, "let it settle to the bottom again,
    then you will see your reflection.
In order to observe yourself better, remain in the wilderness."
    Thus spoke the recluse.
They took his word, they followed that salutary advice.
It isn't that social positions are not to be countenanced.
Since law cases do exist, and people die and get sick,
we must have doctors, we must have lawyers.
We won't lack these aids, thank God:
the honors and profits involved all convince me of it.
And yet, caught up in these community functions, a man is unmindful
              of himself.
O you whose attention is totally monopolized by the public,
    magistrates, rulers and ministers,
you who can't avoid being troubled by a thousand dire incidents,
who are dismayed by bad luck and corrupted by good luck,
you don't see yourselves, you don't see anyone.
If some felicitous moment allows you to think about such things,
    a flatterer interrupts you.
This lesson will be the end of my book:
may it prove useful to the generations to come!
I offer it to kings, I propose it to wise men:
    Could I possibly conclude in a better way?

# Alphabetical List of French Titles

An opening definite article is not counted in the alphabetization, and appears within parentheses at the end of its entry.

# Alphabetical List of French First Lines